WELCOME TO MY WORLD

An Ed Turner, P.I. Novel

Glenn Eric

Beachfront Entertainment

ISBN-13: 9781892339713
ISBN-10: 1892339714

Cover design by: RolffImages

Printed in the United States of America

WELCOME TO MY WORLD

By a route obscure and lonely,
Haunted by ill angels only,
Where an Eidolon, named Night,
On a black throne reigns upright,
I have reached these lands but newly
From an ultimate dim Thule—
From a wild weird clime that lieth, sublime,
Out of Space—out of Time.

From Dream-Land / Edgar Allan Poe

1

Take it from me. Life's a bitch. Doesn't matter who you are, what you are, where you come from, what your dietary preferences. Doesn't matter if you are animal, vegetable, or mineral. Nope, doesn't matter what sort of lifeform you are or aren't, or even if you are a lowly isotope. Life's a bitch.

Let me repeat. Life. Is. A. Bitch.

I puffed on a Camel and stared out a window which hadn't seen the touch of a squeegee in all the forty years or so of its existence—through one toxic cloud of pollution into another, you might say. Yep, it was one of those southern California days the Department of Tourism prefers you don't talk about.

Not that I could've seen far anyway. My second floor office window looks across the narrow street into another grimy office window, this one belonging to an accountant. You ever look into an accountant's office window? No? Lucky you. Talk about boring. I'd rather watch the proverbial paint dry on a park bench. I've done both. Believe you me, paint drying trumps peeping on an accountant anytime, day or night.

I live and work in LA's Toy District. I kid you not. And no, I'm not into toys, although some of the enterprising folk here have built fortunes out of the toy biz. Good for them. I liked the district because the rent was cheap. My rarely-seen landlord was an Asian gentleman. He and his family owned about thirty or so of the buildings in the immediate vicinity, so I've been told. Not exactly the hip and upcoming place to live, unless you were a Barbie doll looking to shack up on the cheap with Ken. Again, all I care about is the cheap rent. Then again, some of those toy spaceships and gadgets like laser blasters and light sabers do give me a chuckle every time I lay eyes on them. And I lay eyes on them a lot.

And I've never seen so many aliens in my life, anywhere! And that's saying something. Of course these aliens are all artificial, with plastic limbs and fake hair, cotton- or bean-stuffed or air-filled, and lining the streets and stalls from top to bottom. Yep, a real toy lover's paradise. Angelenos are a weird bunch. Then again, half of them are considered aliens too—by the other half, I might add. Just because they come from one side or the other of some imaginary line. Can you imagine that?

As for the myriad dolls the vendors are hawking daily, uh, no thank you.

I puffed some more and somebody or something banged on my office door. Rattle-rattle. Not a quality build. I rent two rooms. Office in front, bed and bath in the rear.

I ignored the knock on the door. I hate it when people knock. It's so…intrusive, you know?

I puffed, quietly cleared my throat so whoever or whatever was out there wouldn't hear me. Would go away. So I hoped. I was also hoping I wasn't on my last cigarette because that would mean I'd have to run down to the shop in the lobby. Anna Ping charges an arm and a leg for a pack of smokes. And her prices on alcohol are astronomical. Sometimes I get the feeling she's taking advantage of me just because I'm not from around here.

More knocking.

More ignoring.

A hand turned the brass knob. At least I assume a hand did because the knob rotated, the door swung open, sounding like a baby porker taking a first gander at the big bad world, and a young woman peeked tentatively inside. So it wasn't an incorporeal spirit with exceptional motor skills.

"Can I help you?"

"Mister Turner? Ed Turner?"

"That's me. You come to tell me my name?"

I prefer old movies, especially old American cinema from the forties and early fifties. Life was simpler then, everything was. Everything was black and white too. I preferred my reality like that. Black and white. Cut and dry. These days everything's all rainbow connection—yellows, reds, purples, greens, blues... every damn color of a well-lit prism and some shades that haven't even been invented yet.

Take this young woman blocking the doorway for instance, blue jeans, red sneakers with chunky white laces, and a black Blink-182 tee shirt. What was that all about? Had she set a record or something? Blinked one hundred eighty-two times in a row? If that was for the Guinness record books, it was a strange one even for them. Even stranger to print yourself up a tee shirt boasting about the dubious feat. I, for one, was unimpressed. The only Guinness I care about comes in a bottle. Well, comes in cans too.

Loads of black hair trailed nearly to her waist. And the lower half of said hair shimmered bright blue. I placed her somewhere in her thirties maybe—same age I'm shooting for myself. Then again, she might've been fifty, she might've been twenty. I'm not much good at pinpointing age but I'm working on it.

"What is this, a prank?" I leaned forward. "Like one of those TV gag shows?" She also dragged a scent into the room with her. I caught hints of water lotus, orange blossom and strawberries, among other toxic molecules.

"Huh? You mean some sort of hidden camera thing?" Her eyes circled the room then came back to me.

"Do I?"

Blue hair and lots of brown skin, if that's even what they call it these days. Everybody is so politically correct. *Politically correct* what a dumb phrase. As if there is *anything* correct about politics.

Personally, I'm on the whiter side of pale with ginger hair, such as it is. I'm not the hairiest critter in town. Her eyes blinked green. So we had that one thing in common. A tenuous connection but it was something. I've learned it's always good to have a link, a commonality, with a potential client—if that's

3

what she was.

She helped herself to a Walmart office chair opposite my desk. The chair was no great shakes in the style department but functional as all hell. I'm a utilitarian kind of guy. Utility is a key ingredient of survival.

She leaned in, spread her arms across my desk, palms up. "My brother is missing."

I let the world skip a beat.

"So?" I said finally. "I got a brother who's missing. You don't see me banging on doors asking people please can you help me find him."

"But—"

"Tell me something."

"Yes?"

"How'd you get those—what do you call 'em?—dreadful blue locks?"

She frowned. A hand, hers, tugged at her locks. "They're called dreadlocks not *dreadful* locks."

"Is there a difference?"

"Yes, you see—"

"You born that way?"

"Of course not, I color it." Her cheeks colored a little at the moment too.

"Suit yourself. Hell, we got people back home with blue skin but I'd never heard of anyone going out of their way to dip themselves in blue paint just because they wanted to be like them." I shrugged, tapped cigarette ash into my palm and licked.

"Ugh! Gross!"

I blinked at her. 182 more times and I'd beat her record. "To each his or her own, right?"

She sighed deeply. "Mister Turner, can you help me or not?"

"The question isn't: *can I? Of course, I can.*" I spent a moment wiping my damp palm against my tan trousers. The word *smudge* came to mind. My best light-blue button-down short-sleeve shirt was tucked in at the waist. I prefer button-down, makes me feel so...normal. Human, you might say. "The question is: *will I?*"

"Then will you?"

"Nah, why should I?"

She fell back in her chair. The chair barely budged. See what I mean? Solid. "Because that's what you do. The sign on the door." She pointed. *Ed Turner, Private Investigator.* Yep, there it was stenciled to the door, looking as fresh as it did the day the maintenance guy sprayed it on with that aerosol can in bold black Latin letters. "Says you're a detective."

I shrugged. "Signs gotta say something. If they don't, are they really signs? Hey." I grinned. "That's a real philosophical poser, isn't it? Aristotelian, wouldn't you say?"

"Aristotle who?"

Okay, so she wasn't a history buff. At least, not an Ancient Greek history buff. I rubbed my hands together. I do that sometimes when my brain gets sunk in an interesting topic. "As an aside, did you know a couple hundred years back your Latin alphabet used to contain twenty-seven letters?" I wagged a scholarly finger. "Not twenty-six, twenty-seven."

"Huh? No, I—"

"It's true. Nowadays they call it a whatchamacallit." I snapped my fingers and glanced at the virtual keyboard feature of my tablet. "This thingie. Ampersand, is that it?"

She drew in a stiff breath filled with resolve. "Mister Turner, please. My brother—"

"Right, missing." I chewed my cigarette butt, rolled it around my mouth, and mulled things over.

"You shouldn't do that, you know."

"Do what?"

"Chew on that-that thing. It's disgusting. And cigarettes have been proven to cause cancer."

I stared at her blankly. Why do some folks always got to tell you what's best for you? "One man or woman's Cancer is another man or woman's Sagittarius, isn't that what they say?"

"Excuse me?"

"Nothing. I thought we were talking astrological signs.

Glad we're not. What a lot of hooey that is!" I swallowed the butt, grinned when she gasped in horror, fiddled with the pack of Camels, tapped out the last one in the pack, and lit it up with a blue Bic. I slipped the lighter in my pocket and tossed the empty pack in the wastebin under the desk.

She waved her hand in front of her nose like I'd just blasted her in the face from outer space with a radioactive cloud bearing death and destruction. If that had been the case, I'm not too sure what good the flitty wave of the hand was going to do her—not all that functional as far as blast shields go. The things I could teach her.

I ignored her rudeness and enjoyed my smoke.

She folded her hands in her lap and straightened. Looked me in the eye. I watched tears forming along the edges of her eyes. Uh-oh, I knew something was coming.

"Please, Mister Turner, help me find my brother." She extracted a white tissue from a packet she'd found at the bottom of her purse and dabbed her eyeballs.

It was my turn to sigh, so I did, pushing another cloud of cancer-filled smoke her way. She chose to ignore it this time, no hand waving. She simply held her breath for a minute.

I slid my electronic tablet closer to me. It's one of those Windows-based jobs. Not an Apple because I can't stand the name. I can't stand apples. I can't stand any fruit, to be honest. Talk about poison. That stuff could kill you. Well, maybe not you but me.

I tapped my tablet to life and punched open my notes app. "When was the last time you saw him?"

Her eyes rolled to the ceiling then came back down. "Maybe three years ago? Two and half?"

I leaned back in my red leather seat. Sure, the sleek black one in the discount office supply store looked cooler but the tufted red one's price had been drastically marked down. No skin off my nose if it makes it look like I manage a brothel, as one former client had suggested. "And only now you're looking for him?"

"No, you don't understand. He lives out of state. Moved to New Mexico several years ago. Los Alamos. So I haven't seen him in a couple of years. But we talk all the time. *All* the time."

"And the last time would be?"

"Three days ago."

"So what's the problem?"

"He's not answering his phone. That's not like him. And when I call his work they give me the run around."

I refrained from commenting that I might not pick up if I knew this woman was on the other end of the line myself. She'd interrupted my idle smoking for this? "How did he sound last time you spoke?"

"That's just it. He sounded upset. Worried." She chewed her thumbnail. What was that all about?

"Upset, worried, why?"

"He said they were trying to kill him."

"They who?" Maybe I should have set up shop as a dentist. Dealing with this woman was like pulling teeth. And I wasn't set up for the job. Maybe I should have purchased a dental chair instead of the desk chair. Was it too late to exchange it?

Her jaw stiffened and she chewed her lip now, all to build up the tension, I suppose. Then like Hoover Dam catastrophically failing without so much as a hint of warning, she blurted "The aliens."

That got my attention.

2

I sat up, snatched the open bottle of bourbon off the dusty bookshelf behind me and sloshed some into my IHOP coffee mug. I didn't stop pouring until amber liquid spilled over the sides and onto my desk. No matter, I'd sop it up later with a straw, or my tongue if that's what it took—after present company departed.

I'm not one for wasting anything. And this anything was bourbon. One of the most precious commodities on the planet. Forget gold. What good was the stuff? You couldn't drink it. You couldn't even eat it. Leastwise, not digest the dumb metal. Bourbon you can drink to heart's content. This particular bottle had been something of a splurge, an indulgence, if you will. A bit on the pricy side. The bourbon's called Heaven's Door. I didn't believe much in heaven but I sure as hell believed in this stuff. I drank. Tried to control my nerves.

"Aliens you say?" I struggled to keep my voice calm and my demeanor on an even keel. Aliens? Los Alamos? New Mexico?

Really, was this one of those hidden-camera gag shows?

I gulped my bourbon and sat the emptied mug on the desktop. Some do yoga or deep breathing exercises. I smoke Camels and drink bourbon. What can I say? To each his or her own. Besides, we all have our own ways of coping with things. You choose yours, I'll choose mine.

"Should you really be drinking so much, Mister Turner? And so early in the day?"

"It's called staying hydrated. That's supposed to be good for you. I read it in a book somewhere." To prove it, I scanned my bookshelves in search of the title in question but had no luck.

I mostly had copies of self-help books, geography, sciences, film history, and a smattering of physics books—those I kept around mostly for giggles. Where was that book that said it was okay to drink more? To heart's content?

"Let's start with a name. You got one?" I asked her.

"Karen. Karen Dalton."

"Are you sure?"

"Yes, of course I'm sure!"

"It's just that you didn't sound sure."

She cleared her throat. "My name is Karen Dalton. My brother is Ken Dalton."

"Okay." I ran a lazy hand across my lower lip. "Tell me more about this brother Ken."

She did. And brother was it good.

"Like I said, he moved to Los Alamos. Got a job there three years ago."

"Doing what?"

Karen Dalton scratched behind her ear. "I don't know. He didn't say exactly."

"Okay. What did he say in general?"

This prompted a bit of shoulder shrugging and feet shuffling. A real song-and-dance girl, this one. "He's a doctor."

"Got it. What's his specialty? Ear, nose, and throat? Foot fungus?"

"Well, he *is* a medical doctor," she admitted. "But he has a PhD in astrobiology too."

I whistled. "Impressive."

"He always has been the brains of the family. Way smarter than me."

I commiserated with my potential client. I'd always been the outcast, second-rater of my own family, such as it was. And not the brightest star on our family Christmas Tree. Is that even a thing? "What is it that you do, if I may ask?"

"Graphic design. But that's just something I fell into. I have my Master's degree in poetry and poetics."

I paused in my note taking. "You're kidding me, right?"

"No, University of Chicago."

"And you paid for this? In US dollars?"

"What's that supposed to mean?" Her back stiffened. Had I said something wrong? Something to offend her?

"Never mind." I pressed my back into my seat and laced my fingers behind my head. "Please, continue, Karen Dalton."

"Anyway, Ken got this job three years go. He'd been working at JPL here in Pasadena. The Los Alamos job offer came as a big surprise to him. Other than that, he wouldn't tell me much. Not even who his new employer was. He only told me it was something he simply couldn't pass up. Within two weeks, he was gone. Sold his condo, stored his car, packed up all his things and moved to New Mexico."

"Do you have his current address?"

"No. He wouldn't tell me. Said it was top secret. I thought he was being mysterious for nothing. Teasing. Now I'm beginning to wonder. You know, every time I suggested I pay him a visit, he came up with a reason why it wouldn't be practical."

"Think," I persisted. "He must have told you something. Did you ever write him? Forward his mail?"

"Oh, yes."

"Okay. Now we are getting somewhere. Where did you address his mail, for instance?"

"A PO box in Los Angeles, I'm afraid. I don't know what happened to it or where it went after that."

"Oh," I said, unable to hide my disappointment. "He didn't mention a town? Maybe the names of some friends or colleagues?" If so, I might be able to trace him through them.

She chewed on the question a minute before spitting out an answer. "About a year ago, he did mention something called Groom Lake." She laughed. "Ken joked that it was Area 51, you know? Like the place with the top-secret alien conspiracy stuff." She laughed some more.

I did not laugh. No, I did not.

Nor did I point out to Karen Dalton that Area 51 is in

Nevada, not New Mexico. Curiouser and curiouser. And not in a good way.

I caught the clatter of footsteps mounting the stairs down the corridor. The steps stopped next door. My nearest neighbor imported handmade toys from Vietnam. Sounded like he had a visitor. Personally, I couldn't understand how he stayed in business. Never seemed to actually sell a damn thing.

"So will you help me? He's all the family I've got."

"Really?" My brow quirked up all on its own volition. "Most people I've met have a set of parents lying around. Maybe a sibling or two."

She shook her head sadly. "Mine have passed."

"Passed?" I tapped my pencil against the tablet's glass screen. I know, a complete waste of time and utterly useless here. But it did give me something to do. "Like a test?"

Her brow furrowed like a row of Martian canals. "What? No! I mean, they're dead. And I have no other siblings. No more brothers and sisters. Maybe a couple of distant cousins somewhere..." She trailed off as if she'd reached a dead end in her head.

"I see."

"I can pay you."

"I would expect you to." Just so long as she didn't think she could get away with paying my fee with several stanzas of free verse, or a flimsy, stapled chapbook of her collected opus. And I don't do barter, leastwise not with a graphic artist. I had no need for graphic artistry at that time. "I would expect, say, five hundred US dollars per day?" I had no idea what the traffic might bear but five hundred a day sounded bearable to me.

The corners of her eyes tightened. "I-Yes, that would be acceptable." She clamped her hands over the black handbag resting on her lap. "Do you take Zelle?"

"What form of currency is that?"

"It's not currency. It's a way to exchange money between banks."

"I don't do banks, I'm afraid. Too many rules and

regulations." And they're sticklers for IDs.

"Of course," she said but she did not sound like she meant it. "I'll have to go to the ATM."

"A money machine?"

"Yes, a-a money machine." Karen appeared flustered.

"No matter." I stood. I've learned this is a good way to get the other party to do the same. "Pay me when we find your Ken."

Karen stood. See what I mean? People are so predictable. "And if you don't? Find Ken, I mean."

Her question caught me off-guard. "Is that an option?"

That stumped her.

3

The Toy District is not merely a great place to buy toys, it is also a great place to get lost. Literally. Take it from me, I must've done it a hundred times, and I live here.

Then again, it's also a great place to get lost figuratively. And that's also what I love about it. All the hustlers and bustlers, the myriad toys, the colorful and crammed shops and stalls. Yep, a great place to get lost. To be lost.

I purchased a single-serving carton of cold noodles and shrimp from a street vendor and slurped it up while waiting for the next Metro bus. Trust me, there's always a next bus.

Sure enough, this one finally showed up, twenty minutes later than scheduled, but what's time anyway? Personally, I've never believed in it. Tit for tat, it doesn't believe in me either. I'm okay with that.

I dumped my trash in the nearest can and squeezed into a seat next to a gent the size of sofa. He hadn't finished his lunch, a meatball sub which he clamped tightly as if fearful I'd snatch it from him. If only he knew...if I thought I could get away with it, I'd have had my hands all over it. Cold noodles and shrimp is only so filling. A meatball sub would've made quite the dessert.

As he polished off his man-sized sandwich, I squinted into the sun and watched the city pass by. I grew drowsier with each passing mile and only shot awake as we came to a stop. Then it was a subway ride and another bus. I do not possess an automobile. So public transport it is. Mixing and mashing with the denizens of public transport. A curious and multicolored, multi-scented stew of all shapes and sizes. Some I'd never seen before. Many I wished never to see again.

And what's with all the tattoos? I've spent years, blood, sweat and tears—well, no tears because I don't cry, although I do sweat bourbon—trying to fit in, not look or seem different. All to observe some people go out of their way to do the opposite.

And people think *I'm* queer.

Rather, they would, if they knew me.

I tumbled out of the bus. I don't like to sit still for too long. Especially on public transportation because they refuse to let me smoke or drink.

It was late afternoon and JPL loomed ahead of me. Ken Dalton's last place of local employment, according to sister Karen. I wondered what secrets it might hold.

I'd promised Karen Dalton that I would start my investigation right away and here I was, a creature of my word. Now, if I could only figure out what to do next.

NASA's sprawling Jet Propulsion Laboratory complex sits in the northern tip of Pasadena, at the foot of the San Gabriel Mountains. What came next was that I joined up with a cluster of about thirty business-dressed men and women exiting their own private bus and tumbling onto the hot sidewalk. Late summer in southern California can be oppressive. The group proceeded at the behest of a blue-suited guide to the Visitor Center. I had no idea what their business or intentions were but they were moving in the right direction for my purposes.

They hustled us inside to a blessedly chill sixty-eight degree lobby, handed out visitor passes and led us to a large room where we stood idly chatting amongst ourselves until an austere blonde tour guide, with a walk like a stork, instructed us all to follow her, stay on the path and do not, definitely do not at threat of prosecution—or dismemberment, I supposed, judging by the threatening tone of her voice and psychopathic slant of her eyes—go off the prescribed path.

Which I did the first chance I got. And that chance came quickly. The tour group consisted of a bunch of real estate agents. Why they wanted a tour of one of the most sophisticated and state-of-the-art, federally-funded research-

and-development centers devoted to earth sciences and robotic space exploration was way beyond my understanding. I barely had any interest in the tour myself.

No, what I wanted was to get a look at Ken Dalton's old personnel files and workspace. Maybe learn a thing or two about the man and his work.

Of course, why JPL wasted time providing a tour to a group of realtors was way, way beyond my understanding. Was JPL thinking of selling? Going condo?

I made no pretense of stealth. Look like you fit in and you fit in. That's my motto. I slipped the visitor pass lanyard off my neck and into the front pocket of my trousers and got busy.

After several failed twists and turns, I discovered something called Human Resources. To my surprise, it did not contain everything you'd need to assemble and sustain a human. Rather, it contained every stupid little iota of data about everybody in the place, past, present and...no, no future. I supposed they were not technologically advanced far enough for that yet. Would they ever be?

I threaded my way down gray carpeted passages filled with four-foot-tall gray boxes until I found an unoccupied cubicle. Unoccupied but not unused. Some creature named Sylvia, according to the small plaque affixed to one wall, called this little gray nest home five days a week. Poor woman. I'd rather be trapped in a windowless escape pod for five days with nothing to cast my gaze upon but an AI-controlled interstitial space monitor. Especially an AI-controlled interstitial space monitor that kept insisting it was sentient. And if you've ever been, for lack of options, forced to stare at one of those, even for five minutes, you know how dull that can be.

Sylvia liked cats. And comfy button-down sweaters. Dozens of cat photos, all featuring the same Siamese, dotted the three-sided cubicle. Three sweaters, one yellow, one blue, and the other dark gray draped the back of her swivel chair.

Lucky for me, she also loved black licorice twists. She kept an entire jar, one hundred and fifty pieces worth, according to the label, within reach of her computer keyboard. Which I helped myself to. Both. The computer keyboard and the licorice twists.

I shoved a stick of twisted pleasure into my mouth and bit. Ecstasy! Who or what doesn't like black licorice? I'd smear it all over my body, bathe in the stuff, were it possible.

Were it possible?

Something to think about...

But I couldn't get distracted. I was in Ed Turner, Private Investigator mode. I needed to get investigating. I needed to get out before Sylvia returned from wherever she'd gone and found me ensconced in her work nest.

I tapped the keyboard and the screen blinked to life. "If only creating all life was this easy," I said under my breath, cognizant that others lurked nearby, busy toiling in their own work nests. Ears ever alert for possible skulkers like myself. This was a high-security facility, after all. Not that these walls contained much of interest to me.

I quickly found the historic personnel files directory and typed in Ken's name. I found him under Dalton, Kenneth.

Bingo!

I scanned quickly, memorizing every smallest detail. I've heard such an ability called eidetic imagery. I call it being normal.

And that's what Ken Dalton's life had been. Normal. Ho-humping-hum normal. Sure, a bright enough guy but nothing unusual. No blue dreadlocks. Nothing that presages a phone call with him telling his kid sister that aliens are out to murder him.

I tapped my fingernails on the built-in gray plastic desktop.

Great work record, rarely a sick day, impressive advanced degrees, including the one in astrobiology from the University of Edinburgh. He'd been working on several projects here at JPL. Projects with such whimsical, yet unrevealing—no doubt for security purposes—names like Wishing Well 2, High Price To Pay, and a third titled Unicorns & Dragons.

Interesting but useless to my investigation into where Ken

Dalton was now and what had happened to him.

Was he alive? Was he dead?

If he was dead, was an alien to blame?

4

I pictured myself theoretically having to break this grim news to Karen Dalton. *Sorry, Karen, your brother's been done in at the hands, tentacles, claws—insert nefarious appendages this space—or whatever else you might imagine, of an alien.* Yeah, she wasn't going to like that.

But let's not get ahead of ourselves. This investigation had a long way to go before I'd admit defeat. Or that Ken Dalton was dead.

I twiddled my fingers some more. Stared at Sylvia's cat. Meowed at Sylvia's cat. Not loudly but enough.

Enough to know that I was going bonkers.

Oh-oh!

I was getting high. Crap. Of course, I should have known. Should have known better too than to gorge on six licorice twists in the space of mere minutes. Black licorice is to me what catnip is to Sylvia's cat—a gateway drug!

What can I say? Something about the molecular makeup of black licorice that binds with a neuronal receptor in my midbrain that makes me do my happy dance. Makes me not be able to not do my happy dance. I know, that's a lot of negatives and double negatives—and all for something that makes me so absolutely, positively happy.

My vision gets all fuzzy too, like my rods and cones start filtering light through sharp tiny prisms that turn the light beams into many-colored magic only I can see.

"Who are you?" a stern voice demanded. "Why are you seated at my desk?"

"S-Sylvia?"

"Who are you? What are you doing seated at my desk, young man?"

I fought to keep my eyes fixed on the far-side-of-middle-age woman confronting me. Apparently, Sylvia possessed a fourth sweater because she was wearing a green cotton-blend button-fronted sweater now. Her hands were thrust into its deep pockets. Was she packing heat?

Her hair squirmed as if alive and appeared to be composed of salsa dancing purple-and-orange snakes. This I knew to be an artifact of my licorice-based high. "Oh, hey, Sylvia. Boss sent me to check on the status of that report." I may not know much about the workings of an office but I know enough to know that there is always a boss. And there is always a report due.

"Report? What report?" Sylvia's hands dropped to her sides. She wore a long tan skirt that fell to her ankles. Due to my weakened—or heightened, depending on your point of view—condition, that pleated skirt appeared to be cascading like Niagara Falls. Why weren't her feet getting wet?

Sylvia interrupted my hallucinogenic—in the best way—thoughts. "Oh, right. I've been compiling the sick leave data all morning. You can tell Mister Etsitty that I should be able to send it up before the day is out." Sylvia sounded a bit put out. Her Mr. Etsitty must be a bit of a harsh taskmaster.

I stood. "He'll be happy to hear that, as am I." Relief flooded her face as I sidestepped around her and made my escape.

And ran into Karen Dalton coming up the hallway near a pair of restrooms split by a water fountain holding an out-of-order sign.

"Karen? What are you doing here?"

"Same as you, I suppose. Looking for clues."

"That is supposed to be my job. That is why you hired me. And I told you I would be checking out Ken's previous place of employment."

"I know. Sorry." Karen clutched a cardboard box to her chest.

"Never, never apologize. It's a sign of weakness." I was

paraphrasing John Wayne who said something along those lines in Tie A Yellow Ribbon, a marvelous film of the Old West. A film whose only flaw is that it was shot in Technicolor rather than glorious black and white.

"Sorry."

I shook my head. "What's in the box?"

"Some personal belongings of Ken's. Someone new is ensconced in his old office."

Bummer, I'd find no clues there. I'd considered it a longshot anyway.

"The department secretary said he forgot a few things when he left. Been sitting in a storage closet gathering dust all this time. Told me I should give them to Ken next time I see him. I didn't tell her I had no idea if or when that might be."

Tears threatened so I changed the subject. "Anything of interest in the box?"

Her eyes peered inside. "Not particularly. Couple of mugs, a water bottle, a pen I gave him one Christmas. An ET paperweight," she lifted it from the box and held it out.

"Ew, hideous."

"Yeah." She dropped the monstrosity back in the box from whence it had emerged. "Some notebooks, some—"

"Any licorice?"

"Huh?"

"Never mind. Not important." I really, really should know better. "I'll take the notebooks. You never know, they may hold some clues. You can keep or dispose of the rest."

"Fine." She handed me the thick notebooks. I'd peruse them back home. "Did you discover anything?"

I looked over one shoulder then the other. The effects of the licorice seemed to be dwindling. "A thing or two. Nothing I care to discuss here. Who knows who might be listening." I arched my brow meaningfully.

"Right." Karen glanced at the corner where the wall met the ceiling. I noticed a tiny camera up there. "We could go somewhere for coffee."

"Coffee and licorice don't mix."

"Huh?"

"Not important. You mentioned that your brother sold his condo."

"That's right." She jostled the box in her arms.

"You also mentioned that he stored his vehicle? Here in town?"

"Yeah, not far from his old condo. A private storage facility. Why?"

"Since we're here in the area, it wouldn't hurt to have a peek inside."

"You think his car might hold some clues?"

"Maybe." I was also thinking that it might hold his rotting corpse—I'd seen it in a film once—but no point in telling Karen that. She'd probably only get upset. "Might you have a key to this vehicle?"

"I think so. Here." She thrust the box into my arms and rummaged in her pockets. She came up with a keyring bearing half a dozen keys and fobs, and a knitted string of pink yarn about four inches in length. "Yep. Here it is. This one." She gripped the fob between thumb and index finger.

"Marvelous. And have you a vehicle of your own that will take us to his car?"

"I own a Vespa."

"A scooter thing?"

"Yep. But I Ubered here."

"Then let's Uber there."

And we did.

Arriving in a warehouse district not far from where Karen Dalton indicated her brother's condo was situated, we entered the storage facility yard. We strolled down a row of metal accordion doors until she came to a halt. "I think it's this one." She paused, looked down the long row, counted the doors aloud and bobbed her head. "Yep, it's this one." She dropped her cardboard box o'Ken stuff to the concrete and fiddled until finding the key to the storage locker door.

She slipped the lock from the latch and pulled. "Give me a hand?"

I grunted and gripped the lower edge of the door which she'd managed to budge a few inches in the right direction. Up. The door fought us. "Probably hasn't been opened in years." Unless a murderer had opened it recently and locked Ken inside for an eternal car ride. This was beginning to seem less likely given the door's resistance.

I gave it another shove, careful not to overdo it. Karen is not tall, perhaps five foot eight. She's still got me beat. I'm five-six, five-seven when the moon is at perigee—that damn rock hanging in outer space affects me like it does the tide.

I whistled.

"Nice, huh?"

"No. What a heap."

"Are you serious?" Karen Dalton replied. "This is a first generation Tesla Roadster. Ken loves this thing. It's his baby. He was one of the first adopters. This electric car was a big splurge for him. He made a big deal about it. Joked that he spent more time fooling with this car than he'd spent on dates."

"Hmm." I stroked my chin. Her comment said something about her brother. I wasn't sure what but it was something.

"Guess that's why he keeps paying to store it all this time rather than sell it. Electric cars are the future, you know?"

"The future? You really think so? The same crummy little batteries that you stick in your TV remote control? That's what you think is your world's future?"

"Huh?"

"Consider this. The car weighs maybe thirteen hundred kilos and the battery pack probably accounts for thirty percent of that weight. Do the math." I planted my hands on my hips. "Going EV, it's gonna take a battleship's worth of batteries to send a man to the moon again. And then some."

"I don't think that's what—"

"And don't get me started on the environmental impact of mining lithium and cobalt. Air pollution, water pollution, groundwater pollution, soil erosion. Do you know it can take upward of one hundred thousand gallons of water to extract enough lithium to produce one battery?"

"No, I never knew that. Are you s—?"

"Have you considered the vast quantities of the diesel fuel those machines doing the extraction drink on a daily basis? And, do you know these machines must move upwards of half a million tons of earth just to scrape together enough lithium for one battery?"

"N-No, I didn't know that either but—"

"What's all that dirty activity doing to your precious environment? Your wildlife? I've read seventy percent more carbon dioxide is emitted producing a battery versus an automobile. Shouldn't you all just ride bicycles?"

"I'm sure there must be...I mean, everybody says—"

"Of course, everybody says. That's the answer to every ugly truth. Pardon me." I gently moved her aside and threw open the driver side door and peeked inside. A stale blast of warm air assailed my nostrils. The car, black on black, was remarkably clean. Looked freshly vacuumed. I scrounged around the glove box. Nothing but a registration form and an expired insurance card.

I sat in the driver's seat and gripped the steering wheel, gave it a jiggle and grinned. "Hop in, Karen Dalton."

Karen smiled. "Growing on you?"

"You might say that." Although the Tesla had several marks against it, like a cramped interior and the lack of a rear seat, the car did have possibilities. Such as no longer having to pay for bus fare. "And stealth black. What's not to love? Well, except for that whole battery thing." I was relieved, for Karen Dalton's sake, not to see the rotting corpse of Ken Dalton plopped behind the steering wheel.

Karen's eyes snapped from the Roadster to me.

"Let's see if she starts," I said. And it did. "Remarkable. And you say neither you nor your brother have driven this vehicle since he left JPL?"

"Nope."

"Interesting. Hop in."

"Are you sure?" Karen wavered. "I'm not certain Ken would like you driving his car. He *never* let me drive it."

"Your brother is either dead, murdered by an alien as you say he told you, or—" Her mouth flew open and I threw up a hand to stop her. "Or he will be happy when he learns we have used his fine vehicle in our pursuit of finding him. Besides, vehicles need exercise. They're like dogs that way."

"Like dogs?" Karen looked hurt then looked angry. "What the hell does that mean? And you're not exactly Mister Sensitivity, are you?"

"Sorry."

"You said never to say sorry."

"Tell that to John Wayne."

"I'm going to tell it to Ken."

"That's the spirit," I said as Karen Dalton, cardboard box and all, squeezed into the passenger seat. "Let's not surrender hope that your brother is alive."

I heard a throaty growl.

5

Karen Dalton, butt on the corner of my desk, left leg kicking and right leg swinging, spoke, "Find anything?"

I leaned back in my seat, rubbed my eyes. "In the first place, I don't know how you do that." Light was fading. I reached over and flicked on the desk lamp.

"Do what?"

It was late. Dark had dropped on the Toy District and all Los Angeles. A soft yellow light glowed in the accountant's office across the street. The accountant's chin sagged against his flabby chest. I caught a glint of drool at the corner of his lips. An accountant's life is not an easy one.

"Move your legs like that. One leg going this way, one leg going that. Don't think I could do it." I stretched out my legs and gave it a shot. I knocked over the wastebasket.

Karen snorted.

I scowled and let the trash stay on the floor. It was trash after all. I picked up the bourbon and filled my IHOP mug. My stomach growled and I wished I had some chocolate chip pancakes to go with the drink. When was the last time I'd eaten? I mean, except that cigarette butt earlier, of course.

I savored the bourbon, swished it around my teeth. Better than any mouthwash you can buy. Ken Dalton's notebooks spread across my desk. My stomach again cried for attention. "Buy you a burger?"

"Plant-based?"

"Not plant, burger. B-u-r—"

"No, No. I mean is it a plant-based burger? I'm trying to be more plant-based. Go vegan."

"Be more plant-based? Is that even possible? You are meat, after all." I squinted, took a closer look at Karen Dalton. "Aren't you?"

Karen Dalton hopped off my desk and backed to the office door. "What's that supposed to mean?"

"Do you think an animal wouldn't eat you given half a chance?" I rubbed my hands together. I was on a roll. "Including your precious kitty?"

"What makes you think I have a—" Karen Dalton threw her hands in the air. "No. I give up. You're impossible. I don't know why I bother to—"

"There, there, Karen Dalton. Don't get your bananas in a bunch. I mean no offense. *I'm* not going to eat you." She was giving me a look that told me she thought otherwise. "Bourbon?" I extended the open bottle, a clear gesture showing that my intentions were good. I don't offer my best bourbon to just anyone, let alone someone I may be contemplating eating.

"No, thank you."

"Look, go Dodgers, I can understand, but go vegan? Why?" I love baseball. Name another sport where spectator beer guzzling is considered part of the game, de rigeur even.

"It's healthier. And kinder to animals."

"Aren't people animals?"

"Well, sure, I guess you could say that." She stood behind the Walmart chair, kneading her forehead between her thumb and index finger. Was she using the chair as a shield? It was sturdy but not that sturdy. Hardly, here we are in the Roman Coliseum and, oh no!, here comes that ugly, armed gladiator material.

"I think science says that."

"Okay," Karen Dalton admitted.

"And don't animals eat other animals? Is that not what they are, you might say, designed to do?"

"What's your point?" Karen Dalton snatched the bourbon off my desk by its neck.

I gasped as she helped herself to the Flying Saucer Diner

mug I kept in a place of honor on my bookshelf. Picked it up in Roswell, New Mexico many moons ago. That mug was a collectible! And the diner itself... Coffee out of this world. The rhubarb pie was excellent too.

"Careful with that!" I begged.

She fell into the chair with her drink and drank. "Five hundred a day and what do I get for it? So far today? Nothing."

Geez, was the woman drunk already? What a mouth on this one.

"You didn't even ask me for a picture of Ken. Aren't you supposed to do that? Isn't that what all detectives are supposed to do?" She slouched sideways in the chair and crossed her legs. The mug safely nestled between her breasts. Yes, she had breasts. Two of them and they were not inconsequential.

"As a matter of fact, Karen Dalton, I've learned quite a bit. I'd say your money is being well spent."

"Such as?"

"Such as? First, to answer your question, I saw several digital photos of your brother at JPL." I tapped the side of my skull. Not too hard, I'm sensitive there. "I know exactly what he looks like."

"Whoop-de-do. Big deal."

I gave her a frown. "You don't know much about electric vehicles, do you?"

She returned the frown. "I know you forced me to practically steal my brother's."

"Ha-ha. Very funny. EV batteries, if not charged, probably lose something in the region of two to three percent of their stored energy per month. Per month," I repeated for emphasis. "Multiply that times thirty-six months give or take and your brother's batteries should have been flatter than—" I cast about for an analogy and the only thing that caught my eye was the IHOP mug. "A pancake."

"That analogy makes no sense."

I shrugged. "It's all I could come up with by way of—"

Karen Dalton sat up in the chair. "No, that the batteries

weren't dead. The car should never have started."

"But it did. And I saw no charger cable attached to the vehicle."

"Weird." She drank more Heaven's Gate. This woman was running quite a tab. I reached for the bottle but she beat me to it and poured herself a refill.

I glared.

"What does it mean?"

"Not sure." I didn't have enough data to make a guess, let alone come to any solid conclusion. I flipped open one of Ken Dalton's cloth-covered old JPL notebooks. "Pages and pages are missing from his notebooks also. If you look closely, you can see where the pages have been carefully removed. Cut out with a razor, I'd surmise." I showed her.

"I hadn't noticed."

"Don't knock yourself. I have an eye for these things. There are vague diary entries concerning his work. Nothing helpful, I'm afraid. Some of this reads like fan fiction, fan *science* fiction. The question is: who removed the missing pages and what did they contain?"

"Yeah," she said slowly. "You know, Ken always was a science geek, his phrase not mine. And loved all things science fiction."

"Aliens?"

"Sure, he loved all that stuff too. Aliens, time travel—"

I snorted. The things some people believe. Time is an observer-specific phenomenon. I might consider temporal elasticity, at best. I lit a Camel, having succumbed to purchasing a fresh pack at blackmail prices downstairs before we'd come upstairs.

Karen Dalton yawned. "Now what?"

I made a pained and ugly faced. "I hate saying this." But with nothing to be found in town at his old haunts, that meant driving to...

"What?"

"I'll have to go to..."

Karen Dalton's brow rose. "To?"

"New Mexico…"

"Great, let's go!"

"No, no." I waved my hands at her. "Not us, me." Not that I wanted to go.

She narrowed her eyes at me. "Why not me?"

"Must I remind you that you are paying for my services? I work alone." I puffed furiously on my cigarette. It glowed bright red and orange like a hot-burning rocket ship fuel tank. "I'll be taking your brother's Tesla, of course."

"Why?'

"I do not have a personal vehicle, remember?"

"No, why drive? That's hundreds of miles. It'd be faster and simpler to fly."

"I prefer land-based transportation."

Karen Dalton smirked. "You're afraid of flying."

"No, I'm not." Sounds funny, I know, but I have a fear of flying.

"Have you ever tried taking something?"

"Told you. I took a plane."

"No, I mean something to help you on the plane."

"Oh, sure. I got drunk once. That didn't work out so well for me."

"What happened?"

"I told you, I got drunk. Then they stopped serving me. They said I was drunk."

"No shit." She looked at me in wide-eyed wonder.

"Then they kicked me off the plane."

"Kicked you off?"

"Landed in a tiny county airport in the heart of peach country and booted me right out. Couldn't fly out again until the next day. You ever spend the night in Georgia? Surrounded by nothing but stinking peaches!? I thought I was going to die!" I shivered at the horrible memory.

Karen Dalton stood. "Fine." She slammed my flying saucer mug on the desk with a little more force than I felt necessary.

29

"But I'm driving."

"No, no. I travel alone."

"Not in Ken's car, you don't. I'm responsible for it. See you first thing in the morning, Mister Turner."

With that she was gone.

I chewed my cigarette butt and washed it down with the remains of my bourbon, contemplating Karen and Ken Dalton. Trying hard, trying desperately not to contemplate New Mexico.

Ken Dalton. Missing.

Astrobiologist!

I'd dug around on the Internet. Karen Dalton's brother didn't have much presence there. She'd told me he wasn't into social media. Karen was. I found all sorts of silliness featuring her. Boy did that girl like to Instagram!

Personally, I don't do social media. Seems to be about the most serious social disease a person could catch. And I confess, I am a bit of a germaphobe. You'd be too if you were in my position. This world's full of germs! Sometimes I felt like an Aztec in the midst of the Spanish Conquest. And once infected, it would be almost impossible to recover. Social media disease is like a virus that lives inside you forever. I've got enough of those little buggers already.

I gave up, undressed, and crawled into bed. Killed the light. I pulled the bedcovers to my chin.

New Mexico, Roswell, aliens, crashes, abductions, Los Alamos, Nevada's Area 51, Groom Lake, Wright-Patterson Air Force Base in godforsaken Ohio...

I woke up in a hot sweat. No need to panic. No need to panic. Nope, no need to panic.

But the Southwest? New Mexico? Was I really going back there?

Voluntarily?

6

"Explain to me," Karen Dalton said with what I detected to be more than a touch of disdain. "Why did we come here?" Hands planted on hips, she squinted at the broad and empty expanse of sun-soaked desert. "A bunch of cheesy tourist shops in some nothing desert town?"

"Nothing desert town? I'm not sure the denizens of Roswell would be happy to hear you characterize them thus."

"Okay, goofy then. Goofy desert town. Alien souvenirs and statues everywhere. Not even the locals take themselves seriously." She stuck her hand over her forehead in a failed effort to lessen the sun's impact. A ball of elemental fire approximately 93 million miles away and it'd burn your nose as soon as look at you.

"Why are we here?" she couldn't help grumbling again, toes kicking hot sand.

"I thought it was important to see."

"Not to me."

I ignored the remark. Besides, I felt it important to begin at the beginning, even if she didn't understand what that meant. "And I, Karen Dalton, do take this town very seriously."

"Whatever. You know, I'm missing work for this. I had to call in sick. My boss was pissed."

"Coming along was your idea. Suffer the consequences." I turned slowly, memories flooding back. Storms, bright lights, explosions, flashes, people running everywhere. Weapons pointing everywhere. Cages and chains. Drugs. Threats. Torture.

"I'm suffering you," she mumbled.

I continued to ignore her snarky remarks.

Nearly forgotten fear oozed from every pore.

"And five hundred dollars a day." She crossed her arms over her chest. "I am not paying for this. My brother was never even in Roswell, at least not to my knowledge. I told you Los Alamos."

"Fine." Cheapskate. "But I needed a new mug." And the shipping and handling charges nearly doubled the cost of one. Who'd want to pay that?

Karen snarled at me, giving it her best impersonation of a feral Doberman. "Are you going to start that again?"

"You cracked my mug."

Karen got in my face. "For the last time, I. Did. Not. Crack..." Pause. Point finger in my face. "YOUR FUCKING MUG!"

"I can see we're going to disagree on the matter." Nonetheless, her actions had resulted in a crack on the underside of my collectible Flying Saucer Diner mug, hair-thin, I admit, but a crack is a crack is a crack. Good thing the mugs hadn't been discontinued.

"So now what?" Karen wanted to know. Dressed in a white-linen cami and snug jeans, she'd twisted her long locks into a knot. She insisted on wearing brown leather sandals rather than a pair of sensible shoes or hiking boots. I often wonder what it is with the female of the species that makes them want to torture their feet to the extent they do. Unprotected toes, five-inch heels that make them appear to be falling on their faces. Why?

Being the smarter of the two of us, I'd dressed in khakis and a polo shirt, both boasting SPF 50 protection. And the I ♥ ALIENS snapback hat I'd picked up at Jupiter Jems, a Roswell souvenir shop and self-serve ice cream parlor, fit my head perfectly. I wasn't the one having to use an appendage as a sunshade. How primitive.

"To the Tesla," I answered. We'd parked the Roadster a couple hundred yards back along the side of the deserted highway.

Karen plodded to the car, feet slugging through the hot sand. "Ow! Should've commandeered a fucking camel not a Tesla!"

I felt no sympathy. Besides, I was still a little miffed that she'd thrown a hissy fit when I'd suggested buying the *I Brake For Aliens* bumper sticker and affixing it to the Tesla's rear bumper.

On the other hand, I could have used a camel but not the kind Karen meant.

I floored the accelerator, happy to see Roswell, New Mexico, and environs in the rearview mirror. That place gives me the heebie-jeebies...

And nightmares.

7

The Los Alamos National Laboratory might be world-famous but I'd have known it anyway. Learned about it the hard way. Sitting at approximately 7300 feet above sea level, on the Parjita Plateau of the rugged Jemez Mountains west of Santa Fe, Los Alamos was considered home to the atomic bomb. In some sense, and not a good one, it felt like my home too. And this wasn't a homecoming I was looking forward to.

We parked in the sprawling visitor lot of the main campus and proceeded to the entrance. The LANL serves as a world-class science research and development facility. Hundreds of scientists, support staff and a steady stream of visitors run around the various LANL locations day and night on a regular basis. In addition, the LANL is home to nearly two thousand student interns, from high schoolers to post-docs. So getting in wasn't hard.

Getting answers was. We were shuffled one office to the next to the next. In each, we were told clearly and, at the third, rather forcefully, that Kenneth Dalton did not work there, had never worked there and, as far as they were concerned, had never, EVER, existed.

"Well, that was helpful," Karen Dalton moped as we returned to the Tesla.

"I recognize you are being facetious, Karen Dalton," I replied, plopping down on the blistering hot seat. Black leather interiors are a poor choice in a hot, sunny climate, which Los Alamos could be at times. "But, contrary to what you may be thinking, we have learned much." I headed us down the mountain.

"Like?"

"Like that your brother not only exists, but that his existence and, by extension, his work and whereabouts are highly important to the people of the lab."

"Ah." Karen Dalton grinned. "You think they doth protest too much?"

"Precisely."

"So now what? This is starting to get expensive, motels, food, lodging."

"Cheer up," I countered. I thumped the steering wheel with both hands. "At least you're not having to shell out for dinosaur-rot-based fuel."

"No but I am paying your fee."

"Progress," I chose to reply. "We are making progress."

"Could've fooled me. Cuz I'm not seeing any."

"Sometimes," I said, hurtling past a slow-moving convoy of drab olive military vehicles, "it's the progress you can't see that is the most revealing."

Karen Dalton banged her head against the window. Not too hard. I discerned no cracks in the glass.

"We'll check out the county's public records. One thing I've learned is that most all private citizens' transactions, personal data, and doings are publicly available." There's something weird about that. "Usually at no charge, too. That should make you happy."

Parking at the county office was free too. As a bonus, they had two EV charging stations. I plugged the Tesla in. You never knew when you'd come across another. Especially out here in the southwest, an expanse so great and empty you could measure it in lightyears. "Be simpler if we could buy cheap replacement batteries at Walmart," I commented, watching the device kick into action. "Or one of those dollar stores. There's always one of those around."

"Why don't you just break down and buy a car? A gas guzzler. And stop your complaining?"

"Ha-ha. You are quite the wit. Let's apply some of that

mental energy to sleuthing, shall we?" I palmed open the door and she slipped past me.

"What are we looking for?" Karen Dalton asked as we settled ourselves at a free computer in the lobby of the downtown Los Alamos County Assessor's office.

"For any property your brother may have owned in town. He had to live somewhere." I left unsaid that he might have been living in quarters on the LANL campus, someplace unlisted. Such places without a doubt existed.

I dug around in the computer records. "One Dalton but not a Kenneth. Muriel?" I looked at Karen hopefully. "Any relation? Muriel Dalton, age sixty-seven?"

Karen rubbed her eyes. "Nope, none I know of." She yawned. "Maybe we should quit. Wait for Ken to call. I'm sure there's a good explanation for everything."

I planted my hand on Karen Dalton's shoulder. "If we quit now," I whispered, others lurked, "we may never learn what happened to your brother. You may never see or hear from him again. Is that what you want?"

"Of course not!"

"Shh!" I admonished. "Then we must continue. The journey ends when we find Ken. Dead or alive."

"Must you? Again? Dead or alive!? Do you have to keep saying that?"

"Okay, maybe I shouldn't have said that last part." Not aloud anyway. I pulled her to her feet. "We'll get something to eat. Plant-based, if you like." Anything to make the woman feel better. I can be sensitive. "Then we'll check into a motel for the night."

"And tomorrow?" She shuffled along beside me to the exit.

"Tomorrow," I said, still keeping my voice low. I had no idea who or what might be listening and was taking no chances. "We head for Area Fifty-One in Nevada."

Karen Dalton swiveled her eyes at me. "You're joking?"

"Oh, Karen Dalton," I said with a sad shake of the noggin. "Never, never joke about Area Fifty-One."

I found a motel advertising vacancy on the outskirts of town. Actually, it was more a hybrid motel and bed and breakfast. One look inside at my room for the night and I wanted to vomit up my breakfast—and I hadn't even had my plant-based dinner yet!

After checking us in, I located the perfect spot for our plant-based dining, a quirky spot downtown called the Bathtub Ring Brew Pub.

"This is your idea of trying to appease me?" Karen's eyes virtually spat contempt as she took the joint in. "What, they brew their beer in a bathtub? Gross."

"Trust me. I perused the menu online. Small but serviceable. Plenty of beer on tap—plant-based by its very nature, I might add—and a reasonable selection of meat and meatless choices."

"Okay but you're paying."

"I insist on it." Crap. Now I was going to have to shell out good money for this so-called food.

We stepped inside. It was dark, made darker by the low brown-stained pine ceiling and plank walls. All six tables were occupied. The bar was filling up too. A ballgame played on the widescreen TV. All eyes were glued to the Diamondbacks versus White Sox game. Inning five and all tied up two-two. The White Sox made me think of beer, Falstaff, to be precise. I muffled a sigh. How I missed Falstaff beer, a brew once synonymous with the game. What was that slogan on their label? *The Choicest Product of the Brewer's Art.* How succinct. How elegant. How true! And a mere two bucks a case or so back in the day. And those were the days.

Karen scooped a folded paper menu of copy-machine quality off a round two-top table near the front window that also offered napkins and flatware. And two dead houseflies. She scanned the selections, cursed some, and wadded up the menu. "Let's get this over with. Where do we order?"

"At the counter, I would say." I led her to the bar. A man, with a dirty white apron tied round his waist, appeared to take our order. He communicated our wants to a woman visible through a small opening in the wall. A few minutes of waiting and our food was shoved out the same opening and into our hands.

During that time, no one had entered the pub and no one had departed. With no other option open to us, we carried our dishes and glasses to the empty billiards table near the juke box towards the rear and pulled up a bench.

No one complained.

I dropped my cap on the beer-stained felt. Still no complaints. I was beginning to like this place. I glanced wistfully over my shoulder at the television, wishing I was sitting in the stadium behind third base rather than at this billiard table seated metaphorically behind the eight ball. Wishing I had a Falstaff in hand.

In the corner next to the hall leading to the Stallions and Fillies, a man in droopy jeans—red underwear showing like a flag of pride—whacked noisily away at a light-flashing Space Invaders pinball machine. From the sound of his cursing, I guessed the aliens were winning. Go aliens!

"Tell me about this Area Fifty-One." Karen Dalton stirred a french fry around in her light beer, chewed the fry, swallowed the fry, then chugged some french-fry-infused beer.

I watched in awe. Such desecration! I mean, who does that to beer? Nonetheless, in an effort to blend in, be like the locals, I followed suit. I dipped a french-fry in my dark ale, and swished it around. Then I upped the ante by swishing my half-pound burger, smothered in cheese and onions and mayonnaise, around in my glass.

It was Karen Dalton's turn to watch in awe. And I must say she was very good at it. The taste, however, when I sank my teeth into my rare burger was not so good. "Lesson learned." I dropped the soggy burger down on my plate.

"Area Fifty-One?"

"Right. What isn't there to tell about Area Fifty-One?" I began. "It's everything you've read about and more." The only thing worse than Area 51 was Area 52. But there was no point telling that to Karen Dalton. She'd only worry more. Besides, the knowledge could put her life at risk.

"I haven't read anything about Area Fifty-One. I've only heard and seen vague mentions in TV and movies. Told you, I'm not much of a sci-fi fan. And I don't believe in fairytales."

"Well, your brother was, is, a scientist." Whew, I'd slipped there and might have pissed her off yet again. Good thing she'd missed my little faux pas. I continued quickly lest she pick up on my words a beat late. "And I'd say he's mixed up in some very classified, very high-tech sci-fi worthy enterprise. Let's keep our voices down," I suggested. "Los Alamos has ears, Area Fifty-One too." And it might just have Ken Dalton too, if my hunch was correct.

"They'd have to have ears the size of Dumbo the elephant's," scoffed Karen Dalton. "Besides, who can hear anything over the roar of the TVs?"

"Let's not take unnecessary risks."

"Fine," Karen Dalton replied. "What makes you think we'll find my brother at this Area Fifty-One? He never mentioned the place. Not even once."

"I am not surprised. It's not the sort of thing one brags about." I settled back in my seat with my half-empty glass. "Believe you me, all roads lead to Area Fifty-One."

"And you really think that's where we'll find Ken?" Karen Dalton blew a shot of air out her nostrils and bit into her meatless burger. "And whatever aliens are trying to murder him?"

"Yes. Besides, what other choice do we have?"

"None." She pulled a few more salty fries into her mouth and chewed.

"Excellent."

"So," she said after a moment of silence that I was enjoying immensely. All these days on the road together. Karen Dalton could talk up a storm. Any minute of silence, however brief, was a blessing. She chewed her lip. "So," she repeated.

"Yes?"

"You don't actually believe in aliens, do you? I mean, the whole thing's crazy."

"Ken seems to believe. Are you saying you think your brother is crazy?" I nibbled at my burger, avoiding the soggy bun and focusing my attention on the meat. I was dying for a cigarette and pined for the days when smoking was allowed in such fine establishments as the Bathtub Ring.

"No, not at all." Karen Dalton frowned and pushed the remains of her burger around on her plate. I was paying for that atrocity and she'd barely eaten half. How annoying. "I just don't buy this whole aliens thing. I don't know what was going through Ken's head when he called me. I don't get it. I really don't get it." She grabbed the orange number five billiard ball and hurled it down the green baize pool table surface. The ball bounced off two rails, crashed into the red-striped number eleven. Both bounced into opposing corners pockets. Clack-clack. "You think he might've been on drugs?"

"Does he have a history of this?"

"No, not at all."

"Right. Then," I said, choosing my words carefully, "let us assume that your brother was in full possession of his faculties when he called you in distress." Or very, very drunk.

"Okay."

"Then we must keep our minds open. We must accept, at the very least, the premise that Ken believed he was being targeted for death by aliens."

Karen Dalton shook her head. When it stopped shaking, she aimed her glass at her mouth and quickly guzzled its contents.

"Shall I order us a pitcher?"

"So fucking crazy."

"Uh-uh." Was Karen Dalton suffering a breakdown? "Open minds, remember?" I mean, what the hell, I'd just said that! "We must prepare ourselves for what is to come and what we may uncover. We may see and hear things that are new to us.

Strange things. Extraordinary things. Open your mind, Karen Dalton." I gently tapped my finger against her throbbing temple. That pulsating blue vein of hers worried me. Was it about to burst through her skin? Was she in need of a doctor? Emergency medical care?

How would Karen Dalton react were she to learn other... things?

"I'll try." She slipped the black plastic triangle used to rack up the billiard balls over her arm and twirled it round her elbow.

I stretched my hands out across the pool table and angled closer to Karen Dalton. "Good. That's all I ask. I must warn you however, we—"

Karen Dalton jumped to her feet. The triangle flew through the air like a black UFO and struck a bar patron in the back of his bushy head before clattering to the floor. Humans 1, Aliens 0. He did not appear appreciative. "Hey! That's Ken!"

I jumped to my feet. Jumping to one's feet can be contagious. Had we found brother Ken? Was our case about to solve itself? Was I about to be unemployed?

I followed the imaginary line of her trembling finger. That line led to the bartop, across the bar, through the bartender, and landed on a rather poor photograph of Ken Dalton thumb-tacked to a corkboard behind the cash register, along with nearly a dozen other scruffy and boozed faces. "Now, now. Remain calm."

"Right." Karen knocked me down and raced to the bar. So much for keeping a low profile—although my profile, technically, was quite low at the moment, considering that I was sprawled across the floor. I could only hope we weren't being watched by the wrong people. I especially hoped that I was not under surveillance. That would spell an end to everything.

I picked myself up and rushed to the bar where Karen Dalton was busy making a spectacle of herself. Nobody was watching the ballgame now. All eyes were on my agitated companion. Karen slapped her hands down on the counter. "What's that?" she demanded.

The poor barkeep, a skinny fellow wearing baggy jeans, a

cowboy shirt and bolo tie, and the aforementioned apron, gaped. "What's what, lady?"

I caught a whiff of cologne. Better still, I caught a whiff of tobacco. Even a whiff is better than nothing when you're dying for a smoke. I inhaled deeply. Marlboro. No matter, it would do in a pinch.

"That. That photograph!"

"That?" He tossed his red bar towel over his shoulder and dared a step in the direction of the electronic cash register. "Just a bunch of pictures. Freeloaders. Troublemakers, you know. You cause a ruckus or try to skip out on your tab, your picture goes up." He looked pained. "That's where the boss says to keep them. So's whoever's on duty knows not to let them in the pub."

Karen Dalton narrowed her eyes at him. "Why is my brother's picture on your board? He's no freeloader and he sure as hell is no troublemaker!"

The barkeep barked out a laugh. "You kidding me, lady? That brother of yours nearly wrecked the joint. Must've caused a thousand bucks' worth of damage." He slapped the damp towel against the bar. "Should've seen him. Drank up a storm and then started hollering that the aliens were out to get him!" He threw up his hands and wriggled his fingers wildly. "Woo-woo. Aliens!"

The patrons perched on the barstools guffawed.

Karen Dalton balled up her hand and pulled back her elbow. I grabbed her fist. "Now, now." Turning to the bartender, who looked more surprised than scared, I inquired, "When exactly did this dramatic incident occur? Can you tell me?" Karen Dalton snarled at me.

"Can I tell you? Sure, I can tell you." He came closer. "But it's going to cost you." He extended his right hand, calloused palm up.

Karen Dalton leapt at him. "Why, you lousy—you think I'm going to pay you to—"

I pulled her back and gave her my hardest stare. "Pay the man."

"Pay the man?"

"Pay the man." I turned to the bartender. "How much?"

"Twenty."

"Twenty!?" shrieked Karen Dalton.

"Make that forty," the bartender said with a smirk.

Huffing and puffing, Karen Dalton extracted a twenty and two tens from her bag and dropped them in a wet ring on the bar. "Now, answer the man's question."

"He came in here maybe two weeks ago." His hands shot out rattlesnake quick and the money disappeared down the front pocket of his jeans. "It was a Friday. I know because I was working. Yeah, two weeks ago Friday."

"And he hasn't been in since?" I asked.

"Nope, hasn't been in since. Like I told you, he's not allowed. He comes in again, we throw his ass out. You tell him that."

Karen threw up her fist again and he inched backward.

"Did he leave alone?" I pressed. "With friends?"

The bartender broke into a toothy grin. "He didn't leave alone but I wouldn't say he exactly left with friends."

"Who then?"

"Some guys in dark suits."

"Guys in dark suits?" A twinge walked up my spine.

"Yeah, the kind you don't want to mess with." He made a show of zipping his lip. "And that's all I'm going to say about the matter."

Karen and I bumped shoulders on our walk out to the Tesla. "Guys in suits," she spat. "What do you make of that?"

"He said suits, not little green men." I opened her door for her. "Not aliens, that's for sure." What I did not tell her was that guys in suits could be much, much scarier.

8

I waited impatiently until Karen Dalton was safely ensconced in her first-floor motel room and hopefully sound asleep before making my next move. That move was my Johnny Cash move. Yep, it was time to go all Man In Black.

In my tiny adjoining room, I threw my suitcase down on the bed, unsnapped the latch, and changed into my black trousers and threw on my black leather bomber jacket. Sadly, the snazzy and cheeky I ♥ ALIENS snapback hat would have to remain behind. A bit too blingy, with its red lettering and rhinestone heart, for this covert night maneuver. No accessorizing for me.

Still, who was I kidding? Not me. The outfit probably wouldn't do a damn thing towards keeping me from being discovered—the enemy was too good for that, too sophisticated —but it was the thought that counted. Besides, the outfit made me feel good. Made me look good too, so I noticed in the mirror over the washbasin.

There's a whole other side to the LANL that regular folk, those without the highest of high security clearance, never see. A whole *underside.*

That's the side I was going to. I waited until it was good and dark, midnight dark, before stealing out in the Tesla, grateful that the vehicle ran near silently, seeing that it was parked right outside Karen Dalton's motel-room window. Poor but troublesome woman. Things would've been so much easier for both of us, and safer for her, if she'd stayed in LA like I'd wanted her to.

I stopped at the convenience store round the corner to top

up the tank. Not the Tesla's, it didn't have one. Besides, I'd helped myself to some Tesla juice back at the county public records office. No, it was my tank that needed topping up. I'd be climbing up into the cold mountains to a location you wouldn't find on any travel maps. I required a certain degree of fortification for this trip. I laid out some cash for a carton of Camels and a quart of the fine establishment's lowest price bourbon.

Back in the Roadster, I took an invigorating swallow, took a second to be sure, then snugged the bottle up under the passenger seat where I hoped it wouldn't come to any harm. I ripped open a pack of Camels and lit up. Relished the cloud of death as it wrapped its arms around me.

I inhaled deeply. Inhaled deeply again. Puffed and puffed. I held the cigarette tightly in my lips. Fortified, I hit the road. Ready for action. Ready for Los Alamos.

The question, the big unknown, was whether or not Los Alamos was ready for me. If the answer was yes, I could be in Big Trouble.

If memory served, and it did, I'd find a small unmarked gravel road skirting a postage-stamp-sized mesa. Remember postage stamps? I remembered a whimsical 1965 run of Hungarian space exploration stamps that were simply magical. Childish and fanciful, of course, but was there anything human that was not?

The Tesla handled the road with more confidence than me. With no streetlights and fearful of running the Tesla's headlights, I had only the million stars above to guide me. Where was the moon when you needed it?

According to the Tesla's primitive instrument cluster, the outside temperature had plummeted into the forties. I only hoped the car and me, its sole occupant, didn't plummet down the side of the mountain. This was not guardrail country and I had no experience driving under these conditions. At least, not on the ground.

Relieved and, I confess, somewhat surprised, I found the small wooden shack carved onto a rocky ledge of mountain to be just as I remembered it. Maybe a little the worse for wear, but then, aren't we all?

The shack appeared empty. It also appeared to be nothing more than a simple wooden shack. Perhaps, a prospector's humble old abode in his search for gold or other precious metals. As humans like to say—dolphins may say this too but I've not yet mastered the tongue— appearances can be deceiving. Who was I to disagree? Hell, I was practically the poster boy for the slogan.

And this shack was anything but and the only telltale sign of this was the small silver finger of an antenna visible beside the dummy stone chimneystack. Everything was deception. Behind that pine cladding a thick layer of concrete and steel kept the world at bay.

I killed the motor, zipped up my jacket, and sat silently watching. My warm breath bounced off the windscreen. Splattering quickly disappearing clouds. I saw no other persons outside. Nor were any vehicles present. None of this surprised me.

I kept hoping no surprises waited for me inside.

I imagined sensors out there watching, waiting, ever alert for intruders, trespassers, even lost hikers off the beaten path. Were their hidden eyes on me now? I had to take care, be cautious about using my abilities. The more I employed them, the more I revealed myself, became more vulnerable to detection. Made it all the more likely they would sense my presence. That could spell disaster for me and my objectives. And Karen Dalton's brother—assuming he yet lived.

I unfolded myself from the Tesla and approached the skinny door. The door was four-inch steel too. As if that wasn't enough, a high-tech electronic lock kept unwanted visitors out.

Unfortunately for the lock, I wanted in. Not owning or even knowing how to use traditional lock-picking tools—no doubt this lock would prove immune to them anyway—I was forced to resort to other means.

I only hoped those other means didn't raise any alarms. I had no choice but to try. I'd promised Karen Dalton that I would do everything in my powers to find her brother. I had no other choice. Sure, he might be in the vicinity of Area 51, as I'd suggested to her. But he might be closer. Far closer. And there was only one way to find out.

Ignoring the slight warning tremble of my fingers, I concentrated until I heard the heavy lock turn. I glanced over my shoulder. No sign of life. Or death for that matter.

And no audible alarm.

With a sigh of relief, I twisted the handle, held my breath, and stepped inside. A chill blast tickled my ears and neck, colder inside than it was out on the exposed mountaintop. A lone automatic light, covered in a protective steel-wire cage, came to life, casting a dim glow. A steep, long, and dimly-lit concrete staircase descended to the bowels of the earth. Possibly continued on down to Hell. I'd never tested the hypothesis.

And I didn't plan to tonight.

Wishing I'd brought a flashlight, I followed the stairs downward. My shoulders brushed the cold stone walls of the tight narrow space. In places, short as I am, I had to crouch to keep from cracking my skull against volcanic rock. Los Alamos is ancient volcano country and the mountains here let you know it.

I fought the vague ghostlike memory of being suspended in a vat of warm fluid, stranded in isolation for a long bar top time, how long I couldn't say, that walked with me. The memory pressed down on my shoulders. Each step grew more arduous, more burdensome.

My ears caught the distant sound of a drip. I paused and pulled in a slow breath through my nostrils. My sense of smell is superb, like a dog's really. I smelled peaches. Was it my imagination playing a trick on me?

I continued on. Several minutes later, the stairs ended and the floor leveled off in a small poured-concrete hallway. Two windowless doors to my right, one to my left, and one straight ahead.

I stopped and listened. Heard only the slight hum of the air recyclers doing their job. If I remembered correctly, to be honest, I'd been a bit fuzzy at the time, only one of the doors was real. The others were dummies. None would be locked. This was the easy part.

And the hard part.

I was pretty certain the first door on my right was the correct door. All the others would set off alarms and activate traps. I closed my eyes a moment and concentrated, allowed my feet to move of their own volution. I opened the first door. When nothing bad happened and no bogeyman launched out to eat me, I stepped inside.

And I wished I hadn't...

Uniformed hands grabbed me and roughly pushed me to my knees. I winced, both at the pain their fingers digging into my shoulders caused and the impact of my knees against the concrete.

"What do we do with him?" asked voice number one. He sounded young to my ears.

"Put him in storage until morning," snarled voice number two. "No point waking the brass." This one sounded even younger. Not a good sign or signal, as the case might be. Younger oft times meant more brash. More likely to pull the trigger. And although I hadn't yet laid eyes on the pair, I was certain they each had a trigger to pull.

"Yeah, we don't want to do that again. Not without good reason."

"Yeah and this old runt sure as hell don't qualify as a reason."

Old? Youth can be so arrogant.

"Turn around runt."

Before I could even think how I might comply, strong hands spun me around on my knees. My hands flew out to protect my face as it hurtled dangerously toward the floor.

"How you suppose this runt got in here?" The first soldier kicked me in the knee with his heavy military boot. I couldn't imagine what shape my knees would be in by morning.

"How'd you get inside?" snarled the second soldier who, to my surprise, turned out to be a woman of Asian descent by the looks of her. She had a deep voice and a pair of evil eyes made larger by her prescription glasses. The two of them had sharp military haircuts. A few doodads and ribbons stuck to their drab uniforms but I had no idea what they meant—except that I was in trouble.

The female of the pair withdrew her handgun and aimed it at my face. Yep, I was definitely in trouble. "You going to answer my question or shall I shoot your ass?"

"Surely, you wouldn't shoot an unarmed man. Who, I might add, is making no sign of resistance, would you?"

"You've entered a top secret military installation."

Soldier one sucked in his gut and added, "We are fully authorized to use brute force."

"*Deadly* force," said the female, waving her gun in front of my nose. Apparently she wanted to put a fine point on it. Not that that had been necessary. I got the point. Oh, I got it, alright.

"That won't be necessary," I promised. I gave a little grin but it was wasted on the pair. What had I gotten myself into?

"On your feet, asshole."

Asshole? Was that a step up or down from runt?

Once again, hands forced me up before I could react. Never letting go, they led me down a brightly-lit corridor, LED fixtures spaced every eight feet, with a polished-concrete floor. Several twists and turns later, without having passed or heard any other persons—alive or dead—the pair tossed me ignominiously into a bare concrete-floored room a scant six-by-eight feet in size. No windows, not a stick of furniture. No place to sit or stretch out, no sink, no toilet, no reading material.

The door slammed shut behind me. Blink.

No lights.

I stood in the dark contemplating my fate.

Should the Man In Black sing the Folsom Prison Blues?

I counted to 10,000 and then put my hand on the door. I concentrated all my attention on the lock, hoping that the energy disturbance would go unnoticed. I had no choice. I couldn't stay there forever. Couldn't let them capture me like that again. The lock turned. I opened the door and peeked out.

Nothing.

No guards. No guns. No monsters or bogeymen.

So far, so good. Relatively, at least.

I straightened my jacket at my waist and considered my options. I pulled out my cigarettes—the morons hadn't even searched me. Had the military lowered their standards that far? If so, that could work in my favor. I knew better than to light up and have the delicious odor give me away, so I planted one in my mouth and chewed it like a stick of licorice. Of course, that made me wish I had a stick of black licorice but I also knew it was best that I did not. I settled for the sweet and savory tang of raw tobacco on my tongue.

Enough waffling. I needed to pick a direction. So I did.

No point going back the way I'd come, assuming I could actually find it. I wasn't quite sure on that point. Besides, I hadn't come here simply to turn around and leave. I wanted access to an office, a lab, any place with running electricity down in this secret subterranean maze. Electricity attached via cable to a computer. A friendly computer, one inclined to spit out some answers, such as: Hey, Ken Dalton, are you here?

9

I swung to the left. The floor dropped two steps then continued downward at a slight slope. I felt eerily alone. Not a sound followed me. Where had my captors disappeared to? Not that I cared to see them again.

Alone. With the weight of hundreds of tons of earth crushing down on me. Been there, done that. Feeling like a so-called proverbial babe in the woods—or in my case cave—subterranean secret lab. I'd basically come into this world with nothing, barely the clothes on my back, such as they were. Clothing swapped against my will for what amounted to a prison uniform.

Like so many people, I'd started with nothing. Unlike those many people though, I'd had to pretend to be something that I wasn't. Hide what I really was. And to this day and—it was impossible to say how many more days to come—that would continue to be my lot in life. My fate.

"Ed?"

I froze. My vision blinded by cascading memories, I'd let my guard down. Run into trouble. Now what?

I turned slowly in the narrow hallway to see a man in a gray onesie gaping at me. Swept back jet black hair, sharp brown eyes, medium build, and rich brown skin—the kind you get when you cross genetics and the great outdoors.

Did he mean me harm? His only weapon was the mop he gripped by its bright yellow fiberglass handle. Water dripped lazily from the gray mophead into an equally bright yellow bucket riding on casters. Was I about to participate in a gunfight at the Los Alamos corral? Of course, I had no six-gun, merely a pack of Camels, missing a single cigarette. This man had a mop. He could literally mop the floor with me.

I decided it might be time to say something. Keeping my hands splayed and my arms raised, I said, "Yes?"

"Hey, aren't you Ed? Ed Turner?" Those vivid brown eyes peered through me.

"Do I know you?"

It's me, Joseph. Joseph Aguilar." He released his hold on the mop. The mophead plashed into the bucket, splashing droplets in an arc, some landing on his polished black workboots but most on the floor. The scent of strong soap and ammonia reminded me of Jupiter. "Joe. Little Joe." He beamed. Always a good sign.

Cocking my head, I gave him a closer look. "Joe? Oqwa Aguilar's grandson?"

"That's me." Joe threw himself into my arms and we embraced.

"It's so good to see you again, Joe. All grown up too. You were nothing but a toddler the last time I laid eyes on you."

He playfully slapped me in the chest with both hands and said, "And you, Ed, you never change." He winked broadly. Had a grin to match. "Not that we'd ever want you to!"

"Right. You work here, Joe?"

"Yes, maintenance crew." He tapped his name patch. "Crew chief, actually."

"Congratulations."

Joe shrugged. "It's a crap job but steady. And the pay's good. Best you can get around these parts. Village needs all the help we can give her."

I nodded. Joe and his family dwelled in the nearby San Ildefonso Pueblo. Wonderful people, warm, welcoming. They'd done much for me, given me hope and help. Especially Joe's grandfather Oqwa, back when I'd needed help the most. Throughout the pueblo's nearly thousand-year existence, it's been home to many remarkable artists— potters and painters alike.

"What are you doing here, Ed?" He looked at my clothes. "You should not be in this place. What if they find out?"

My turn to grin. "I'm afraid they already did." Joe sucked in a breath as I explained. "Two rather rude military type locked me in an empty storeroom."

Joe whistled softly. "Lucky they didn't shoot you." He dropped a hand on my shoulder. "I've seen some things, Ed..."

"I suppose it could have gone worse then. Those two might have blown my brains out."

"Hey, you're right. And I'd have had to mop your brains up off the floor. You've saved me some work. And a messy job at that."

"You're welcome," I said. "I believe they intended to keep me locked up until morning and then turn me over to whoever is next up the food chain."

"General Grant is top of the food chain around here, Ed. And you do not want to meet him." Joe glanced nervously up and down the hallway. "Nor Doctor Allison. She's the top dog as far as research goes in this hellhole. And I do mean top dog. The bitch would just as soon gnaw your femur off as look at you. Practically kicked me in the ass for forgetting to empty her wastebasket one night. She catches you here, man, I don't even want to think about what she'll do."

I frowned. "Probably cut me into a million pieces, slap those pieces between glass slides, and take her time studying them through her microscope."

Joe nodded. "It's as if you know her already."

"Speaking of knowing..."

"Yes?"

"Do you know a Doctor Dalton? Kenneth Dalton?"

"Sure, I know Doctor Dalton. Hell, his lab's next door to Doctor Allison's."

I tugged his sleeve. "Will you take me there?"

Joe's brows rocketed upward. "You want to go there? Now? What the hell for?"

"I'm in town with Ken Dalton's sister, Karen Dalton. Have

you met her?"

Joe shook his head. "Never."

"Okay, I didn't think so." I didn't take Karen Dalton for a liar but it never hurt to check people out. Verify their stories. And I've heard some doozies over the years. "She's here in town with me. She hired me to find her brother Ken."

"Huh?"

"She's worried about him, Joe. She has not seen him personally for three years. Ever since he moved out from California."

"California."

"Right. Ken called Karen several days ago."

"So what's the trouble? I mean why come all the way to Los Alamos. Why come to this place?" he more pointedly wanted to know. "I mean, Ed, you know what will happen if they catch you."

"I know, I know. But I promised the woman I'd find her brother. Make sure he's okay. She's very, very upset. Concerned. He hasn't answered his phone or returned her calls since their last conversation."

"Okay. Doesn't sound like a big deal to me. Not big enough to haul out yourself here to New Mexico. Not that I'm not happy to see you," he hastened to add. "In fact, Doctor Dalton often went away, sometimes for weeks at a time."

"Do you know where he went?"

Joe's lips moved as he chewed over the question. "Nothing specific. He mentioned Nevada. Think he's got a lab up there too. So does Doctor Allison."

"I'm not surprised." The dots were beginning to line up. And I didn't much like the picture those lines were beginning to reveal. "Any place else?"

"Just home. Dalton mentioned that."

"Pasadena?"

"Yeah. Mentioned in passing once that he has a place there that he escapes to whenever he gets the chance. Hey!" Joe's face lit up. "You look for him there?"

"No." I frowned. Why had Ken Dalton kept this a secret from his sister? Sure, the woman could be annoying. But still, she was his only family. On the other hand, Karen Dalton could have lied to me. Then again, the question was why? Why would she pay me to help her find her brother then lie to me about his condo? Nothing was making sense. I was dying for a Camel. Washed down with a liter of bourbon.

And a licorice stick.

"Karen Dalton told me he sold his condo when he took the job out here."

"That's weird."

I agreed. "You want to know what's weirder?"

"What?"

"You know what he said in that last conversation Karen had with her brother, Joe?"

Joe licked his lip. "What, Ed?"

"He said he was worried that *aliens* were trying to kill him." I let the significance of my words hang in the air. Watched Joe's face go through various contortions.

"Aliens," he finally whispered. "Shit." He rubbed his arms.

"You know anything about that, Joe?"

Joe's head shook slowly side to side. "No. Nothing. You know they keep things sealed up pretty tight around here. Besides, I don't want to know all that goes on—or is lurking—down here."

"Probably best that you don't."

"Yeah." Joe kicked his mop bucket a couple of times. "Okay, Ed. I'll lead you to Doctor Dalton's lab. Won't do you any good though. You won't find him there. Not now."

"The doctor doesn't work late nights? Doesn't like to burn the midnight oil?"

"No, that's not it, Ed. Hell, that man put in all kinds of hours. Never seen a guy so dedicated. Excitable too. No, that's not it. You see, I haven't seen Doctor Dalton around these parts for more than a week."

That worried me. "Not at all?"

"Nope. His office is clean. No trash. Nothing. I just figured he was off somewhere. Like I said, it happens sometimes. Maybe he's in Pasadena or Nevada."

"Maybe." Personally, I was beginning to wish I was sitting in a bar somewhere watching a ballgame and getting drunk. Where was the client who'd pay me five hundred bucks a day to do that? I mean, come on, already. Shouldn't the American Dream apply to me too? Sure, I may not strictly be an American and, strictly speaking, watching baseball and getting drunk may not be everybody's idea of the American Dream but a dream's a dream, right? To each his/her/its own?

"Come on, I'll show you but stay close and if we see anybody..." Joe frowned. "I know, I'll say you're a new hire. Try to look...janitorial."

I quirked my brow. "I'll give it my best." To prove it, I pushed the mop bucket along ahead of me, using the mop handle as a steering column. All this rig needed was a handful of triple-A batteries and it'd be a compact Tesla.

Joe led me to Ken's lab. "This is it."

I tried the handle. "Locked."

"Sure." Nonetheless, Joe gave it a jiggle. "Pretty typical even down here. Sticklers for security, you know?"

I knew.

Joe extracted a ring of keys from his pocket and thrust one in the key slot. He eased open the door, reached to his right, and flipped a switch. "This is it," he said as the overhead row of lights flickered to life.

I stepped into the long rectangular lab. No windows, of course, being subterranean. But a good-sized space for an underground lab. Lots of equipment, lots of computer power. Evidence of big resources. That meant big budgets. Whatever Ken Dalton was involved in, the folks forking out the bucks must've considered his work even more valuable than much of the other secret experiments and researches being conducted in secrecy here.

A map of the Milky Way adorned the wall behind his

standup desk, atop which sat a model replica of the Starship Enterprise, original version.

I flipped the well-worn pages of a paperback edition of A Hitchhiker's Guide To The Galaxy. Was Ken planning a trip? "Everything appears intact." No signs of struggle, alien or human.

"Told you." Joe fiddled with a stack of papers on the corner of the desk.

"Like he left work one day fully expecting to be back the next." I peered in his wastebasket. "Empty."

"It's been empty more than a week, Ed. Like I said, the doc's been a no show."

"Has Doctor Allison or anyone else commented on his current absence?"

"Not a peep. Not to me anyway. Hell, no surprise. I'm just the janitor to them. I'm not so sure they see me even when they're looking straight at me, you know?"

I knew. "Are you familiar with the Bathtub Ring Brew Pub?"

"Sure, I know it. Been there myself now and then. Lot of the locals do."

"Including LANL staff?"

"Sure, I guess so. I've noticed some. Why?"

I related how Ken's sister and I had spotted a photograph of Ken Dalton on the pub's wall of shame and why. "That was two weeks ago. The bartender told us he left accompanied by some men in suits."

Joe whistled and scratched his temple. "That's some weird shit."

I settled behind Ken Dalton's desk, The computer was an Apple but I had no choice but to suck up my revulsion. I hit the spacebar on his keyboard. The screen sprang to life. Interesting, no local password protection. That didn't mean the machine wasn't protected, not in a facility like this. No, it only meant that protection was handled higher up the network. Folders dotted the screen. I scanned them quickly. "Any other weird shit, as you say, going on?"

"Hell, Ed. You know what this place is like. This is weird shit central."

I frowned. Joe was right. I tapped a few keys. "Let's see what brother Ken has been working on."

Joe planted his feet in front of the map of the Milky Way and studied it. "Space sure is a big, ain't it?"

"You have no idea, Joe," I said distractedly. "You have no idea." But digging around in Ken Dalton's files, I came up with some of disturbing information about aliens. One alien in particular. And that about stopped my heart. I couldn't be sure though. I needed to dig deeper.

"Uh-oh."

I glanced up from Ken's computer. "What's wrong, Joe?"

Joe stared warily at his cellphone. "I just got a text warning of a security issue. Goes out to all employees when it's big."

"Security issue?" I pulled up a file and studied complicated rows of biological data.

"There's been a possible breach and all staff are to be on alert." He typed in a hasty reply.

"What sort of breach?"

"My guess, Ed?" Joe swiveled me around in Ken's black mesh-backed desk chair and looked me in the eye. "You."

10

Joe hoisted me to my feet. "Come on!" The chair clattered as it struck the concrete block wall behind me.

"No." I pulled free. "You go, Joe. Go about your business. Pretend you don't know me. Never saw me. I don't want to get you in any trouble." I cursed myself. Either my earlier captors had come checking on me and noticed my escape or Ken Dalton's office, specifically his computer, was under surveillance. And, like an idiot, I tripped a security alarm when I started snooping on it.

Maybe both.

"Ed, my grandfather wouldn't leave you behind and neither will I." Joe quietly opened Ken's office door and glanced furtively up and down the hall.

"You've got to, Joe."

"No, to do so would be to dishonor my grandfather, my family. Would you have that on my conscience?"

"Okay," I sighed. "But if we get caught—"

"We won't. Come." He waved me on.

Disappointment shadowed me. I'd hoped to snoop some more. Ken Dalton had a lot of secrets to which I wanted answers. I'd also been hoping to dig around in the good Dr. Allison's office. As head of research, who knew what important pieces of information she might be holding onto?

Perhaps I'd never learn... After tonight, the powers that be would be ratcheting up their security another notch. Keeping at bay the powers they did not want escaping or entering their clandestine domain.

Like I said: Life. Is. A. Bitch.

"Faster," urged Joe.

I struggled to keep up. "I can only go so fast with a mop bucket tagging along, sloshing dirty water all over my best shoes."

"Huh?" Joe looked behind at me. "Shit on a stick, Ed! Leave the damn bucket!"

"Gladly." I shoved the bucket to one side.

We surged ahead, approached a junction. I laid a hand on his shoulder. "I hear footsteps, Joe."

Joe pressed me against the wall. "How many?" he whispered.

I held up four fingers. "Assuming they are bipedal," I whispered back, "that would equal two humans. Perhaps my original captors. And I remind you, they're armed."

Joe gulped. "Makes sense. Not more than a skeleton crew at this hour. Even for security."

I heard Joe's heart pounding. Poor guy. What trouble had I landed him in?

Oh, brother. And I did mean *brother*...

I shook myself. No, it wasn't possible. I mean, are impossible things even possible?

I sniffed, wished I had a couple of twisted sticks of black licorice to tickle my neurons and, if not ratchet up my nerve, at least make me too loony to care. "I'll handle this, Joe."

"Don't do anything stupid," Joe told me.

So I did.

I blurred around the corner. Let my guard down. Let myself be me. Not a smart thing to do. Without a doubt. Not now. Not here.

And not any easy thing to do. I've become used to being something I am not, odd as that sounds. I'd been keeping up an illusion for a very long time. That takes a lot of energy. Takes its toll...

Sometimes it's all I can do to remain human. *Ish.*

I faced my recent captors. The two did not like what they saw. Not one bit. Should I feel offended?

The woman pulled her weapon but her nerves got the best of her and the gun clattered to the floor unused. Good. Bullets like me far more than I like them.

The young soldier beside her gaped. "What the hell, Neela! Get your shit together!" He hollered but he looked just as scared and trembled every bit as much as she did. His hands shook so hard he couldn't even manage to draw his gun from its leather holster.

I raised my arms and swept towards them. You'd think they'd seen a ghost. Probably wished they had—would've preferred it.

Although in some ways they really had seen a ghost... I had half a mind to yell "Boo!" but resisted.

Neela scrambled for her weapon on the floor, fumbled it once again. "Shit, this is not worth it!" She retreated down the hall, chasing her partner who was already rounding the far corner, his feet slapping the concrete hard. His screams were giving me a headache so I was happy when he turned the corner and his fright-filled cries faded away.

Joe leapt around the corner. "Ed? You okay?"

I smiled. I was my old self once again. Or was I my new self? Whatever. I was the self Joe knew and was comfortable with. "Yes." A little weak but nothing to worry my friend about.

"You took a hell of a risk."

"It was worth it. I think I've bought us some time. The question is, can you get me out of here?"

He nodded. "Come."

A ten-minute fast walk down cold empty corridor after cold empty corridor, led us to an unmarked gray elevator door. He scanned his ID under an electronic reader and the door welcomed us—or at least him. Me it tolerated. The tiny elevator led us to the surface and disgorged us on the verge of a small unlit parking lot. The signage on a pair of squat buildings, including the one we'd exited, stated this was a physical plant station. Red brick clad both buildings. The buildings were otherwise nondescript and windowless. I shivered in the night air.

We climbed inside his dusty blue Ford pickup. A helicopter flew to the north of us, heading our way. "Looks like company's coming." Joe shifted into gear. "You got a car around here or did you come in your flying saucer?"

"Very funny." I explained where I'd left Ken Dalton's Tesla.

"I'll get a buddy to pick it up. Deliver it to you."

"Thanks." I dropped my key fob into the plastic tray between the seats. "You've saved my life, Joe."

Joe smiled as he careened down the mountain at a speed I wouldn't have dared even if I'd been in a NHTSA crash-test approved flying saucer. "Grandfather Oqwa told us many times how you saved his life. I thank you for that."

"It was nothing."

"Nothing? He was dying from the inside out." He lit a cigarette, drove with one hand. The expression *speed kills* came to mind. "Because of you, he lived another twenty good years. Healthy years. Lived to see his grandchildren. Like me."

I grabbed the arm holding the lit cigarette and held it steady while I ignited a Camel from the orange glowing tip of his. I planted my cigarette between my lips and sucked. I shut my eyes—if we were fated to crash headfirst into a granite mountain, I didn't need to see it coming, I'd feel it when we struck. That would be soon enough. I leaned back in my seat and pondered the future.

Funny I know, I may not believe in time but I did believe that the clock was ticking. For Ken Dalton. And for me.

11

Karen Dalton and I split Los Alamos the next morning. Only one of us was well rested. I'd keep her in the dark regarding last night's little adventure. What she didn't know wouldn't hurt her, at least, I hoped it wouldn't. Hurt can blindside you. And it hurt like hell.

Nothing more to see or do in Los Alamos. And the town makes me itchy. Gives me night sweats.

Nightmares.

Took me places my mind did not want to go.

Besides, last night's adventure had been like poking a stick inside a hornet's nest. Remaining in town another day was not an option. Not a good one anyway. Besides, we were hot on Ken Dalton's trail.

Well, lukewarm anyway.

Joe Aguilar deposited me at the motel around three in the morning and I'd tumbled into bed, not bothering to pull back the covers or undress. Ken's sporty Tesla was waiting for us when we got up. A quick breakfast at a waffle joint and we hit the highway with two large to-go cups filled with hot coffee—hers dark as a melted bar of 85% cacao, mine filled with plenty of cream and even more sugar to balance it out. Funny as it sounds coming from me, there was something unnatural about Karen Dalton.

A big red sun eyeballed us for hours, looking down on us like the universe's least stealthy UFO.

The highway shimmered in the heat. Karen navigated and I drove. Her grumbling and lousy sense of direction drove me crazy. When she'd discovered my stash of bourbon under her seat, she'd unceremoniously rolled down her window and tossed the nearly-full bottle along a stretch of brown dirt outside of Nageezi—a census-designated-place it takes all of three seconds to pass through.

But we didn't pass, we stopped and filled our bellies at a chuck wagon with a huge black barrel-shaped wood smoker sitting out front on four-foot in diameter spoked wooden wagon wheels. Its smoke stack sent up a steady stream of inscrutable black clouds. Inscrutable but smelled damned good. I swear, I'd caught scent of that slow-burning mesquite from ten miles away even with the Tesla's windows up and the AC running full blast.

I ordered baby-back ribs. Karen Dalton nibbled an ear of corn, seeing as how that was the only vegan option. Some sort of cola, the proprietor proudly said he'd concocted himself, served to wash the ribs down. The best way to describe the beverage would be to say...*caustic*. The sort of fluid you'd use to scour the rust off the chrome front bumper of your fifties Cadillac. The Tesla had no such thing. Karen Dalton spilled a drop or two on her feet and I could still see the red welts on her bare flesh. Like I've said, why the hell don't women wear practical footwear? I mean, brown loafers. How can one go wrong with brown loafers? They're low to the ground and the color of dirt, for pete's sake.

As for me, by the time I'd finished my homebrewed *cola*, my teeth hurt and I'm pretty sure they had lost all their protective enamel coating. Come to think of it, maybe it had been the whole chuck wagon thing that had given her the idea to chuck my bourbon out her side window earlier.

Such thoughts, when not thinking about Ken Dalton, alien killers, Los Alamos, and Area 51, filled my head for two miserable days on the road, made the worse for having to keep stopping and recharging the damn EV. With the Tesla and I equally about out of juice, we finally reached the barely there town of Alamo, Nevada.

From Los Alamos, New Mexico, to Alamo, Nevada. Some hidden meaning there or mere coincidence?

Driving across empty desert and over desolate, unfriendly mountains while dodging big-rig drivers—all of whom let us know they were in a big hurry—was not my idea of fun. Although it did beat hoofing across that same lifeless void while being chased by every branch of the military plus those lunatic alien hunters and ufologists. Hell, a two-day march across the Martian landscape held more pleasure. And superior scenery.

I was worn out and my back ached something fierce. Then again, the last time I'd made this journey, conditions had been far, far worse. Poor roads, cramped quarters, and a truck whose shocks stood in shockingly poor condition. So who was I to complain?

I steered into the unpaved yard of the Lil' Green Man Motor Court. I'd telephoned the day before and booked our rooms for the night. "Home sweet home." Modest yet serviceable. The scattered lights of tired mobile homes dotted the flat landscape.

"This is it, huh?" Karen Dalton sagged against the passenger side window. She stared at the mangled and pin-holed picture of her brother. She'd swiped it from the Bathtub Ring Brew Pub moments before our being summarily ejected. On the plus side, I hadn't paid for our dinner and drinks prior to our being tossed out. A penny saved and all that.

"Afraid so." Cheap motels had become a signature feature of our adventure. Neither of us could afford better. Not that better could be found in this god-and-alien-forsaken country.

"Better not be another waste of time."

"It won't be. I've a good feeling about this."

"That makes one of us."

"Trust me." I patted her knee. "All roads lead to Ken."

She muttered something obscene.

"By the way," I said. "You might find this interesting."

"I doubt it."

I sensed the woman's hunger and fatigue. We'd have to find somewhere to gather nourishment sooner than later. Before she bit my head off, vegan or not.

I plowed ahead as we approached the motel office. "The Lil'

Green sits at one end of the Extraterrestrial Highway stretching for over a hundred miles, finally petering out in Tonopah, to the northwest. Tonopah, I've read, boasts an establishment called The Clown Inn, if you can believe it." Karen Dalton mumbled something about not caring or believing and I continued. "Featuring the world's largest private collection of clowns and clown memorabilia."

Mind blowing, isn't it? Sheesh, and people think aliens are creepy! Have you seen some of those clowns running around loose in the world? I grabbed the door to the office and held it open for Karen Dalton. I chose to believe that the elbow that crashed into my ribs as she passed had been an accident.

"Not far from here sits the Alamo Impact Breccia," I continued against her wall of stubborn silence. "Not many folks today even know what that is. But four hundred million years ago, give or take, that impact had been big news. Trust me, when those objects hit, the whole world knew it."

My monolog appeared to have little positive impact on her mood. A pack of stale cookies would have had a more positive result.

The sign clinging to the front door by means of a slim chain and yellowed suction cup noted the establishment remained open twenty-four hours a day and that aliens must wear shoes. Cute. The signage included that earthlings were welcome.

"Earthlings welcome? What about me?" I said.

"Huh?" Karen Dalton asked.

"Never mind." Kitschy alien and UFO-inspired souvenirs for sale, everything from toy aliens dolls, tee shirts, pens and pencils, plastic alien meteor globes—tiny flying saucers suspended in water with teeny-tiny meteors that went this way and that when you gave the thing a shake, which Karen did—thermometers, underwear, and goofy maps of Area 51 crowded the 1970s-era paneled shelf space. I also spotted maps indicating the exact locations of the upcoming alien invasion of Earth. Good to know. A mix of wooden bins and milk cartons under the side window offered stacks of CDs and videotapes offering stories of alien abductions. A poster advertising Green Flying Saucer Tours conducted in a ratty jeep—dolled up to look like a flying saucer no self-respecting ET would ever be caught dead in—made of water-colored paper mâché, MDF, and aluminum foil was taped to what was probably a storage closet. Or a time machine, or a portal to another dimension. In these parts, one never knew.

Spindles peppered with sun-faded postcards flanked the entrance. Karen spun one lazily and the screech of rusty metal sent a lance of pain between my ears. I caught the lingering aroma of tobacco and beer that filled the air and infused the old walls. Quite homey, actually.

I checked us in and asked where I might plug in my Tesla, Ken's Tesla. Having no charging station, the clerk loaned me a dusty orange extension cord. He explained that I could run it from the outlet behind the ice machine near the door. "Excellent," I said.

"Cheer up," I told Karen as we headed to our tiny rooms on the second floor. "Did you see the sign? Free wifi and intergalactic toll-free calling."

She slammed the door to her room in my face.

Going to my own room, I discovered as much dust inside as there'd been outdoors.

I sat down on the bed then stretched out. I stared at the ceiling for a while. All that popcorn was making me hungry. I strolled downstairs in search of food and found the clerk half-asleep behind the front counter. He was a healthy looking brown-haired fellow with a beaklike nose. He was wearing a short-sleeve red plaid shirt unbuttoned just far enough to reveal the underlying white V-neck tee shirt, and clashing gray trousers over cowboy boots. Age? I was guessing mid-fifties.

"Evening." I scanned the antique snack machine while searching my pockets for loose change.

"Howdy." He yawned, not afraid to reveal a mouth filled with yellow teeth. "Help you with anything?"

"Hungry." I dug out a few quarters and shoved them in the coin slot. "Any good places to eat around here?" I was not going to ask if there were any vegan establishments. What would he take me for? I was trying to fit in, for heaven's sake.

"Sure, you got a couple of options." He smiled. "You like chicken?"

"It'll do." Eating things covered in feathers doesn't exactly tickle my fancy. But if I'm anything, I'm adaptive. Peering through the smudged glass of the vending machine, I made my choice and pushed the appropriate button: A8. A packet of peanut butter crackers surrendered to its fate and dropped to the stainless steel tray at the bottom of the machine. "What is my other option?"

"Go hungry."

"Excuse me?"

His smile got bigger. "Because that's it. Chicken."

"Ah, understood." The man was attempting humor. Probably used the same joke on every guest who spent a night at his motel. I juggled my cellophane-wrapped snack. No way Karen Dalton was going to buy my argument that chicken was vegan. Sure, she had a degree in poetry but that didn't make her stupid. Except with her money. "Fried chicken it is."

"You'll find The Chicken Shack just up the road." He pointed opposite the direction we'd arrived from.

"Thanks." I leaned my hands on the counter. "More importantly, does this town have a liquor store?"

"What's your beverage of choice?"

"Bourbon but beer will do."

"I got both in back. Six pack and a pint?"

I pulled out my wallet. "You are a saint, sir."

"Name's Samuel Hitchcock. Call me Samuel." He disappeared in back and returned with a six-pack of Busch beer and a half bottle of bourbon. Samuel dropped everything on the counter. "What do you say? Twenty for everything?"

"Can't argue with that." Hell, back home in my building, Anna Ping would've charged me double the price. I forked over the money. I could probably bill Karen Dalton for this anyway. After all, she was the one who'd thrown out my previous bottle of bourbon. She owed me for that at least.

"One more thing."

"What's that?"

I extracted Ken Dalton's photograph from my pocket, the one Karen had ripped off the wall at the Bathtub Ring Brew Pub. I'd managed to borrow it when she wasn't looking. The photo was in rough shape. I was hoping the same could not be said for its subject. "Ever see this man, Samuel?"

"Sure, I seen him some nights. Used to come in once in a while. Get drunk at the bar."

Drunk? Again? "Bar? I thought there was nothing around but chicken?"

Samuel spread his arms.

"Oh, this one." I tapped the counter with my knuckle.

"You got it. Man's name's Dalton, right? Some kinda scientist?" I nodded. Samuel smiled proudly. "I've got a good memory. That Dalton had a lot on his mind. Troubles, you know?" He unscrewed the bourbon I'd just paid him for and poured some into a coffee-stained mug that said *Property of Holiday Inn*. He took a sip and handed the mug to me.

"I'm beginning to think I do. Thanks." I drank.

"So what's your interest in him?"

"His sister's worried about him. She's here with me."

"Gotcha." He closed the bottle and slid it to me. "So that's the lady who walked in with you, said nothing, and was pulling a face like she'd just walked into a hot men's room smelling of warm piss earlier?"

"You pegged her. But I wouldn't say that to her face," I added quickly. Samuel certainly had a way with words.

"You know, Dalton came here with a lady a couple of times."

"A lady?"

"Yep."

"Not his sister?"

"Nope, not his sister. Unless he's got another he's sleeping with."

"Let's call that a no."

"Okay, no it is."

"Did you get this lady's name?"

"Nope, don't know her name. Never said. Pretty though but not much of a talker. Not much of a drinker either. Me, I don't trust a person who won't have a drink with you."

This was a man after my own heart. "When did you see Dalton last? Do you remember?" Ken Dalton was sounding more and more like a man with a bad habit or three and serious troubles. Alien troubles? Murdering alien troubles?

"Shit. Must've been weeks ago. Wasn't looking so good either. Looked like he'd been kicked around by a mule. Then those MPs come and got him and that's the last I seen of him."

"Could you check your computer?" I nodded at the device. Not an Apple.

"I could but Dalton asked me not to register him."

"Didn't you find that odd?"

"Sure. But I don't ask questions." Samuel scratched his chest hair. "Especially when a man is paying cash and giving me fifty extra for my trouble."

"Wise, I'm sure." Although this kind of wisdom—practical as it might be—was hampering my investigation.

Samuel stepped from behind the counter and crossed to the front windows, peered through the mullioned glass. "Thought that might be his car. Don't get many like that around here. Nice." He rubbed the glass. "Yeah, sweet ride. Of course, it's no pickup truck."

"Sure, what is?" I said in an effort to be companionable. Then I had a thought. "Like to take it for a spin?"

The corner of Samuel's mouth quirked upward. "That?"

"Yep. Classic Tesla Roadster. Trust me, you press the pedal to the metal in her and she'll push your spine through the seat."

Samuel chuckled. "Might be fun." He faced me. "What's the catch?"

"No catch. A simple tit for tat."

"Okay, so what's the tat?"

"You can take a spin in the car and..." I popped open a chilled can of beer and handed it to him.

"Thanks." He drank.

"And in exchange, you let me borrow your pickup truck."

"My truck?" Samuel made a face like I'd just asked to date his underage daughter. Maybe take her to Vegas for the weekend.

"That is your fine vehicle?" I pointed to the dusty red Chevy pickup visible through the window, nestled up against the office, sitting under the eave. Signs of dried dog slobber painted the driver's side window.

"You going to take good care of it?"

"Of course. I am an expert driver. Ask anyone." Except Karen Dalton.

He scratched his thigh. "I suppose that could work."

"Fine, fine. There is one catch however. I almost forgot." Sometimes lying comes so easy. "I would like to borrow the truck *later*."

Samuel squinted suspicion at me. "How later?"

I shrugged. "Let's say one o'clock."

"One in the morning? What the hell you want to borrow my truck at one in the morning for?"

"Let's just say I'd like to drive out and park someplace... quiet," I said. "Do some stargazing."

He looked at me blankly. A sparkle of comprehension and a big leering smile followed. "Oh, I gotcha. You and the sister." He chuckled. "Fine, you got a deal. Don't burn up all my gas." He handed me a pair of truck keys attached to a black leather keyring bearing the Chevrolet emblem.

I handed over the key to the Tesla and we made plans to exchange keys in the morning.

I was seeing stars in my future.

And hoping none of them went nova.

12

Shiny Chevy keys jingle-jangling in my right hand, I climbed the stairs and knocked on Karen Dalton's door after dropping off the bottle of bourbon in my room. There'd be no more tossing good bourbon out car windows if I could help it. I'd plucked a couple cans of beer loose and snugged one in each pocket of my leather jacket.

The door flew open. "What?"

"Napping?" Her eyes were puffy and her hair akimbo. She'd changed into a pair of black sweat pants, a bright yellow tee shirt, and pink flipflops. Affix a pair of antennae to her head and she'd be Queen of the Bees.

"What do you want, Ed?"

"I brought food."

Karen Dalton looked at my hand. The one holding the peanut butter sandwich crackers. "I found these." I extended the package.

"No thanks." She swatted my hand. "Now if you could only find my brother."

Working with this woman really required a thick skin. Fortunately, mine is. I tried again. "Peanut butter crackers. Two months past their sell-by date but dates can't kill you." I shoved the crackers at her. "Go on. Take them. There's no finer food than the peanut," I declared. "Besides which, you should be happy. It's plant based."

That got a response.

She punched me.

"Oof!" Thick skin, yes. Abs of steel, no.

Then she took my crackers.

"Come on in," Karen Dalton said, disappearing inside. She flopped down on her bed and ripped the cellophane off the crackers using her teeth. She plucked two sandwich crackers from the package and chomped down. She extended the package to me.

I took one to be civil. She needed them more than I did. But I really do love peanut butter. In return, I offered her a beer. She didn't refuse.

"So this is dinner?" Karen Dalton licked whole wheat cracker crumbs from her lower lip. Drank some beer. My meager supply was dwindling quickly.

"Merely an appetizer. There's a chicken joint up the road."

Karen Dalton grunted her disapproval.

"What? Thighs and wings for me. Cole slaw and french fries for you."

"Pass." Karen Dalton looked at her beer can as if she was studying for an end of semester exam at Budweiser U. "Ken would never have let himself become drunk. He never drank. Period."

"People change."

"Not Ken."

I shrugged. We all need our delusions. Who was I to burst Karen Dalton's Ken bubble?

I peeled back the corner of the heavy curtain. Moths and mosquitoes danced round the yellow light outside the door. "He's out there somewhere."

Karen joined me at the window. "I hope so."

We gazed out into the darkness. A blanket of stars covered the night sky. "'As the moths around taper, as the bees around a rose, as the gnats around a vapour,'" she whispered, one hand clutching the curtain. "'So the spirits group and close, round about a holy childhood, as if drinking its repose.'"

"Where did that come from?"

"Elizabeth Barrett Browning. Victorian poet."

"I see your degree in poetry is paying off in spades."

"You want me to punch you again?" She made a fist and

aimed it at my solar plexus.

"No. No." I threw up my hands, palms out. "Only a joke."

"I hope you're a better detective than you are a comedian."

"For your information, I had an interesting conversation with the clerk downstairs."

"Really? Him? I find that hard to believe." She tugged at her long blue braids. "Looked at me like I was nothing but a piece of meat."

I ignored her not very flattering opinion of Samuel. And the fact that she was indeed a piece of meat. Afterall, we'd been down that road before and it had led us nowhere. "Turns out Ken has been here."

"Ken? Here?" She yanked my arm, sloshing cold beer all over my shirt. I felt it pool at the elbow. "When? What did he say? Why was he here?"

I pulled free. "Not only are you wasting beer—and the only thing worse than wasting beer is wasting bourbon—you are asking question after question without giving me a moment to answer you."

"Sorry." Karen wiped her hand up and down my shirt. "Sorry, I'll get you a towel." She ran off and returned with a paper-thin white terry towel. Interestingly, the towel also bore the name *Holiday Inn*.

I patted myself dry. *Ish.*

She threw herself down on the bed. "I hate the desert. Let's go home."

"We could but remember the only reason we're here, and that we'd gone to New Mexico in the first place, was because you said Ken was out here. And that aliens were going to kill him."

"I did not say he was in New Mexico."

"Did so. I remember distinctly you saying—"

"Put a lid on it, would you, Ed!" She tossed her empty beer can at the television. It crashed off the screen and fell dead on the tatty tan carpet.

"Fine." I planted my hands on my hips to show I meant business. "But you know I'm right." Never good to let a client think you're wrong. It could lead to a lack of confidence—quickly followed by a cessation of fees.

"Here we go again," Karen Dalton sighed. "No, I did not. I *never* said that. I said Ken told me he took a job in New Mexico. But the next time I talked to him he admitted he was in Nevada. West of Vegas." She pointed a finger at me. "We only went to Roswell because you wanted a stupid mug!" She kicked her heels into the mattress. "Should've come here in the first place. Maybe Ken would have been here. Whatever. We should go home now!"

"And yet here we are," I said calmly.

"Yeah. Maybe I should post a selfie. Make everyone jealous of all the fun I'm having."

"Let's hope your brother is here too. At the very least, we can be sure he's been here." Assuming Samuel hadn't lied to me. Always a possibility but what would he have to gain by it?

That got her attention. "You really think he's out here?" She leaned into the headboard.

"I think we need to find out. Let me remind you, it's been days since you heard from him. He called to say he feared aliens were out to kill him. Time could be of the direst essence."

"So how you figure on going about finding him Mister Five-Hundred-Dollar-A Day detective?" Her anger was peaking again. Time for another peanut butter cracker?

I glared at her. "I've often heard the expression 'you're beautiful when you're angry.'"

"Oh?" Karen Dalton held herself up with her elbows.

"Yes." I considered her in silence. Face angry red, toes kicking, veins throbbing. "I'm not sure who coined the expression but it definitely does not apply here."

"Oh…" Karen Dalton rolled over, turned her back on me.

"We go tonight," I said in a clipped tone. "At the bitching hour."

"I believe you mean the *witching* hour," she told the pale yellow wall inches from her nose.

"Believe you me, I know *exactly* what I mean. Getting up and driving blindly out into the desert at one o'clock in the morning is a bitch. See you at twelve forty-five."

"Where exactly are we going?"

After a pause, I said, "Into the belly of the beast."

"The belly of the beast?" Karen Dalton snorted. "What the hell does that even mean?"

"It means Mister Five-Hundred-Dollars-A-Day is going to earn his fee…and then some." I laid my hand on the doorknob. "If you like, you can remain here. Get some beauty sleep. You need it."

"Ha-ha." She leapt from the bed. "I am not letting you out of my sight."

"Really?" I hoisted an eyebrow. "Watch this!" I didn't slam the door on my way out but I let it know in no uncertain terms that I was pissed off.

I returned at twelve forty expecting to drag an obstinate Karen Dalton out of bed kicking and screaming. Been there, done that with others. Yes, I have quite the way with the ladies.

To my utter surprise, Karen Dalton stood waiting for me. "Come in!"

I did.

"I'll be ready in a sec." She combed her hair in the heavy-framed mirror behind the TV. She tossed her brush down on the dresser. "So where are we really going? You never actually said."

"You didn't exactly give me much of a chance." Not that I'd really wanted to explain my plan. Nor was I really sure I wanted her tagging along. Still, although the woman was a pain, she might come in handy. Besides, I wasn't sure how safe she'd be if left alone. It's a big desert out there. Easy to disappear in. Like Ken Dalton maybe.

"I told Samuel we wanted to do some stargazing. I suggest you bundle up. The desert is cold at night." Karen Dalton hadn't changed clothes since I'd departed earlier. In lieu of desert camo, the sweats and tee would do fine for our purposes, as long as she kept that bumblebee-yellow tee shirt hidden.

"Stargazing?" Karen Dalton had the whole skepticism pitch down perfectly. She braided her hair into three long ropes. A lesser creature might have been tempted to strangle her with one of them.

"I'll explain as we go. Time is critical, not that I believe in the concept. Bring your hoodie." The black hoodie was perfect. Fortunately, she'd brought a pair of white lace-up sneakers minus the laces—when had that become a thing? Still, not exactly hiking-in-the-desert wear but they were a, no pun intended, step up from flipflops and open-toe sandals.

"Yes, boss." She snatched her hoodie from her open suitcase. While she zipped up and did some last minute primping in the bathroom mirror—did she think we were going to a black-tie gala?—I opened the paper sack I'd carried in.

"What's inside the bag?" she said, glancing at my reflection in the mirror. "Desert survival supplies?"

"To paraphrase WC Fields, always carry a flagon of *bourbon* in case of snakebite. Furthermore, always carry a small snake." I pulled out the dwindling supply of bourbon. "One out of two isn't bad. In baseball, I'd be batting five hundred. That's damn good." I squeezed in beside her and poured a quantity into a plastic cup beside the bathroom sink. "Have some." I held out the cup.

"No, thanks. And who's WC Fields?"

I grinded my teeth. "Your loss. Trust me, you're going to need it." I downed the contents of the cup and quickly refilled.

"If I get bitten by a rattlesnake, I'll definitely have some. In fact, you can pour it over the fang marks. Maybe it'll counteract its deadly venom."

"I'll be happy to. And thanks."

"For what?"

"You've given me a reason to bring the bottle." I shoved the bourbon inside my black leather bomber jacket for safekeeping.

She locked the door behind her and we moved quietly down the concrete steps.

I headed for Samuel's pickup truck.

"Hey, what about the Tesla?"

"Samuel and I made an arrangement to temporarily swap

vehicles." She flinched. "I thought the truck better suited our purposes. Not to worry." I'd watched the motel man race wildly up and down outside the highway for nearly an hour earlier in the Roadster before retiring to his quarters. "As you can see," I nodded towards the dusty Tesla sitting askew near the road, "the Tesla appears none the worse for wear."

"Man, Ed, Ken is going to be pissed. He hates strangers driving his car. He barely tolerates me."

"He'd have to be alive to be pissed so let's hope he is."

"Asshole," she whispered.

"Everybody's got one," I said, cheerfully. It's a wonder what a little bourbon and beer can do for one's spirits. Spirits for spirits, you might say.

The pickup sat unlocked. Probably more horse thieves than truck thieves around these parts. I climbed into the driver's seat and she hopped in on the other side. "Smells like dog in here," she complained.

"Dog probably complains it smells of humans," I replied, thrusting the key in the ignition, and cranking the starter. The back of my head bumped against the polished wood stock of the double-barreled shotgun mounted horizontally across the rear window. Blocked a good chunk of my vision but it certainly made a statement. Was the thing loaded? Might the shotgun come in handy?

I'd never actually fired a weapon but how hard could it be? Just point and shoot, right? Simple. Like a Polaroid camera.

On the Chevy's dashboard, a suction-cup-mounted berobed Jesus bobbled beside a suction-cupped little green man with big blue bug eyes and wearing only a futuristic loincloth, kind of like Tarzan, 2077. The pair appeared to be getting along harmoniously. They probably made better traveling companions than Karen Dalton and myself.

As I drove, I heard a tin of chewing tobacco rattling in the door pocket. Steering with one hand on the wheel, I popped open the lid, extracted a handful and shoved it in my mouth.

"That's disgusting." Karen Dalton fiddled with the radio.

Mostly fuzz but she finally landed on a country radio station and left it there. Randy Travis serenaded us with a lyrical vision of a honkytonk moon. Quite beautiful. And apropos. Where was this poet's Nobel Prize for the literary form?

I smiled and chewed. Yum. This chewing tobacco stuff was delicious. But the debris it left on my tongue was disgusting and annoying. And I thought fruit stones were bad! I waited until Karen Dalton's attention was drawn to the view out her own window, rolled down the window on my side and spat the wet wad out. I've tasted better sawdust.

Karen Dalton laughed. "Serves you right."

I rolled up the window and veered off the highway. A vast sandpile with some mountains in the distance and not a manmade light in sight.

"What are you doing?"

"This looks like as good a place as any." We bounced up and down as the pickup traversed the desert sands. I killed the headlights.

"What did you do that for?" Karen Dalton planted both hands on the dashboard to steady herself as the pickup bravely bucked blindly forward. Jesus and the little alien held on as best they could. "I can't see anything. You might hit a boulder!"

"A rock more likely. I think I'd spot something the size of a boulder even in the dark. But we can't take a chance of being spotted. Where we're going isn't exactly...how can I put this...? Legal."

"Oh, brother." Karen Dalton's teeth rattled.

I pressed on the brake and cut the motor. "Here we are." We listened to the engine cooling. Counting off the minutes. Tick tick tick.

I pushed open my door, climbed out of the Chevy, and hastily closed the door behind me when the overhead light popped to life, exposing us to any and all eyes. "Get out and close the door quick. And quietly. Better yet, climb out your window."

"Fine." With a couple of grunts and a string of curses, Karen Dalton unfolded herself from her seat and squirmed awkwardly through the Chevy's window. She sort of leapt, sort of fell, to the ground. She dusted off her elbows and knees and looked up. "It is beautiful…but scary, if you know what I mean?"

"I do."

She crossed in front of the pickup to my side. "What we're doing…"

"Yes?"

"It-It isn't going to be dangerous, is it?" Karen Dalton pressed closer. "I mean, there isn't anything dangerous out here, is there? Like rattlesnakes and scorpions?"

I chuckled for her benefit. "The most dangerous thing around here? Some say it's the Air Force. Some say it's the aliens. And still some say it's the cows."

"Cows?"

"Lots of open range out here, as you can see. A cow will kill you good and dead if you hit him or her just right. And they got brown ones for the daytime and black ones for nighttime. Bam!" I slammed my left fist into my right hand. "You never see them coming."

"Thanks for making me feel better, Ed. I knew I could count on you."

"My pleasure." I can be oblivious when I choose to be. I unfolded my copy of the alien invasion map from my inside pocket and studied it.

"You bought one of those things?"

"I thought it might come in handy. Even the most wrong things can be right. Sometimes."

"Including you?"

I reassembled the map as best I could. "Why the hell don't these things ever go back together right? I swear, sometimes I think it would be easier to reassemble a rocket ship!"

"Ed?"

"Yes?"

"Focus, huh?"

"Right." I shoved the crumpled mess down my pocket. "Now follow me. And be as silent as possible. No talking."

Talking probably didn't matter but she didn't know that. And the silence would be bliss for a change of pace.

"Fine."

"One second." I reached over and adjusted the hood of her hoodie over the top of her skull, pushing as much of her hair underneath as possible. I pulled the hoodie string taut and knotted it. All that brilliant blue hair! Her head looked like a ginormous blueberry! I tugged the zipper of her jacket up to her neck.

"Satisfied?"

"It'll do. Have you ever thought of cutting your hair? Maybe losing the blue?"

"Have you ever thought about what you'd look like with a black and blue eye?"

"What?"

"A *black* eye? Surely, you've heard of it. Maybe even been on the receiving end of one?"

I had. "Point taken." I turned and headed into the nothingness. "Let's march. And stay close. A body could easily get lost out here."

Or disappear completely.

13

"We must've walked a mile," Karen Dalton complained.

I stopped and glanced at the stars. A splinter of moon hung in the air. I spotted Jupiter, Saturn and Mars, mere motes in the Milky Way. "More like a mile and a half, I'd say."

"Great."

"Cheer up." I pointed. "See that horizontal line?"

"Just barely. What is it, Stonehenge? We've walked far enough."

"It's a fence."

"Whose fence?" She leaned her hand against my arm, yanked off her left sneaker, thumped it against her thigh, dumped out a sand dune and screwed the sneaker back over her foot—an operation she must've performed on one foot or the other a dozen times or more over the course of our night march.

"The sooner we get there, the sooner you'll see." I picked up my pace.

"So what's your story," Karen Dalton asked, not two minutes after I'd asked her to keep quiet.

"How do you mean?"

"I mean I've been stuck in a car with you for days and days on end and you never really talk much about yourself. All I know is weird stuff."

"Like?" I marched on, hoping against hope that she'd tire of speaking soon.

"Like you hate flying, hate fruit, drink too much, chew cigarette butts," she said with clear disgust, "and never sweat."

That got me. I missed a step, tripped, caught myself, and continued. "Don't I?"

"Not that I've noticed."

"Well, how about that."

Karen Dalton doubled her pace and followed me shoulder to shoulder. "Come on, what's your story, Ed? Why so private?"

"I'm a private eye. It's part of the job description."

"Ha-ha. No, really."

I sighed. The woman never shut up or gave up. "There's not much to tell."

"Right." Step-step. "You married?"

"No."

"Girlfriend?"

"Nope." The shadowy outline of the fence grew nearer.

"Family in LA?"

"Nada."

"Born in California like me? Got family there?"

I shook my head in the negative.

"In the US then? I haven't picked up any particular accent. Although you do talk funny."

I let that pass.

Step-step-step. "In the world? Have you got any family at all?"

"Again negative. I have only myself. And it's better that way."

"That's a funny thing to say."

"I'm a funny guy." And my shoes were filled with sand. "There it is."

Karen Dalton whistled. "It's no Great Wall of China but I bet it works just as well at keeping the marauding hoards out."

"And the tourists."

"But why put a big security fence out here? Must've cost a bundle. I don't see any Mongols running around. Nothing but fucking desert."

"You think?"

She hung close as we approached. The fence stood out clearly now and extended endlessly in both directions. "We are about to enter Area Fifty-one."

"Area Fifty-one?" Her fingers dug into my shoulder. "Is that really a good idea? What happens if we get caught?"

I gazed up at the top of the eight-foot tall barbwire-decorated, electrified-steel fence. "All hell breaks loose."

"Seriously, Ed. This is no joke. You see the sign." I did. Such signs were spaced every hundred yards or so along the fence. "Restricted Area. No trespassing beyond this point," Karen Dalton read. "Photography is prohibited. Use of deadly force authorized. *Deadly force*," she repeated for emphasis.

"What would you suggest? We can't go knocking on their gate and asking them politely to let us in. You hired me to find your brother. Keep him from being killed."

"But I didn't hire you to get *me* killed." She turned on her heel and headed back to the pickup.

"Okay," I said as loudly as I dared. There was every possibility that the landscape held as many listening devices as it did cacti. "But give up now and you may never find Ken. He may die because of you." Cruel, I know, but it had the desired effect.

Karen Dalton marched up to me, eyes slatted, nostrils flaring. I expected a punch and braced my muscles, so I was surprised when all she did was bite down on her lower lip before cursing me out.

"Are you done?" I asked as she paused to catch her breath.

She nodded.

"Learn that colorful language in poetry class, did you?" I reached into my jacket and pulled out the bourbon. I unscrewed the cap and pulled the neck to my lips. Karen Dalton snatched the bottle, wrapped her lips around the neck and sucked like a clumsy baby elk attached to mama's teat.

When she handed the bottle back, it was empty. I tossed the bottle into the darkness. Yeah, yeah, pollution and all that. Bottles are glass, the sand is glass. Ashes to ashes, dust to dust and all that. It's the cycle of life, bourbon bottle style. "Was that really necessary?" I asked morosely.

Karen Dalton smirked. "Absolutely. Now, let's do this." She

gazed up at the fence and burped. "How the hell *are* we going to do this?"

I stroked my chin. "Let's hope you're not as heavy as you look."

"Excuu-sse me?"

"Never mind. Perhaps the less you know the better."

"Listen—"

"Over we go." I held my hands out to her.

"You mean?"

I nodded.

"Oh no. You want me to go first? I think not." Karen Dalton backed away from the fence again.

"Do you trust me?"

"No, I don't trust you!"

"Too bad. Such a pity." I grabbed Karen Dalton at the hips and threw her over the barbed-wire fence. She landed with·a splat. I think they call it a belly flop. I believe I was supposed to say to remember to tuck and roll. Drat...

"You asshole!" she screamed from the other side, coughing up dust and rocks.

I closed my eyes for a moment and concentrated. Then I jumped. It was a risky thing to do but I had no choice and could only hope I hadn't given myself away.

I landed three feet behind Karen Dalton.

She spun quickly around. "Why did you do that? Wait." She blinked. "How did you do that?"

"Good calf muscles. Spin class. You should try it sometime."

She narrowed her eyes at me and climbed to her feet. Good, no broken bones. The effects of the bourbon might have saved her from serious injury. A worthy sacrifice of perfectly good alcohol.

"You-You..." She rubbed her fists into her eyes. "For a second there, I thought I saw... I mean, you... You looked different somehow. Like, like, like I don't know what. Like you weren't all there."

"The desert can play tricks on you," I explained. "Even at night. Especially at night. Now, we really should be very careful and very quiet from here forward. Stick close."

Karen Dalton cocked her head and looked at me long and hard. "Fine," she whispered as she pointed at me. "But you owe me an explanation."

"No time for explanations now. Fish or cut dates, isn't that what they say?"

"No, that's not what—"

"So let's get fishing. I hate dates."

"Adding that to my list of weird things I know about Ed." She scribbled with an imaginary pen in the air and finished up with an invisible check mark. "Check."

I took a peek at Mars and veered to the northwest. We stumbled along. We managed about one hundred yards.

And then the lights came on.

A wall of harsh LED vehicle headlights seared our vision. A million of them, more or less. Okay, less. But still plenty. But not so much that I couldn't discern the dozen or so automatic rifles waiting to Swiss cheese us. And I don't do dairy. Well, unless it's in the form of ice cream.

Karen Dalton screamed and threw her hands up higher —any higher and her sharp fingernails would've scratched the cheek of the Man in the Moon.

A black helicopter shrieked across the sky and descended rapidly, like a tornado. A beam of brilliant white light shot down, practically gluing us in place.

"I suggest we don't move."

"I couldn't move if I wanted to," replied Karen Dalton. "And I think I might've peed myself."

Our meet-and-greet army stood mutely.

The black helicopter dropped a dozen yards from where we stood, kicking up a sandstorm forcing us to shut our eyes. I opened my eyes once more as the rotors thudded slower and slower then ceased.

All the while, the vehicles circling us drew tighter.

Two uniforms, handguns at the ready, and a third suited man between them, hopped out of the chopper and halted in front of us.

"Bring them," ordered the man in the suit and tie without so much as a how do you do.

The first uniform holstered his weapon over his shoulder and dropped a thick gray canvas sack, smelling of grandma's slippers, over each of our heads.

"Ed, do something!" urged Karen Dalton.

"In good time," I said. "For now, I suggest we cooperate."

"Listen to the man," quipped one of the uniforms. "Live longer that way."

"Of course, you'll spend the rest of your lives in prison," the other uniform chuckled.

"Quiet!" I recognized the man in the suit as our speaker.

"Yessir!" both uniforms snapped.

Karen Dalton whimpered as they led us to the unmarked helicopter. The two strapped us in blindly and the helicopter rose quickly. "I feel like a bag of groceries," I dared to say.

That earned me a harsh slap from an unseen hand.

Within minutes, the chopper fell back to earth and wobbled to rest. We were helped out and guided silently down a steep metal stairway. Several twists and turns and we were shoved into a cold room. My guess was that we were one hundred feet or more underground. That was a lot of sand and rock between us and freedom.

All the while, Karen Dalton and I hadn't shared a word. She did squeeze my hand so hard at one point during the copter ride I was pretty certain she'd shattered my phalanges, two through four.

Rough hands pressed our butts down on a hard bench—I prayed it was a church pew but knew better—and those same hands yanked off the canvas sacks from over our heads. I blinked under the bright lights overhead. For people who operated in the dark, these people sure liked their lights.

Karen Dalton blinked too, eyes all agog and mouth gaping.

Although there wasn't much to see, a spartan and windowless room, not much more. The uniforms departed, closing the door behind themselves. She looked a little worse for wear. Her hoodie was filthy and her hood had fallen from her head. I noticed a new tear in the knee of her sweat pants. Of course, that might have been my fault when I'd sent her flying head-over-heels across the fence without warning her first.

Tuck and roll, tuck and roll. I really needed to remember that.

A woman in a fitted navy jacket stared at us, looking as animated as a department store mannequin. Deep brown hair, imprisoned within a tight bunch in back of her skull, extended from blonde roots. Her almond eyes judged me and Karen Dalton, seemed to bore into us from an unfathomable depth. She folded her hands atop the desk across from us. Pale skin told me she wasn't a sunworshipper. I wondered what she did worship.

She represented the upper echelon of the upper echelon, no doubt. And I had a name for her. "Doctor Marcia Allison, I presume?"

"How did you know?" Although her eyes barely flickered, I saw I'd surprised her.

"Lucky guess." Okay, I had to give the Internet a jigger's worth of credit. After my little foray into Ken Dalton's underground lab and learning from Joe Aguilar of Dr. Allison's existence, I'd done my research. Scouring the Web back at our hotel, I'd discovered a photo of her at an LANL function. Then, like now, she wasn't smiling. Not the type, I suppose.

Karen Dalton burped loudly and slapped her hand over her mouth in embarrassment.

"Is she drunk?" demanded Dr. Allison. I shrugged. Apparently she smelled the bourbon too.

"Wait, Ken's boss?" Karen Dalton gasped with a mix of something between awe and confusion.

"The one and only." I crossed my legs.

"You were trespassing." Marcia Allison leaned into her leather chair, swiveled slowly side to side. "You could be shot for being here."

"I'm looking for my brother." Karen Dalton clenched her hands tightly. "That's all. You don't have to kill anybody. Ed, Mister Turner, is helping me locate him. I hired him."

Dr. Allison very nearly smiled. "Mister Edward Turner of Los Angeles. Private detective." She fiddled with an Air Force-issue pen she plucked from the desktop. "The general hasn't been able to dig up much more about you. He's not happy about that."

"My apologies to, General Grant, is it?" She refused to confirm but I knew I was right again. "Tell the general there is not much more to tell. I've led a rather unremarkable life."

Her smile bloomed. "I'm sure you are being humble. We all have a story. A past."

Karen Dalton cleared her throat. "About my brother, Ken?"

Dr. Allison swiveled her eyes, like gun turrets, on the speaker. "Karen Dalton, poet slash graphic artist slash sister."

Karen Dalton gulped. "Is-Is Ken alright?"

Ken's boss let the question hang in the air a minute. "Yes, yes, Ken is fine. Perfectly fine. We're not monsters. We're all on the same team."

"Could've fooled me," I said.

"Listen." The pen twirled in Marcia Allison's fingers. Funny, I didn't picture the good doctor as the high-school baton-twirling cheerleader type. "Things in the lab were getting tense. Ken's been under terrific pressure. My fault, I suppose. I am his boss. I suggested, strongly suggested, that your brother take some time off. Attend the retreat."

"Retreat?" I asked.

"A private retreat. One reserved for special people, special circumstances. No computers, no telephones, no outsiders, and no outside communications of any kind. I assure you, your brother is perfectly safe there, Miz Dalton. Everybody on the team was getting a little nuts. I feel that way myself sometimes."

"What exactly is Ken Dalton working on?" I enquired. "I mean, it must be quite…special, shall we say, to cause him such distress."

Dr. Allison cocked her brow at me. "Are you asking General Grant to execute you here and now, Mister Turner? Because if I answer your question—"

"You'll have to shoot me afterward," I concluded.

"After having you dig your own grave first," Dr. Allison answered. "With a trowel."

"What about aliens?" Karen Dalton asked.

"Like little green men? Venusians? Don't make me laugh," Dr. Allison said. She set her pen down carefully. "You sound like one of the goofy locals. They're common as Joshua trees. You don't seriously believe that nonsense, do you?"

"But Ken told me that aliens were trying to kill him," Karen Dalton explained. "He telephoned me last week. He sounded really worried."

Dr. Allison threw open her hands. "You see? That's what I'm talking about. It's the pressure we've all been under. He was behaving erratically. Started drinking… Who knows? He might be doing drugs."

"No, Ken wouldn't do that," snapped Karen Dalton.

Ken's boss answered with a shrug. "Maybe he was succumbing to all the local weirdo mentality. Getting caught up in the preposterous hysteria that stretches over Los Alamos and Groom Lake like a cloud of crazy." Dr. Allison chuckled. "My personal opinion? They're all schizo."

"My brother is not schizo!"

"So what happens now?" I asked.

Karen Dalton shot me a warning look.

"You may not wish to learn what they intend to do with us," I said. "But I see no point putting it off."

Dr. Allison pressed the back of her head against her chair and chewed her pale pink lip. "Now," she stated, eyes never leaving me, "you two return to the Lil' Green Man Motor Court. You pack your bags and you go back to Los Angeles."

"But Ken—" Karen Dalton started.

Dr. Allison threw up her hand like a stop sign. "Ken will

contact you when he is...ready. Believe me, we all want what's best for him. He's the best of the best."

Karen Dalton sniffled. "He'd better be okay."

"He is. I promise."

Why did her promise not impress me? Quite the contrary, it had the opposite effect and left me feeling unsettled.

"Now," Dr. Allison rose from behind her desk. "The general's men will escort you to your motel. I suggest you leave as quickly as possible. The general is not your friend. Give him an excuse and he'll bury you both."

"No!" Karen Dalton jumped to her feet. "I won't! Not without seeing Ken!"

"Karen," I said gently. "We must. You heard the doctor. Ken isn't here. Besides, we've no choice. I'm sure Doctor Allison will do everything in her power to reunite you with your brother." I turned to Ken's boss. "Isn't that correct?"

"Of course," Dr. Allison managed to exude the best fake smile I'd ever seen. And I live in Los Angeles, surrounded by actors and hustlers of every ilk, so that's really saying something.

I clasped Karen Dalton's shaky hand and looked her in the eye. "Trust me."

She sobbed, chest heaving in and out.

General Grant burst in. "You're letting them go!?"

"Yes," replied Dr. Allison.

"No!" The general's face burned red. "This is a top secret facility."

"They haven't seen or heard anything, General."

"I still say lock them up and throw away the key."

"And I say your men are escorting the two of them back to the Lil' Green Man Motor Court where they will pack their bags and return immediately to Los Angeles."

"But—" The general sputtered, unused to, and unhappy with, taking orders from a civilian. The fact that it was a woman irked him all the more.

"I assured them that Doctor Dalton is perfectly fine and

would contact them as soon as possible." She smiled at both of us. "In fact, it's against the rules and it won't be easy, but I'll get word to him within the week. I'll insist he give you a call, Karen. That should ease your concern."

"You promise?" Karen Dalton asked.

"Yes. Hell, I'll order him to, if he gives me trouble."

General Grant gaped and fumed but kept his lips sealed.

Dr. Allison threw open the door. "General?"

With a sour look at the doctor, General Grant roughly shoved me through the doorway. Karen Dalton took up the rear. Our friends in uniform waited outside in the nondescript hallway. They dropped the same smelly canvas sacks over our heads and out we went.

14

Dawn greeted us on our return to the Lil' Green Man. Our captors had provided us with private yet less-than-luxury transportation in their unmarked black helicopter. Our hoods came off.

Samuel ran outside, shirtless and shoeless, hollering like WWIII was breaking out in front of his eyes, as we touched down in front of his office with all the stealth of a giant pink elephant, clutching a cherry-red umbrella in its trunk, tumbling down from a cumulonimbus cloud.

Or perhaps he thought the black chopper carried aliens come to ferry him back to display in their zoo on Zeta Reticuli.

The proprietor gripped a forty-four Magnum revolver with a six-and-a-half inch matte stainless steel barrel in his right hand. He pointed the barrel at the copter's windscreen. The two uniforms tucked their automatic rifle butts up to their shoulders and took aim at him from inside the chopper.

A real Area 51 standoff. Were Karen and I about to witness the Gunfight at the Area 51 corral? Who did these soldiers think they were, Burt Lancaster and Kirk Douglas?

The pilot radioed for orders—Dr. Allison and General Grant had declined to join us on our excursion—nodded to himself, then told the uniforms to dump us.

"Out you go!"

A kick in my posterior sent me falling from the helicopter. Karen Dalton landed on the ground at my side. I grabbed her and scrambled away from the rotating blades. "Come on! And keep your head down!"

I'm fond of my head and didn't want to lose it. I'd been

growing oddly, surprisingly, and annoyingly fond of Karen Dalton's head too, so better she should keep hers also. Plus, she represented a paycheck. I don't get a lot of those.

"What the hell is going on?" Samuel screamed above the roar of the chopper. We watched as it shot straight up then veered to the west. He stuffed his weapon into the waistband of his baggy gray Jim Beam pajama bottoms.

"Sorry about the commotion, Samuel. You remember Karen Dalton." The poor thing had her arms wrapped around my waist like competing pythons. I pried her loose.

"Not your fault. Goes with the territory. Living out here, you've got to put up with the vermin." Samuel coughed a good healthy smoker's cough. "What the devil you doing with those-those devils?" He shook his head, spat, and headed for his office.

We followed.

"The military offered to give us a ride home," I explained. I was dazzled by Samuel's hairy belly, more so by his hairless belly button. I'd never seen an outie before. Looked like an alien lifeform worming its way out of his stomach. This world never ceases to amaze me.

"I wondered what the hell happened to you." Samuel threw open the door and stepped into the motel office.

I smelled coffee and burnt toast.

"After I found my Chevy sitting out by the road and all. And no sign of you two." Samuel helped himself to a mug of brew. "You folks want some?"

"No, thanks," Karen Dalton managed to say. She was shivering and appeared on the verge of catatonia.

I glanced out the front window. I hadn't noticed but, sure enough, Samuel's pickup truck had returned to the roost. Compliments of military security, no doubt. I was happy to see that I hadn't cost Samuel his truck. And that the military hadn't confiscated it. Free of bullet holes too. I'd been feeling bad about leaving his treasured vehicle abandoned in the desert. I suspected losing a pickup truck was akin to losing a child in this world.

"Enjoy your stargazing?" Samuel looked from me to Karen.

"I think I've seen enough stars to last a lifetime." She yawned big and loud. "All I want now is to see a bed."

"I know the feeling," I replied. I patted my pockets. No truck keys. "Keys in the truck?"

"Keys in the truck."

I said goodbye for the two of us and Karen and I headed to our rooms. She paused outside the door to room 207.

"Don't worry. If you're thinking there might be soldiers waiting inside to kidnap us again, there won't be."

Karen Dalton glanced sourly at her drape-covered window. No telling what was inside. "Better not be. And that bitch better be telling me the truth. She better tell Ken to call me. And soon." She shuddered and I sensed a wall of tears hiding behind a dam might break loose. Get my feet all wet.

"Good night," I said. Better to go now, before the proverbial floodgates broke open. Let her cry in the peace and comfort of her own room. Well, her own Lil' Green Man Motor Court room, such as it was.

"Wait." She gripped the cuff of my jacket between her thumb and forefinger.

"Yes?"

Before I knew what was happening, Karen Dalton pressed her sandy dry lips against mine. She kissed me. Stuck her tongue down my throat. I gasped. Sucked in a lifesaving breath.

She pulled away. Blinked. "Sorry."

"No need to apologize. All in all, it wasn't the worse thing anyone has ever done to me."

"Gee, thanks." She punched me in the gut. But not hard. I mean, I could still breathe. She reddened. Was that shame or mere embarrassment?

"Better get some sleep," I said. "It's been a long night."

"What about what Doctor Allison said? About us leaving town straight away? Won't the general be pissed if we don't leave pronto?"

"Sure but we need rest. The general's just going to have to

be patient a little longer. We'll get some sleep, some food, plant-based, if you must, then hit the road. Deal?"

She answered with a peck on my cheek. "Deal."

"Goodnight," I said softly. "Karen." I waited until she went inside and I heard the sound of her locking her door. Afterward, I leaned over the wobbly railing, lip up a Camel, and scanned the desert. There was so much going on. And not much of it made sense.

The world could wait. I chewed and swallowed my cigarette butt—wouldn't want to litter, would I? I returned to my room, crawled into bed, pulled up the covers, and shut my eyes. The loud asthmatic hum of the wall-mounted AC unit lulled me to a restless sleep.

It was the sirens that woke me. I sat up quickly and rubbed my eyes. My mouth felt like I'd been chewing wet sand. I teetered to the window and threw open the curtains.

Two sheriff department vehicles and two unmarked sedans swarmed the parking lot, lights flashing. What on earth? Had I been wrong? Had General Grant arrived to boot us out? Worse, to bury us?

I slid back the security chain on my door and stepped outside. I'd slept in my clothes, too tired to undress, too tired to care. "What's going on?"

A young man with greasy brown ponytail, blue shirttails hanging loose over tight blue jeans, clutching a baby swaddled in a pink blanket, hurried along the corridor. His bare feet slapped the ground. "They say it's some dead woman. That's all the cops will tell me." He gently rocked his crying baby. "Police, what assholes," he said before slamming the door to his unit.

The young man's opinion of authorities seemed to be the popular one around these parts. The fellow was probably a UFO nut and conspiracy theorist, most tourists this far out were pretty far out themselves. Not much else to see or do around these parts otherwise. Perhaps he'd come to have his newborn child baptized in a ritual to be conducted by the High Priestess of the Court of the Venusian Sun Queen. I'd buy a ticket to watch that.

I pulled on my shoes and hurried downstairs where I found Samuel leaning against the whirring ice machine. "What's going on? A guest said somebody died?"

Samuel pulled a face. "You might say that. Then again, you might say got herself murdered."

"Oh?" I looked around quickly. "Karen—"

"Nah, relax, Ed." The proprietor patted my arm. He wore a brown denim pants, a Lil' Green Man Motor Court tee shirt and cowboy boots adorned with tooled five-point stars at the toes. "Not your lady, Karen. I'm sure she's fine. This is another woman."

"Glad to hear it." I breathed a sigh of relief, surprised to discover my heart racing.

"Didn't look too long dead neither."

"You saw her?"

"Yeah. Mel found her."

"Mel?"

"Part-time maid, part-time girlfriend."

"I see. Came in this morning to do her thing. Mel went to dispose of some trash a little bit ago, like she always does, and found the poor thing sitting next to the dumpster out back. Told me she thought the lady had passed out drunk or on drugs or something. Tried to rouse her. That's when Mel realized she'd snuffed it."

"Wow." I glanced at my watch. Nearly three in the afternoon. The way the building sat, the body would have enjoyed some morning shade but by afternoon, well, the effects of all that hot sun on the body would not be beneficial—even to the dead.

"Yeah, wow." We stopped to watch an ambulance roll into the parking lot and a couple of EMT types roll out its doors. I smelled beer on Samuel's breath.

"We got a rule of thumb around here," Samuel spat.

"What's that?"

"Aliens are good for business. Police are bad for business.

Make the guests nervous."

"People here are suspicious of cops?"

Samuel smiled. "Yeah. And the feeling's mutual. Cops are suspicious of them."

"How's your girlfriend taking it?"

"Okay, I hope. I haven't talked to her since she came running into the lobby like a crazy person. Screaming that the aliens had finally done it."

"Done it?"

"Murdered one of our guests."

"I see," I said. But really, I didn't.

"You might find this part funny."

I doubted it but asked, "What?"

"The woman's the one you were asking about."

"Asking about?"

"Yeah, you know, the woman who came in here a time or two with Dalton."

"Wait, the murdered woman Mel found is the same woman that Ken Dalton sometimes came here with? Are you sure?"

"Sure as sure can be. Saw her myself. After I got the old lady calmed down I ran around back to check it out. I didn't want to be calling the authorities if I didn't need to. Mel has quite the imagination. Might've been seeing things. She does sometimes. Then again, the lady might've just been sleeping off a bender. You know what?"

"What?"

"I could see straight away that lady wasn't going to be waking up from any bender. Not in this lifetime," Samuel added rather nonsensically, although his words did make a certain sense to me.

"Did you notice any signs of a struggle? Or violence?"

"Nope. She was just slumped against the back of the motel, chin tucked into her chest. She wasn't mutilated by no aliens, if that's what you're thinking, Ed."

It wasn't but there was no ruling out the possibility. The universe can surprise you so it's best to leave your mind open to the infinite possibilities it holds. "When did she arrive?"

"The dead lady?" Samuel shrugged. "No idea. Hell, I didn't know she was here. Like I told Sheriff Pack, she wasn't a guest."

"Did the sheriff tell you anything? The victim's name?"

The proprietor shook his head in the negative. "Assholes haven't let me talk to Mel since they showed up. Questioning her, I guess. Fat lot of good that'll do. Mel didn't see nothing more than what I already told you and them."

"They around back?"

"Suppose so. Want a beer?"

"Yes," I answered. "but it will have to wait. I believe I'll take a look at this mysterious dead woman."

"Suit yourself. I mean, you can try but the authorities will probably tell you to go to hell."

I cracked a smile. "Not to worry, they tell me that on a regular basis."

Samuel retreated to his beer stash and I worked my way behind the motor court from which I heard sounds of commotion, including a healthy amount of arguing and cussing. I surmised none of this emanated from the dead woman's mouth.

Four uniformed cops paced the rear of the motel. Two of them worked together cordoning off the area with crime scene tape. The third busied himself taking photographs. Maybe of the victim, maybe of alien spacecraft. His call. The fourth man, standing around looking self-important, I identified as Sheriff Pack.

A metal Quonset hut erupted from the earth some ten yards or so back from the motel. A glancing peek through the hut's folded open double doors revealed Samuel utilized this as a storeroom for his motel supplies and ancillary workings. Near the door stood a white washer/dryer combo whirring and belching their way through the day. I also spotted boxes and boxes of toilet paper, hand sanitizer, canisters of milk powder, ammunition for weapons of various calibers, cereal, freeze-dried dinners, and other everyday essentials for the imminent apocalypse. And two whole pallets stacked emu high with cases and cases of bottled water.

The recently-arrived EMTs stood near the green dumpster, rolling chrome steel stretcher at the ready. Dr. Allison was interviewing, more accurately haranguing, a dowdy woman somewhere in her late forties, dressed in a frilly white blouse and tight jeans embroidered with pink and yellow peonies, with a waistline nearly as large as Samuel's. Her blonde hair was probably not original factory equipment. Her lips were vivid red, and her cheeks even redder. I suspected that the good Dr. Allison was getting under Mel's skin.

Nobody looked pleased to see me round the corner and approach.

"Hey, you! Get the hell out of here!" barked the nearest deputy, moving in my direction.

Dr. Allison stopped talking at Mel and swiveled. "You."

"This is a crime scene, doofus," furthered the deputy. All the while, his boss was talking on the phone. Whether to some higher authority, his bookie in Las Vegas, or his wife to say he'd be home late and to hold his dinner, I couldn't say.

"Come." Dr. Allison motioned me forward.

I smiled at the deputy. "What can I say? I'm a popular guy."

He looked at me like I was a jackrabbit and he was hungry for raw meat but let me pass.

"Can I go now?" pleaded Samuel's girlfriend, Mel.

"Fine." Dr. Allison snapped her notebook shut. "But we'll be in touch."

Mel muttered some Spanish curse words and stomped off. Probably to complain to Samuel about the poor treatment she'd received and to drink a beer. Quite possibly in reverse order. She flung a few words in my direction but she was wasting her breath. I didn't understand a single word. I speak seven languages—but none of them are useful here.

I stepped over the yellow crime scene tape. "Who is she?"

"You tell me."

"I would if I could." I moved closer to the woman. No

immediately recognizable signs of physical trauma. Looking more closely at her slumped neck, I spotted a small mark, like a fuzzy red star, two or three inches across. Dried blood. I pointed to the mark. "What do you make of that?"

"No idea. Not fang marks so we can rule out vampires."

So Marcia Allison has a sense of humor. Another surprise. "No driver's license or other ID?" I inquired. A funny odor stuck in my nostrils but I couldn't place it. Between the dumpster, the cologne of the nearest deputy, whatever scent Mel bathed herself in, and the stewing body of the victim, the air was a foul mixture best left unsniffed.

"Nothing official," replied Dr. Allison.

"Nothing official? What does that mean?"

"It means there was nothing in her pockets except for this." She waved a tattered business card under my nose.

"May I?"

Dr. Allison frowned. "You may look but don't touch it. This is evidence."

"Of course." I looked at the face of the crumpled white card. "Emily Crenshaw. Alien Resistance Corps, Scout First Class."

Marcia Allison snorted. "You ever hear anything so ridiculous?"

I let the question hang in the air before answering, studied the dead woman closely. "The world's filled with ridiculous things. You've heard of this group?" I had. The dead woman was an alien hunter.

She pushed her hair from her eyes. "One of those fringe groups who believe the Earth's been invaded by aliens bent on our destruction."

"If these mythical aliens invented social media, I'd say they're off to a good start," I quipped. "The question is, does this card belong to her or did she receive it from this Emily Crenshaw?"

"I'm sure Sheriff Pack will figure it out."

"I'm sure." The sheriff or the military or both. "Tell me, Doctor, what brings you here? I mean, if this is so ridiculous...

Not to mention, aren't we a bit out of your job description here? Shouldn't we be leaving this to the professionals?" I indicated Sheriff Pack and his posse.

"Nothing mysterious about my presence. I happen to be in the area, as you well know. And if anything…unusual happens around here, I like to know about it."

"What exactly is it that you are working on that brings you to Area Fifty-one? We're a long way from Los Alamos."

"As are you, Mister Turner."

"Meaning?"

"Meaning records show you spent a night in Los Alamos recently yourself. You and Ken's sister."

We'd left a trail. Stupid and careless of me, in retrospect. Then again, I'd no idea what we were involving ourselves in.

Did she know I'd invaded her lair? Were we playing cat and mouse?

Damn, I hate it when I'm the mouse.

"Anything you'd care to share with me?" Dr. Allison asked. Sheriff Pack interrupted our pas de deux to ask if it was okay to remove the body. Dr. Allison told him to go ahead. "Let's let them do their job." She jostled me away from the crime scene and listening ears. I watched the EMTs cart the dead woman away.

We crossed to the shade of the Quonset hut.

"What about you?" I demanded. "Do you recognize Emily Crenshaw, Scout First Class, if that's who she is?"

"Should I?"

Hmm, here was one of those moments that could make or break a case. Change the course of events. Should I tell Marcia Allison about Ken Dalton and his connection—vague as it was to me—to Emily Crenshaw? For that matter, did she already know?

After considering the pluses and minuses, I decided to spill a bean or two. After all, if Samuel hadn't told Allison or the sheriff yet that he'd seen the woman with Dalton, he was bound to sooner or later. Probably sooner. Why not earn some points in my favor with the doctor? It might help Karen reunite with her brother all the sooner.

"The motel manager mentioned to me that he'd seen the victim here at the Lil' Green Man on several occasions. In the company of Ken Dalton."

Dr. Allison pulled a face. "Yeah, he told me that too."

Whew, I was glad I'd come clean.

"Ken might have shacked up with the woman here but I've never seen him with her. And why he'd pick this dump..." Dr. Allison glared at the back of the motel. True, it wasn't much to write home about.

Her face turned fierce as a lioness defending her cubs. "No pictures!" She hollered. "Sheriff! Get that camera!"

I turned to see who or what was causing the commotion. A zaftig creature clad in a skintight green leotard was snapping pictures with her phone. Green body paint covered every inch of her exposed flesh, making her look like she was ready for St. Patrick's Day on Jupiter. She braved pointy black shoes with three-inch heels. And, although I remembered rabbit ears and their purpose on the back of a 1960s-era television set, were those green knitting needles projecting from the top of her skull? What kind of signals was she receiving?

One of the deputies grabbed her. While he was tussling with her, another deputy snatched the phone from her hand —the one she was using to bang the first deputy upside his head. Everybody was hollering at once, except the woman's companion, a man dressed in a striped caftan and leather sandals. He was much skinnier than her and much, much quieter. Hands at his side, he watched with unrevealing blue eyes.

The woman broke free of the deputies, stepped back out of their reach, and yelled, as the deputy stuffed her phone in his jacket. "Hey, you can't do that! That's against the law!"

"This is a crime scene," Sheriff Pack snapped, looking angry and like he gave a shit for the first time since I'd been on the murder scene.

"I'm Lena Jay. You have no authority over me."

"You can't take unauthorized photos here. This is a crime

scene," repeated Sheriff Pack.

Lena Jay bored into him with hard green eyes. "Appropriating private property is against the law. Tell him, Ernie." Her companion blinked. He had a long, acne-scarred face. His head was topped with spiky black hair.

"So is impersonating a Martian!" Sheriff Pack retorted.

"I am not a Martian." She drew herself up, puffed out her considerable chest. "I am the Queen's royal representative from the High Court of Venus."

"Get her out of here!"

"Yeah, go on. Hop in your flying saucer and buzz off!" One deputy said bravely.

"You can stick a flying saucer up your ass!" Lena Jay snapped.

Both deputies made a grab for Lena Jay but one look from her and they allowed her to walk away unaided, her companion Ernie at her side. "You won't get away with this!" she hollered at the sheriff as she disappeared. "I'm a representative of the Intergalactic Venusian Council. I have diplomatic immunity!"

"What you've got is a screw loose," Sheriff Pack replied, but not so loud that Lena Jay might hear him. I didn't blame the sheriff. That woman appeared dangerous.

While the sheriff and his men were preoccupied, Marcia Allison slipped something into my pants pocket. "What are you doing?" I reached inside.

She stopped me. "Not here," she cautioned. "After we're gone."

15

I knocked on Karen Dalton's door. No answer. And I saw no sign of her. "Karen?" I banged harder. Was she inside? Showering? Sleeping? Slumped over dead in the bathroom with a weird star-shaped marking on the nape of her neck? From which all her blood had escaped?

I have a vivid imagination.

"Karen? It's me, Ed!" Crap. The Tesla sat in the parking lot. She hadn't taken the car and fled. Was the woman hiding from me? Mortified and ashamed because she'd stuck her tongue down my throat?

I hurried downstairs to the front office to fetch Samuel. I'd get him to open her door.

The office was open but empty. I heard voices coming from somewhere in back. "Hello?"

I walked behind the deserted counter and followed the sound of mingled voices, clattering dishes, and the aroma of cooking. Down a narrow hall lined with yellowed newspaper clippings—featuring alien abductions and UFO sightings, thumbtacked to the walls—I spilled into a tiny kitchen. A single paned window—unwashed since its creation fifty or more years ago—looked out at the side yard. The yard held a jumble of busted dressers, split headboards, cracked toilets, chipped mirrors, rusty box springs, dysfunctional minifridges, rolled up moldy carpets, and torn lampshades.

The place old motor court furnishings went to die. And apparently the kitchen was the room from which Samuel and Mel liked to watch it die.

"Hi, Ed." Karen said from the small kitchen table, her

hands wrapped around a mug of hot tea. A half-eaten slice of unbuttered toast sat on a pale blue plate in front of her.

"Here you are," I exclaimed.

"Yeah, I wanted to talk to Samuel. Learn more about Ken."

"Sure."

"Park your ass, Ed." Samuel waved to an empty wooden chair with a padded seat. Mel stood over the stove scrambling up some eggs. My stomach let me know it hungered. I glanced at our other guest, seated between Samuel and Karen.

"I thought the sheriff ran you off?" I thanked Mel for the unasked for pile of scrambled eggs smothered in gravy. Two warm biscuits hovered on the edge of my plate. I stuffed one down my gullet.

"I'm not going anywhere until they give me my phone back. Damn thing set me back nine hundred dollars!" Lena Jay's plate was empty but for bits of egg and pepper, and a drop or two of brown gravy.

"Where's Ernie?"

"Out in the RV. Working on our newsletter."

"I see." But I didn't.

Rather than ask, I dove into breakfast, even though it was well past lunchtime. "Delicious," I said, filling my fork and then my mouth. Nobody cared. I noticed that Karen had bought a new Lil' Green Man Motor Court tee shirt complete with a little green man waving hello. She'd torn off the sleeves. She looked good in it. I gulped some coffee. "Learn anything?"

"Not much," Karen admitted.

"Sorry I can't be more obliging," Samuel said. "Like I said, your brother kept to himself the few times he was here. The woman's pretty much a stranger to me."

"Me too." Mel sat down with a five-pound plate filled with scrambled eggs, several biscuits, two slices of toast and guava jelly, and a pickle. "You want a pickle, Ed?"

"Thanks, no." I poured salt and pepper over my eggs. "Best meal I've had in a long time. We've been eating out of motels and cheap food joints the past week."

Mel nodded. "Nothing like a homecooked meal."

"Tell me about it," Samuel grumbled, stretched his arms out over his head and yawned loudly. "That time you was abducted and I had to fix my own meals, man, that was hell."

"Abducted?" Karen said. "What happened?"

"It was the aliens, wasn't it?" Lena Jay leaned across the small kitchen table, hands gripping the edge.

Mel nodded somberly. "Yes."

"Tell us," Lena Jay begged.

"Must have been six months or so ago." Mel sat back and shuttered her eyes.

I took the opportunity to sneak a biscuit off her plate. Karen shot me a nasty look. "What?" I mouthed. "I'm hungry."

"It was a Tuesday, I remember," continued Mel. "I couldn't sleep. Went outside. You remember, Sammy dear?"

"I remember."

"The sky was so clear. That's what made it so easy to see."

"See what?" Karen asked.

"The lights." explained Mel. "From the flying saucer. Only it really wasn't round like your normal flying saucer. This one was more oval and had a big bump on the back."

"Like an overgrown wart, you said," added Sammy.

"You really saw this, Mel?" I found myself saying.

"Sure as anything. Cross my heart and hope to die." Mel made the sign of the cross.

"And the lights," Samuel prompted. "Tell them more about the lights."

Mel nodded. "There were two rows of yellow lights running around the ship like a belt. I tried to yell for Sammy to come. To see. But when I opened my mouth, nothing came out."

Lena Jay bobbed her head. "That's the aliens. They do that. They can control your vocal cords."

I was pretty sure hysteria could do the same thing but kept my mouth shut. This wasn't my story, after all.

"I was frozen." Mel gulped a slug of coffee then continued. "That's when they hit me."

"They hit you?" gasped Karen.

"With their traction control beam," explained Samuel.

"Traction control beam? Sounds like a car feature." Okay, I shouldn't have said that aloud. Karen kicked me in the shin under the table to make sure I got the message.

"Up I went!" Mel raised her chin and looked at the ceiling. I didn't know what she was seeing but I was seeing chipped beige ceiling paint. It probably contained lead. Maybe fossils from the Precambrian period.

"Up she went," echoed Samuel, pointing a yellow-tipped finger at the ceiling.

"What happened next?" Karen stuffed the remains of her toast in her mouth and chewed big, eyes never leaving Mel.

"They probed and prodded me for days." She laid a hand atop Samuel's hand.

"What did they look like?"

I looked at Karen. Had she really asked that question? Was she buying into Mel's tale? And tale it was.

Mel clutched her fork like a wand. "Not like you or me or anybody human," she said, jutting her utensil at each of us in turn.

"Like what then?" Lena Jay demanded.

"Well...more-more fishy."

"Fishy?"

"Like a dolphin, you know. Flipper?"

"Dolphins are mammals," I pointed out. I should have known better. Karen has a vicious kick. And that one struck me pointy toe first.

"Yep, like your dolphin," Mel went on, not seeming to mind my interruption. "Long gray bodies, smooth as rubber balls. But with two long spindly legs and short stubby hands where a dolphin's flippers would be. Their flesh was cold to the touch. And they spoke Hungarian."

"Hungarian?" Okay, even I was curious now. "How do you know? Do you speak Hungarian, Mel?"

She shook her head. "Not a word. But I'm sure that's what

they was talking."

I have no further questions, your honor—I kept that thought to myself.

"Gone three whole days and nights," Samuel added.

"What did they want? Did they say?" This question came from Lena Jay.

"My recipes, can you believe it?"

I couldn't. I mean, her eggs and biscuits were okay but nothing to write intergalactic home about.

"That's it?" asked Karen.

"Yes, well, no." Mel hesitated. "Sorry, Sammy dear, but you know the next part."

"S'okay. Go ahead and tell them."

Mel blushed. "They-They inseminated me."

Lena Jay spoke up. "Alien insemination! The first step in their domination of Earth!" Her eyes shot around the kitchen. "Where is the alien spawn?"

Preposterous as it was, I found myself looking around too. So did Karen.

"Aborted," confessed Mel. "Never took."

"Thank heavens." Lena smeared a fat hand over her sweaty forehead. Green paint dripped down her eyes.

"Did you ever see them again? The aliens?" Karen rose and snatched the warm tea kettle from the stovetop, refilled her cup, waved the kettle in the, dare I say, *pregnant* air. "Anybody else?"

"I'll take another cup of coffee," Samuel said. "If you don't mind?"

"No problem." Karen topped off his mug and sat. "What do you think, Ed?"

"Unbelievable." Everybody could take that statement however they chose.

"They kept my panties." Mel's face bloomed bright red.

Lena Jay sucked in a breath, taking half the air in the kitchen with her.

"To this day, I don't go anywhere outside at night without a loaded shotgun." Mel stuffed scrambled egg down her throat.

She looked for a minute at her plate like something was missing, which it was—the biscuit I'd helped myself to—then wiped up some gravy with one of her two remaining biscuits.

Lena Jay planted her bony elbows on the table. Plates, cups, saucers, and flatware rattled like the kitchen table was one giant Ouija board and a gigantic dead troll was pounding like the devil to get out from underneath. I held onto my mug to keep it from spilling over. "Where are you and Karen from, Eddie?"

"Los Angeles," Karen said.

"Sure," replied Lena. "But where are you really from?"

"That's it," said Karen. "Born and raised."

"And you?" I asked, hoping to cut off any further inquiry to my past.

"Ernie and I are on a royal tour," Lena Jay explained. "Heard about the murder on the CB radio."

I smiled. "I noticed the RV out front." Decorated with more radar dishes than a nuclear class destroyer. "Yours?"

"We use it while we're visiting."

"When on Earth, do like the Earthlings?" I quipped.

"Ed!" admonished Karen. "Don't poke fun."

"Sorry, I didn't mean any offense." I scooted further from the kitchen table. A body can only tolerate so many kicks in the shin. Starts to hurt.

"No offense taken, honey. Being outsiders, we're used to the skeptics."

"Say…" Mel gaped, a look of fear bathed her eyes. "You-You aren't one of the ones that abducted me, are you?" She dove for the kitchen drawer next to the stove and pulled out a thirty-two caliber semiautomatic. She took aim at Lena Jay's mottled green-and-red face.

Karen screamed.

"No! No!" Lena Jay threw up her hands.

"Now, now. Put that away, Mel," ordered Samuel, taking the situation calmly. I got the sense this was just another day in the life for the man. Mel hesitated, chewed her lip, then slid the gun back inside the drawer.

"Thank you! Venusians would never do no such thing, Mel. I can assure you. We come in peace. Probably the Reticuli abducted you. Nasty brutes," she said with a shake of the head that set her chins waddling. "No one's ever seen one—at least not that they can remember. Reticuli burn your memories out of your brain if you accidently catch sight of one."

"But I remember what they look like," Mel replied.

"Right." Lena Jay chewed her lip and side-stepped the problem. "Must be some other alien species we've yet to come in contact with. Even we Venusians don't know every intelligent species. It's a big galaxy."

"I'll bet," Mel said.

"Rest easy, Mel, we want only to be friends with humans, to live together in peace and harmony. And to develop trade."

"What sort of trade?" I found myself asking.

"Glad you ask." A smile transformed the Venusian's face. She bent and scooped a capacious rhinestoned bag from the linoleum floor. "These." Lena Jay smacked a wrapped chocolate bar the size of a gold ingot on the table. She slid the bar toward me.

"Chocolate?" My eyes lit up. I don't do dairy as a rule but chocolate, like ice cream, was one of my exceptions. A pleasure and I felt no guilt about it whatsoever. I don't believe in guilty pleasures. Why feel guilty about harmless pleasures?

"Nothing like it on earth," quipped Lena Jay.

My fingers hovered over the chocolate bar. "May I?"

"Be my guest." Lena Jay smiled. "Anyone else?" She extracted another bar from the depths of her handbag and offered it up.

Heads shook in the negative. Mel and Samuel stated they were full to bursting. I didn't know what Karen's problem was. But it was her loss. I freed the foil-and-paper wrapped bar of heaven from its covering. The label stated this to be the Venus DeLuxe Dark Deep Space Chocolate Bar. Lena Jay's contact info, including phone number and website details, were listed on the bottom of the wrapping.

I held the naked bar to my nose and inhaled. "Amazing." Frankly, I could have eaten the paper too, infused as it was with the luscious scent of dark chocolate. But being in mixed company—both alien and human—I knew better than to give in to my baser urges.

I bit down and my teeth practically melted into the chocolate bar. I rolled the chunk across my tongue, chewed then swallowed slowly.

"Good?" asked Karen.

"The best," I admitted. "This chocolate bar is amazing."

"Glad you're enjoying it, Ed." Lena stuck out her palm. "That'll be five dollars. Cash. We don't do plastic on Venus."

"Five dollars?" I looked at the green creature with confusion in my eyes.

"For the chocolate bar." Lena snapped her purse shut. "Five dollars each. Of course, if you like, I can sell you a whole case, that's twelve full-size bars, for fifty dollars. Great discount, huh?"

I suppressed a frown and extracted a five-dollar bill from the dwindling supply in my wallet. "I'll start with the one." I'm not made of money…or anything else Lena Jay might recognize.

"Are you sure? I can give you a case of the mixed. That's half Dark Deep Space Chocolate. The other half Alien Almond."

"Tempting. But this will do for now." I patted my gut. "Watching my belt." And my cashflow. So far, I hadn't seen a dime from Karen.

"Okay, suit yourself, Eddie. You know where to reach me should you want more."

I nodded and stood. I'd been conned enough for one day—in more ways than one. "We'll be leaving in the morning," I said to our host.

"Sorry to see you go," Samuel replied.

"Ready, Karen?"

We exited and headed upstairs to her room. Sheriff Pack and Dr. Allison had gone, taking all traces of their passing with them. Including one dead alien hunter.

Sitting on the edge of the bed, I used my electronic

notebook to look into the dead woman's background. "Seems Emily Crenshaw was the woman's real name. Age thirty-two. Never married, no children. Parents in Winter Springs, Florida."

Karen hovered over my left shoulder.

"Started out as a bookkeeper for a small firm in Orlando, Florida. Quit to devote her life to the full-time pursuit of extraterrestrials." I read from her blog.

"What's her connection to Ken?"

"You tell me. Maybe Ken hired her to protect him from these aliens he claims were out to kill him?"

"Maybe." Karen tapped her fingers atop my shoulder. "But he only warned me less than a week ago. According to Samuel and Mel, Ken and Emily have been coming here for months. Why?"

I shrugged.

"Some detective you are."

I was saved from defending myself by a firm knock on her door.

Karen froze.

"I'll get it." I glanced through the peephole and opened the door. "Sheriff Pack. This is a surprise. Can we help you?"

The sheriff, a gaunt man with a military-style haircut and beady brown eyes ignored me and latched onto Karen. "You know where your brother might be, Miz Dalton?"

"Ken? No, of course not." Karen stood on the far side of the bed, keeping her distance.

"That's why we're here, Sheriff. We are looking for Ken Dalton. If we knew where he was, we'd be there. Not here." I frowned at him. "Is that it?" I tried to close the door but he stood in the path of its trajectory.

"I've got a witness who says he saw Kenneth Dalton loitering behind the motel early this morning."

"That's impossible!" shouted Karen. "Who is this person?"

"I'm not at liberty to say."

"Really, Sheriff. Your witness must be mistaken. I have it on good authority, the word of Doctor Marcia Allison, in fact, that

Ken Dalton is nowhere in the area."

"I don't care what nobody says, if I catch the sonofabitch, he's gonna be in a jail cell. If you ask me, he's the most likely suspect I got for the murder of the Crenshaw woman."

"How can you be so certain?" I said angrily.

"How? Because I know everybody in this county. None of them are killers." He folded his arms over his chest. "So it's got to be an outsider."

"Then maybe it was an alien!" snapped Karen. "Like the ones who abducted Mel." She drew closer. "What are you doing about *them*, Sheriff?"

I looked at my client in stunned silence. Had I lost her? Had she gone off the deep end into I-believe-in-aliens land? Were Ken and Karen Dalton part of the lunatic fringe?

I mean, I believed in aliens too, but not the way nor for the same reasons Karen appeared to.

Sheriff Pack smiled sourly in my direction and pointed. "You."

"Yes?"

"I don't like detectives. I especially don't like detectives who got no licenses."

"I've been meaning to get—"

"Samuel tells me you two are checking out in the morning. Do us all a favor, don't find your way back here. And you," he barked at Karen. "Tell your brother I'd like a word with him."

"Join the club!" Karen slammed the door on his nose. Muffled cussing followed. "Jerk!"

I handed her a cold beer. She didn't refuse. We sat and drank in silence on the edge of the bed. My thoughts were filled with questions about Ken Dalton and Marcia Allison. A tangle of mysteries. One of the big questions was how exactly were the two mysteries entwined?

And what about Dr. Allison? She'd made a point of letting us know that she knew where Karen and I were staying when we'd first been snared out at Area 51. Had she or others been following us? Spying on our activity and movements? What had she been doing at the installation in the first place? What was her job? And was that the reason she was here at the Lil' Green Man the minute a dead body showed up?

Not happy or comfortable thoughts.

I thrust my hand in my pocket and felt a small square at the bottom. Curious, I pulled it out. I discovered a tightly-folded piece of paper. "Forgot all about this."

"What is it?" Karen sniffed and pressed against my side.

"It's from Doctor Allison. She slipped it to me earlier when we were talking. Said not to open it with the sheriff around."

"That's weird."

"Everything about this case is weird." I unfolded the paper carefully and read. Nothing on the plain white square but a pair of coordinates written in blue ink. Knowing a thing or two about the world, I knew what these numbers represented. These coordinates pointed to a location in Colorado.

"A bunch of numbers?" Karen sighed. "What is that supposed to mean?"

"It means," I said, "we are going to Colorado." Curiouser and curiouser.

"Why would Doctor Allison give you coordinates to someplace in Colorado?" Her fingers dug into my shoulder. "Do you think that's where we'll find Ken?"

"Could be," I replied. "Only one way to find out." I refolded the square of paper and returned it to my pocket for safekeeping.

"Sure." Karen smiled for the first time in a long time. "Sure, she's helping us. I'll finally get to see that idiot brother of mine." She leapt from her bed and grabbed her suitcase from the corner of the room. "Let's go! Get packed, Ed!"

"Not now." I stood. "We'll leave after dark."

"After dark?"

"Less...conspicuous," I replied. As I departed, I couldn't help wondering... If these coordinates did lead to Ken Dalton, why was Marcia Allison helping us?

16

I rapped lightly on Karen's motel room door. My suitcase stood by my side. She opened up her door. "Ready?" I whispered.

"Yes." She clutched her suitcase in one hand and a bottle of water in the other. Pink peace sign earrings dangled from her ear lobes. More baubles ran up the edges of her ears. She was bundled in her jeans, hoodie, and sneakers.

She was going to need some warmer clothing where we were going. Cold had descended on the desert as the sun had set. It would get colder as our road climbed higher into the mountains.

We tiptoed downstairs. At two in the morning, people can take unkindly to others making a commotion outside their doors. The lights of every room were out. Lena Jay and Ernie's RV sat dark at the far end of the parking lot. Apparently even Venusians need their beauty sleep.

A streak of red shot across the distant horizon over the dark mountains.

"What was that?" Karen blinked, stared at the night sky. "Did you see that, Ed? A UFO!" She tucked her water bottle into her armpit.

"No such thing," I said. "And keep your voice down." What the hell was that? Not the trail of any aircraft I'd ever seen. I shook myself. I was letting Lena Jay and all the other characters of LooneyLand get to me.

"What are you doing? Tesla's this way." Karen tugged my arm.

"Follow me." I tiptoed to the Chevy pickup alongside the office, extracted Samuel's car keys from the pocket of my leather jacket.

I slid the key in the lock on the passenger side and opened the door for her. "Give me your bag."

"You're stealing Samuel's pickup?"

"Technically, is it stealing? I mean, I do have the key."

She raised her brow. "Which I'm guessing you stole from Samuel. Am I right?"

"You're not wrong. Give me your suitcase," I repeated in an effort to cut off further debate about the ethical and legal implications of purloining the proprietor's vehicle. I tossed our suitcases in the truck bed and climbed in on the driver's side. I saw no sign of life from the motel. No Mel and/or Samuel coming out guns blazing to put an end to our modern day horse thievery.

The pickup was clearly the best choice. The Tesla was a rarity and might give us away. I was guessing Dr. Allison was familiar with Ken's car too. Better we drove the Chevy. As for the shotgun, we'd see if it proved useful.

Karen buckled up. "Samuel's going to be pissed."

"I'll send him a Hallmark card." In answer to her laugh, I said, "What? Isn't that what you do?"

"It's what *you* do. Ken's going to be pissed too."

"I can live with that." Gravel flew from beneath the tires. I stepped on the gas pedal once we hit hard pavement. Why not? The highway sign did read: Speed Limit Mach 3, after all. We whistled away, leaving Area 51 behind.

"Listen to that engine," I remarked. "That's the sound of a good old gas burner. Much more dependable. And faster. No recharging stops. Good old fossil fuel. Just as nature intended." My palms slapped the sturdy steering wheel. "A return to the classics. Can't beat it. All those dinosaurs hadn't gone extinct for nothing. No, sir, they didn't die in vain."

"You're insufferable. A relic, you know?"

"I'll take that as a compliment."

We sped along hour after hour, racing down the empty highway, across dark deserts and over even darker mountains. Karen drifted off to sleep. I enjoyed the silence inside the small cab and the sight of the unobstructed Milky Way. I was happy to see that no one seemed to be following us. And out here, in this vast empty space, anybody tailing us on the ground, or from above for that matter, would be easy to spot. I didn't slow down until I saw the sign for the filling station.

Karen yawned and rubbed her eyes. "Why are we stopping here?"

"Didn't you see the sign?"

"What sign?"

"Last chance to fill up before Saturn," I replied. I jumped out of the cab and started pumping. I breathed in heavily. There's nothing like the smell of gasoline to fuel the spirit. Karen was asleep again before I'd even filled the tank and screwed the gas cap back in place.

We drove straight through to Estes Park, Colorado, an eight-hundred mile marathon. My back and shoulders ached. "Welcome home." I leapt from the Chevy and winced. Cold rain poured from a slate sky. I looked at Karen inside the cab. "What are you waiting for?"

"Duh. The rain to stop."

I rolled my eyes. "Fine. I'll park closer to the entrance." I climbed back inside the stifling truck. Fog covered the windows.

"Couldn't have parked any farther," Karen muttered, zipping up her hoodie and flopping the hood over her ears.

I rolled up to the hotel entrance. "Milady, if you would care to exit, I'll find a spot for your royal carriage and see to your bags."

She peered through the tiny rear window. "Our luggage is soaked."

"After a week of traveling, I'm sure both your and my things could use a good wash."

Karen eased herself out of the truck outside the entrance to the hotel. "Better park someplace inconspicuous. By now, Samuel might have reported his truck stolen. The police might be looking for it and us."

"Good point. Maybe I should give him a call. Explain that

we might require his pickup a trifle longer."

"Duh, you think?"

"I'm sensing you disapprove of my actions. I did leave him a note and the keys to the Tesla so it isn't like I left the man stranded. Besides, Mel can always summon up a flying saucer if they should need to run out for a quart of milk or a six pack."

Karen slammed the car door in my face.

I parked the pickup in the first empty slot, wrestled the soggy suitcases from the open truck bed and found Karen arguing with the front desk clerk.

"That's the best you've got?"

"It's all I've got," the clerk said. Red hair spiking up like she'd long-term parked her pinkie finger in a live electric outlet. If the woman had any wits, she was at the end of them. Karen Dalton can do that to a person. And fast.

"Fine. I'll take it." Karen slapped down her MasterCard on the countertop. The clerk took it gingerly and slid it through her machine, then returned it.

Karen turned on me. "The Stanley Hotel? Really?"

"You're always complaining about our accommodations. This is a step up from our usual haunts, wouldn't you say?" I grabbed our luggage. The sprawling white palace on the hill did possess a certain creep quotient. "Luxury accommodations."

"Haunts is right. This place still haunts my sleep. I can't believe you'd pick this hotel, the site—"

"And inspiration," I interjected.

"And inspiration!" Her cheeks blew up bright red. "Of Stephen King's creepy horror novel!"

"Yes, The Shining. Quite a piece of literary craftsmanship, wouldn't you say?"

She chose not to.

"Besides, I thought it would take your mind off..." Guests crowded the lobby. Temporary stick-on nametags identified a hotel tour group of fifty as they were being led through. "Aliens," I whispered.

"What? By making me think about ghosts and

murderers, and all sorts of paranormal misfits, murderers, and psychopaths?"

"You already said that."

"Said what?"

"You said murderers." I held up two fingers. "Twice."

She squeezed my fingers with a vice-like grip.

"Uncle!" I cried. She let go. I shook out my hand. "You're drawing a crowd."

Karen frowned. Indeed the tour had stopped to watch like we were a scheduled part of the show. "Let's get out of here. What room are we in again?"

I checked. "Third floor." We rode the cramped original 1909 elevator upward. I rather enjoyed its rattling ascent and said so.

"Not me," Karen said. "Sounds like bones rattling. Did I mention this hotel is spooky?"

"It's just old. You'll get used to it. In fact, this grand old hotel was built in 1909 by Freelan Oscar Stanley, genius inventor of the Stanley steamer."

"The carpet cleaning guy?" Karen startled as the elevator went bump. "Huh, I didn't even know they had wall-to-wall carpet back then."

The elevator came to a stop. So did my brain. "Seriously?"

"What?" The elevator doors pulled apart.

"Carpet cleaning guy? I'm talking about the Stanley Steamer. A brilliant motor carriage. Ahead of its time, really. The steam-powered automobile, now that's an impressive piece of machinery."

"If you say so." Karen made it clear she was unimpressed.

"You're thinking of a steam-cleaning machine. Stanley Steemer. S-t-e-e-m-e-r."

"How about that," she said dully.

We pushed out of the elevator.

"And I have no idea when the steam-cleaning carpet machine was invented, nor by whom."

"Guess you don't know everything, smarty pants," Karen

quipped as we rolled our suitcases down the deserted hallway. "And look at this carpet. It could use a good steam clean. And I've never laid eyes on a steam-powered car so who's the great inventor now?"

"Ha-ha. I'll have you know F.O. Stanley and his brother held many patents. One of his early designs is for what we now know as the modern airbrush."

"Really?" That got Karen's attention. "I use airbrushes sometimes in my graphic design work."

I rubbed my hands together. "Of note, F.O. was also a gifted violinist and violin builder."

"What kind of music do you like, Ed?"

"Music died when Elvis died," I replied. We came to a stop. "Are you sure about this?" I asked at the entrance to room 317.

"It's the only room free. That's what happens when you don't call ahead and make a reservation. Some kind of festival in town." She applied the keycard to the door and stepped aside. "Go ahead."

"What? Afraid our room might be haunted?" I teased. "Shall I give the room a quick blast with my ectoplasmic exorcism ray gun?"

Karen slugged me in the arm. "Speaking of haunted... You don't believe in ghosts, do you?"

She walked slowly around the room, taking it all in, antique furniture, and heavy brocaded draperies. The air itself seemed a hundred years old. Redolent with age—perhaps commingled with the spirits of long dead guests? Would we find secret panels, trap doors, two-way mirrors, and hidden slashers in the bathtub—shades of the Bates Motel—too? A bit premature to tell but I doubted it.

"I'm beginning to think maybe I do," I replied to her question about ghosts. In the graying light of the fading day, I studied the panoramic view of the distant Rocky Mountain range from our window. Storm clouds threatened their return.

"I mean, I watched The Shining on TV when I was a kid." She toyed with the TV remote control.

"I believe the hotel runs the film twenty-four-seven on a dedicated channel."

"Pass."

"Which bed do you want?" Two double-size four-poster beds split the room.

Karen stared warily at the beds. "I'll take the one no guests have been stabbed to death in."

"I believe that's the one on your right, nearest the bathroom." I threw myself down on the bed opposite and kicked off my shoes. Karen sighed with pleasure as her head hit her own trio of fluffy pillows. Neither of us had the energy to turn on the lights. The room grew darker. I stared at the ceiling. Happy to be stretched out in a luxurious room, on a comfortable mattress someplace other than in alien country. "About that kiss the other day…"

"I was drunk," Karen said crisply.

"No. No, I don't think that was it," I made the mistake of saying.

"I said I was drunk. Let it go, Ed." Her voice ratcheted up a notch.

"But—" I stopped myself before she stopped me by use of force. Yes, I was beginning to figure out Karen Dalton and the workings of her mind. Well, except for that part about the kiss…

Before either of us knew it, we'd both fallen asleep. I awoke in the middle of the night and settled the duvet over Karen, who'd been tossing and turning like a handful of lettuce leaves in one of those lettuce spinning doohickeys. Talk about meaningless inventions.

Crawling into my own bed, I heard a faint whisper and a rustling of fabric. I froze in the dark, pulled myself up on my elbows, and strained my ears. A ghost trapped in the wall? No, the sound seemed to be coming from the door. I tiptoed to it in my socks and pulled it open.

No ghosts. No ghouls. Nobody waiting to plant a wicked chef's knife in my chest. Just a long, lonely, and empty corridor. I didn't know what Karen was talking about—the carpet appeared in perfectly good shape to me, clean as a pin. Is that a thing?

My nostrils picked up the faintest hint of chocolate. I sniffed again and a craving for sweets, any food for that matter—chocolate being at the top of the list at the moment—overwhelmed me. We'd gone all day without stopping to eat, and fallen asleep even while talking about making plans for dinner.

"Ed?" Karen grunted.

"Sorry." I closed the door quietly and fastened both locks. "Go back to sleep."

"Everything okay?"

"Just Jack Nicholson at the door. Wanted to know if you'd like your bed turned down."

"Ow!" I rubbed my forehead with the heel of my palm. For having just been awakened and the room being pitch black, Karen's aim was remarkably accurate. The remote control hit me smack in the middle of the forehead. I heard it but I never saw it coming. Just like they say in the movies.

After breakfast the next morning—ham, sausage, and waffles for me; fruit plate, maple soy yogurt, and bran muffin for Karen (one of us knows how to eat and live right)—we headed out wearing our matching black The Shining tee shirts. I'd insisted on buying us each one down in the hotel gift shop. Karen thought we looked silly but the shirt had been my gift to her so she felt bad refusing to wear it. I thought we looked adorable. She insisted we looked deplorable.

"Adorable/deplorable. Another one of those fine lines one must walk in life. And with my I Heart Aliens hat," I told her, "I'd go so far as to say I look smashing."

"I'd like to smash something," Karen replied. We stood under the awning waiting and watching while the falling rain turned to pelting hail and then to rain once more. After the downpour whittled itself down to a light drizzle, we hustled down the hill to the shuttle stop that would deposit us at the visitor's center.

The concierge informed us Estes Parks offered the free shuttle service with routes running every which way around town, plus one running all the way to the Rocky Mountain National Park itself. With that in mind, we'd left Samuel's pickup in the parking lot of the hotel. It was less likely to be spotted there by the police. Although I did leave a phone message for Samuel, telling him not to worry and that I'd return his pickup the first chance I got. Full tank of gasoline included.

"We can walk from here," I said, jumping down from the shuttle at the entrance to the visitor center. We used Karen's phone to guide us. By the time we were hoofing it, the sun had come out with a vengeance. Angry hummingbirds and even angrier elks seemed to tolerate our presence but made it clear by their stances and stares that they'd be ready to throw down with us at the drop of a hat. The elk glared at us with big, unblinking, silvery-green eyes—talk about alien—as we headed for downtown Estes Park. I'd swear one of the beasts was following us. Perhaps to report our activities back to the head bull of the herd who would then decide our fate and whether we lived or died.

"We're getting close," I said, eyes on her phone screen, watching the numbers move. I was using a GPS tracking app. "Very close." We followed the sidewalk past the visitor's center and under Highway 36. Cars, trucks and tour buses rumbled overhead. Este Park is gateway to Rocky Mountain National Park. Sitting in at approximately seventy-five hundred feet in a bowl that fills with icy water that comes racing down the mountains and flooding out the town and its residence every few years or so hasn't stopped the tourists from coming or the builders from building.

The winding sidewalk continued through the short tunnel. Sun promised on the other end. We stepping inside. Puddles covered the ground and tiny colored lights flitted along the walls.

A muscular young man came whizzing along on a state-of-the-art bicycle, pelting us with water spray.

"Jerk!" Karen's voice echoed through the tunnel.

I slowed. Frowned as I watched the coordinates on the

phone now move in the wrong direction.

"What's wrong, Ed?"

"We passed it."

"Passed what?"

"The spot."

"The spot?" Our voices carried in the damp air. "What do you mean passed it? We aren't anywhere." She spun in a circle.

I shrugged and turned around, walking slowly. She tagged along, feet splashing.

"A graffiti-covered wall in a tiny tunnel under a busy street?" Karen exclaimed. "What is this? A gag? A trick? Did that bitch con us? More specifically *you*, Ed? Was all this just a ploy to get us out of Nevada?"

I ran my fingertips along the edge of the wall, back and forth, up and down. Feeling, listening, sensing.

Karen peeked over my shoulder. "What is it, Ed? A secret door? A passage to some top secret lab? She pushed her nose to the concrete. Do you really think it's possible?"

Pedestrians splish-splashed past us.

"Ken? Ken?" Karen banged her hand on the wall. "It's me, Karen. Are you in there?" She pressed her ear to the cold concrete.

I studied the graffiti while Karen embarrassed herself.

"Aren't people terrible? What do they think they're doing scribbling all over the place? I'll never understand what makes some people do this." She rubbed at the paint. "I'm a graphic artist and I'd never defile public property. And if I did, I'd do a hell of a lot better job of it than this. I mean what is this gibberish?" She pointed.

I paused. Followed her finger. Connected the dots. "That gibberish is another set of coordinates."

Karen gasped. "Are you sure?"

"Pretty sure." I snapped a pic of the coordinates. "Come on. Let's get out of the tunnel. Signal's better outside." We hurried the rest of the way through the tunnel and took a seat on a bench in Riverwalk Park. The walkway follows the Big Thompson River behind Elkhorn Avenue, the town's main thoroughfare.

I performed some mental calculations. Karen contributed by saying, "Well? Well? Well?" until I thought, rather hoped, I'd go deaf. She yanked on my elbow. "So are you going to tell me already?"

I massaged my temples. Sniffed the air. "I smell ice cream. Shall we get some?" Licorice flavored maybe?

"After, Ed. Tell me now, where's Ken?"

"Let's put it this way." I handed Karen her phone. "We're going to need some supplies."

"Supplies? Like what?"

"Food, water. Clothing." I looked at her damp sneakers. "Hiking boots."

Her nose wrinkled. "Ectoplasmic-whatchamacallit ray guns?"

"No." I patted her knee. "Although a can of bear repellent might prove wise." I stood, wiped my trousers. There was ice cream out there in the wilds of Estes Park and I was determined to find it.

"Bear repellent?" Karen skipped after me. "Where exactly are we going, Ed?"

"Far as I can tell, Mummy Pass Creek."

"Mummy Pass Creek? Now you've got us involved with mummies? What the hell, Ed!"

I stopped. "Let's hope it's only bears."

"Oh sure," Karen grumbled as I slid my feet into first gear and cut between a couple of historic brick buildings. "Only bears."

We found ourselves amidst the hustle and bustle of Elkhorn Ave. A trio of elk—mama, papa, and baby—eyed us warily from their vantage on the perimeter of a small greenspace near the police station. Undercover agents?

17

We spent the remainder of the day fortifying our minds and bodies for the next day's excursion to Mummy Pass Creek, a remote region of the Rocky Mountains. And I bought Karen some hiking boots. Sturdy and water-resistant. All paid for with her credit card but, as I explained to her, it's the thought that counts.

It had been my turn to choose our lunch, chocolate ice cream and a fresh-baked, chocolate-dipped waffle cone. That meant Karen got the honors of choosing dinner. She selected Indian food, something which we discovered satisfied both our needs, at least, once I picked out all the brown raisins in my dish.

In between mealtimes, shopping was the name of the game. The summer crowds were out in force, armed to the hilt with their major credit cards. Although, unlike most of the tourists, we weren't interested in tchotchkes, doodads, and whatnots. And neither of us had anyone to mail a postcard to. Cold weather clothing and hiking gear headed the top of our shopping list.

And a blue half-dome tent. Just in case. I had no idea if we'd need it but did not want to be caught unprepared in the rugged Colorado wilderness. From what I'd been able to determine online, Mummy Pass Creek campsite was firmly parked in the middle of nowhere. Not a big tent but large enough for two and our sleeping bags. If a big black bear decided to join us, it was going to be a tight fit. And if Karen decided to kiss me again, I'd deal with that if and when the time came. I had purchased a can of bear repellent spray. Just saying.

Back in our hotel room that evening, Karen unzipped her

jacket and threw it atop her bed. She kicked off her shoes and massaged her feet. "I don't know about you but I am exhausted." She glanced at the bathroom. "I think I'll take a shower. Do you want to go first?"

"Why? Afraid Anthony Perkins is waiting behind the shower curtain?"

"Ha-ha. So funny, I forgot to laugh. Is that a yes or a no?"

"No, I can wait." Some people just don't appreciate humor. "You go ahead. I'll be right back." I opened the door to our room.

"Where are you going?"

"Down to the lobby." I was hoping to find a pack of Camels. Hell, I was hoping to find a herd of Camels. I hadn't smoked a cigarette all day. And, except for the root beer soda I ordered to wash down my chocolate ice cream waffle cone, I hadn't had anything to drink but water. How did people stand the stuff? Dull dull dull. "Want anything?"

"I'm good."

"Okay, lock up behind me."

"You can count on it," Karen said. She'd been bending my ear all day with tales of paranormal mischief and mayhem, some with deadly results. No more Stanley Hotels for us. Next time, I'd book a Motel 6. Simple and clean. And they still allowed in-room smoking!

I wandered into the gift shop. No cigarettes. I asked at the front desk and the smarmy clerk told me in no uncertain terms that they did not sell cigarettes. "The lighting and smoking of cigarettes on hotel property is strictly forbidden, sir."

"How strictly?"

She gutted me with her eyes.

I retreated to the bar. Classic dark woods, a long and generous bar top, and blazing stone fireplace to warm my soul. The fact that the establishment boasted the largest collection of whiskeys in all of Colorado was icing on the cake. Well, something like that. I climbed a barstool and waved to the man on the opposite side of the counter. He'd slicked his hair back with enough oil to qualify as the next Exxon-Valdez oil spill.

A red bolo tie with a softball-sized, polished turquoise stone trapped in a silver cage throttled his neck. I held up a hand. "Bourbon on the rocks, kind sir."

"Coming up."

This being the Rockies, I prayed the bartender didn't take my request literally. A splash of bourbon over a pile of granite and shale would not be appetizing. Or go down the throat smoothly.

A forty-pound sack of flour, or a small meteorite, alit on my left shoulder. I spun around. No, it was neither, it was only Lena Jay. "Hello, Lena Jay! May I call you Lena Jay?" The knitting needle antennae were gone. Her brown hair curled up in a bun atop her head. A skintight leopard-skin leotard struggled to contain her. Thigh-high, chunky-heeled silver boots, not unlike something I pictured the astronauts wearing on the moon, wrapped her feet. Green makeup covered every inch of open skin.

Ernie, her mostly silent companion, clung to her considerable side, like cratered Callisto circling bulging Jupiter. He looked practically...*normal*, I guess was the word, in comparison to Lena Jay. Brown corduroys and an emerald green vest over a white tee shirt emblazoned with a fuzzy blue puppy. The mutt's bright yellow eyes seemed to follow my every move. The caption below the blue pooch read: *Feeling blue? Visit Venus.* "Or should I call you, what was it, Your Royal Emissary... something, something of Venus?"

Lena Jay grinned. "Lena Jay will do." She slapped me playfully but it was enough to make my head spin.

"What a coincidence finding you two here."

"Yeah, small world, isn't it?" Lena Jay flashed me an enigmatic grin.

"Bigger than Venus," I teased. "Not that size matters."

"You really are something, Eddie!" Lena Jay laughed so hard the ensuing gust of wind coming out her throat nearly bowled me over. "Buy you a drink?"

"How can I resist?" Really, how could I? Free drinks. I motioned for the pair to sit and ordered the bartender to make mine a double. Her treat, why not? I wasn't going anywhere and I certainly wasn't driving. And Karen was safely in bed and blissfully unaware of my partying with the Venusians. Would she approve? Probably not.

The earth shook and readjusted its center of gravity as Lena Jay plopped herself down to my left. Ernie slid silently onto the empty barstool on my right.

Lena Jay ordered up a cocktail called Rosemary's Baby while Ernie claimed a beverage with the mouthwatering moniker of Pet Sematary. I imagined something the bartender mixed up in the blender with a little bit of gin mixed in with a whole lot of the ashen remains of cremated cats and dogs.

"What are you and Ernie doing here?" Last time I'd seen the pair of Venusians, they were hunkered down at the Lil' Green Man Motor Court selling overpriced chocolate bars to the natives.

"We're on our way to Yellowstone."

"To check out the sulfur springs," Ernie added.

"Reminds of us home. Plus, we've got a perpetual shortage of arsenic on Venus," Lena Jay explained. "We're always looking for new sources to tap. I heard the hot springs up in Yellowstone contain a high concentration of the element."

I tried to think of something to say that wouldn't come across condescending, incredulous, or patronizing and finally came up with, "Sure, I'll bet."

I rolled some chilled bourbon around in my mouth and swallowed. The heady aroma of alcohol and grilled meats settled over the room. I waved for the bartender. I was going to need a refill soon if these two hung around much longer.

"I don't know about you but I could eat a moose," Lena Jay declared, swilling half Rosemary's Baby in one gulp. "Hey, bartender, a charred Porterhouse for me. And Ernie there," she shouted, looking past me to her companion on my other side, "will have the Alaskan king crab. Right, Ern?"

"Right, Lena Jay."

"You, Eddie? I hear the lamb chops are delish."

"Wool makes me itch," I replied.

"Huh? Never mind, how's about a good old steak? Medium rare?"

"No, thanks." I hoisted my glass. "Everything I need is right here." I rolled the bottom of my glass across the bartop. "Well, everything except for a cigarette."

Lina's eyes lit up like a couple of glowing butt ends. "You hear that, Ern? Eddie's got the urge for a cigarette."

"I heard." Ernie sniffed and drank, one eye on the TV overhead running a repeat of a PGA golf tournament. Boring enough live. Who'd want to watch an old rerun? What sort of person likes to watch a tiny white ball roll around on the grass? Now, baseball, that's the only true sport worth watching.

"Ern's a fellow smoker," explained Lena Jay.

I swiveled quickly. "Ernie, you wouldn't happen to have—"

He beamed. "Out in the RV."

"We can step out for a smoke after we eat." Soon enough, Lena Jay was tearing into her Porterhouse and Ernie was pulling the legs off his Alaskan king crabs.

I settled for doing my darnedest and quickest to empty the bourbon bottle the bartender had left within arm's reach at my request.

Lena Jay burped unapologetically and pushed aside her empty plate. Ernie, white napkin tucked into the collar of his shirt, picked up his plate and licked.

"She was one of the good ones," proclaimed Lena Jay of Venus.

"She?" I lowered my empty glass. The bottle was nearly empty too. Had I really consumed that much already?

"Emily," replied Lena Jay.

"Emily?"

Lena Jay's face darkened. "Emily Crenshaw. You forget her already? Did she mean nothing to you? You murder her in cold blood and don't even have the decency to remember her name?"

"Now, now, Lena Jay." Ernie hastily reached across me to placate the big woman. His eyes darted around the room. Lena

Jay was drawing attention. "Inside voices! Inside voices!" he urged.

Lena Jay's steak knife slashed by within a quarter inch of my nostrils. "She had a name, Eddie. *Emily Crenshaw*. Best alien hunter out there. And she was my friend," Lena Jay sniffled.

"I'm-I'm sorry."

"Are you, Eddie? Are you sorry?"

"I didn't kill her." The room wobbled. My reflection in the wall of bottles bobbled. Was it true? Was there such a thing as too much bourbon? "I-I didn't know you knew her. Didn't know you were friends."

"Speaking of friends." Lena Jay picked at her fingernails with the steak knife. "Where's your girlfriend?"

"Girlfriend?"

"The girl with the blue hair."

"Karen?" I slid off the barstool and shimmied side to side. Was the floor moving? Earthquake? Landslide? I stuck my arms out to keep from falling over.

"She an alien too?" Lena Jay demanded. When had she gotten so ugly? For that matter, when had we boarded a jet plane? Because the bar seemed to be bouncing its way up and down in a thunderstorm.

"Alien?"

"Yeah, like you."

"Me? I'm no alien." I laughed to prove it. Ha-ha.

"Sure, Eddie. What room did you say she was in?"

"I didn't."

"Why are you here in Colorado?" Ernie asked sharply. "What's here? Your flying saucer?" Ernie's words sounded like they were being said by a mouth constructed of gooey mud.

"*Frying saucer*?" I asked the mudman.

"Your friend looks like he's had enough." The bartender smiled broadly.

I stared at him. Blinked. Had his head always looked like a giant orange jack-o'-lantern? How had I not noticed earlier?

"I do believe you're right," Lena Jay said. "Pay the man,

Ern."

The bartender plucked the empty bourbon bottle from the bar top and slid the tab towards Ernie. He scribbled with the provided pen.

Lena tilted her head. "Come on, Eddie." She grabbed my upper arm. "Let's get you back to your room and tucked in." She strongarmed me to the exit. I struggled to remain on my feet. Ernie took my other arm.

"What room did you say you were in?" Lena Jay said.

"Don't-Don't remember. Orange?"

Lena Jay cursed. "That's a color, not a room number. What floor? Floor." She kept me on my feet as we entered the lobby. I saw lots of people. All of them blurry as watercolors in the rain.

"Floor?" I dropped my eyes to the ground. "Right there."

"It's no use," Lena Jay snapped under her breath. "You gave him too much!"

"Sorry," Ernie replied. "I never slipped an alien a mickey before. How's I supposed to know what dose to use?"

"Never mind." Lena Jay dragged me to the entrance. "Bring the RV around. And be quick about it!"

Ernie shot outside. Lena Jay kept me on my feet. "Hang in there, Eddie. Ern's bringing the RV around. You want a smoke, don't you?"

"Smoke?" I looked at her six green bobble heads, swaying like a bowl of snakes perched precariously atop her broad shoulders. "Yes."

She patted my head. "Ern's got a whole case of smokes waiting for you."

"That's nice."

"Yeah, the three of us are going to have a grand time, Eddie. Then maybe you'll remember what room Karen is in. You say she's an alien? What planet are you two from? What star system?"

I beamed uncontrollably. "She kissed me."

"Did she now? Isn't that interesting." The rolling Embassy of Venus lurched up to the hotel entrance. The side door to the

RV popped open and Lena Jay hoisted me up and inside.

18

Lena Jay slammed the door behind us.

The RV was cramped. Filled with boxes of chocolate bars, loose clothing, food and water. A compact dinette occupied the middle section. An unmade bed filled the front.

Ernie squeezed his brows together. He was pointing something at me. He might have been trying to look fierce but being such a pipsqueak, he was failing horribly. "I've got him, Lena Jay."

"Be careful with that," she warned.

"That's not a cigarette." I pointed at Eddie, holding a black gizmo in his hand. "Is that a—"

"Zzzzt!"

From some remote place in my head, I felt myself being lugged to the bed. Lena Jay and Ernie were speaking but I didn't understand a word. Were they speaking Venusian? No, that was impossible. I jolted as the earth began to move. Then I realized it was the RV that was moving, not the ground.

"Down the hill," Lena Jay said. "Park down there in the dark someplace. Away from the lights."

The RV jerked to a stop.

Lena Jay loomed over me. She jammed my legs together and lashed a nylon rope around my ankles.

"Hi," I said. I was feeling woozy. "Camel?" I forced my hand up, pinched my thumb and forefinger together, and brought them to my lips. The universal sign for a smoker in need of a fix.

"Camel," Ernie blurted. "He said Camel. He's one of them Camellarians!"

Lena looked at her companion even as she knotted more

rope up and around my wrists. "He wants a cigarette, Ernie." She rubbed her hands together. "Maybe we should give him one."

"A cigarette now? Really?"

"Sure, you know, like in the movies where they torture somebody with a lit cigarette."

Ernie made tsking noises. "Won't work. You know extraterrestrials are thick-skinned. Fire doesn't affect them."

Lena Jay scowled. "I forgot. What do you suggest?"

Ernie raised a brow. "You know."

"Hold him underwater to see if he drowns? We don't have a bathtub. How are we going to do that?"

"Hotel pool?"

My head cleared. I regained control of my arms and legs. My muscles no longer felt like electrified chocolate pudding. I squirmed and tried to move but Lena Jay had trussed me up tighter than a calf headlining a rodeo.

"We might get spotted. "Can't take the chance." She grabbed me by the neck and shook me like a ragdoll. "Talk to us, Eddie! Who are you?"

"What are you?" snapped Ernie.

"Why'd you murder Emily?"

"She discover what you really are, so you had to kill her?"

"No. I-I told you, I didn't. I'm a private eye hired to find Karen's missing brother. Simple as that."

"Bullshit," Lena Jay replied. "You're an alien. Come here to infiltrate our military and take over our planet. I bet General Grant is one of you. But I got news for you, Mister Alien. We are going to stop you. You and your kind, whatever you are!" She turned to her companion. "Check his wallet."

Ernie dug into my trousers and flapped open my brown leather wallet. "Three dollars and a bus pass."

"No driver's license?" Lena Jay asked me.

"I never got around to it."

"No? You got around to murdering Emily," snarled Lena Jay.

"You won't get away with it!" boasted Ernie. "We are on a

search and destroy mission!"

"Fully sanctioned by the Alien Resistance Corps."

"Alien Resistance Corps?" Everything made sense now. "Like Emily Crenshaw."

"That's right." Lena Jay and Ernie said in unison. I struggled ferociously yet vainly with my ropes. "Ernie, get the stun gun."

"There's really no need," I said. "I'm telling you the truth."

"Maybe we should cut him open." Lena Jay eyed me like a cut of meat.

"Yeah," Ernie said gleefully. "Let's slice him open and see what's inside. I wonder what this alien's got for body parts. Want me to get a knife?"

"Better give him a blast first. The way he's squirming, could get blood all over the bedsheets.

"Good idea." Ernie whipped the stun gun from his pocket. "You ready?"

"Yes." Lena Jay snarled in my face and pressed my shoulders into the mattress. "This time, Ern, hit him where it hurts."

"You mean?"

"Yep. Right in the balls."

My eyes widened. "I'm telling you the truth—" Okay, maybe I was lying but they didn't truly know that.

"You think this alien's even got any?" Ernie chuckled. He waved his stun gun wildly in the air then held it menacingly over my crotch and took aim.

I did not like Lena Jay's evil grin one bit. No, not one bit. I held my breath.

"We're about to find out," she said.

"Zzzzt! Zzzzt!"

My crotch lit up like a bouquet of firecrackers. I saw stars. Hundreds and hundreds of white hot stars. I heard a scream and realized it was me. I thrashed and spasmed.

A loud bang bounced through the inside of the RV. Then I heard Ernie yelling. Lena Jay shouting.

"Hiiiii-yaaa!" hollered a fast-moving blur behind them and me.

"Phhsssst-Phhsssst!"

"Yeow!" Lena Jay bellowed.

"No! No! Stop! Stop!" Ernie threw up his hands.

"Take that, asshole!"

"Phhssst-Phhssst!"

"Alien attack!" Ernie sobbed. He fell to his knees with a thud. "We're gonna die!"

Lena Jay cried and hit the ground next. Her weight hitting the flimsy floor of the RV lifted me off the bed.

"Ed! Ed! Are you okay?"

"Karen? Karen Dalton?" My vision was clearing. I'd never been stun gunned before, let alone twice. Let alone twice in one night. Never in the crotch.

Karen tugged at my ropes. "Too tight. Let me find something."

"Hurry," I begged. I didn't like being trussed up. I liked it even less when monsters like Lena Jay and Ernie were running loose—even if they were temporarily incapacitated.

Lena Jay and Ernie rolled around on the floor of the RV, hands scratching madly at their eyeballs.

"What did you do to them?" I asked as Karen tore through the ropes with a kitchen knife she'd scrounged up in the tiny galley.

Karen grinned and plucked a can of aerosol from the pocket of her hoodie. "Bear repellent."

"Stuff's repellent, alright. I smell capsaicin." I wobbled to my feet, waving my hand in front of my nose. "Stinks." I stepped over Ernie and around Lena Jay. Both were busy suffering at the moment and I was happy to leave them to it.

Lena Jay fumbled forward and grabbed Karen's ankle.

"No!" Karen fell and landed hard.

"Karen!" I shouted.

Lena Jay surged to her knees and threw herself atop Karen. "Spray, Ed! Spray!" Karen yelped.

I picked up the fallen cannister of bear repellent, got within inches of Lena Jay's watery red eyeballs and pressed the trigger. I found the Venusian's ensuing bloodcurdling screams oddly satisfying.

Karen kicked Lena Jay's limp form off herself and I helped her to her feet.

"Let's get out of here before they regain their senses!" I urged. Not that this pair had any measurable sense to begin with. I tossed the empty bear spray can at Ernie. After zapping me in the balls, the man was definitely off my friends list.

"Gladly!" Karen tore outside. I was right behind her. We ran up the dark parking lot, distancing ourselves from the RV as quickly as we could. We paused a hundred feet away and looked back. Karen was huffing, bent over with her hands on her knees. I noticed her lavender pajamas under the hoodie and she was wearing one purple slipper with the puffy white clouds on it. We saw no sign of pursuit.

I did see her errant slipper a dozen yards back. I limped back and retrieved it for her.

"Thanks." She balanced on my shoulder and thrust the slipper on her right foot.

"Thank you," I said, straightening my clothing. Pain rocked my chest and my crotch. All thanks to Ernie and Lena Jay. So much for Lena Jay's comment to Mel about them coming in peace.

"What are Lena Jay and Ernie doing here?" Karen's eyes were on the gaping door of the RV. Light spilled out but there was still no sign of its occupants. Only an occasional moan of anguish. Thankfully, there were no other hotel guests roaming about at this hour.

I explained how I'd wandered into the bar only to have Lena Jay and Ernie join me.

"What were you doing in their RV? And why were they acting so crazy?" Karen tucked her bright blue hair into her hoodie. "I mean, they *are* crazy but I mean crazy even for them."

"They drugged me then dragged me into their RV."

"Drugged you? Why would they do that? Who are those people?"

"Alien Resistance Corps."

"Huh?"

I quickly explained about the ARC and their goals.

"So they're not really from Venus?"

"Don't tell me you believed their story?"

"No but I admit I got the impression they did."

"No, it was all a ruse. What better way to hide the fact that you're an alien hunter than to pretend you're aliens."

"What they are is crazy shitheads."

"Crazy *dangerous* shitheads," I replied.

"Yeah, that." Karen chewed her lip. "But I still don't get why they were torturing you."

"They seemed to believe I might have been involved in the death of Emily Crenshaw. It seems she was a friend. And one of them."

"Like I said, crazy shitheads."

"How did you find me?"

"I woke up around one o'clock. I saw you were still gone and wondered what had happened to you. I went downstairs and asked around. I talked to the bartender who told me you'd left with a goofy couple, one of whom was a big, boisterous woman dressed like she was in town for a cosplay convention and all covered in green paint. I was stumped at first. But it didn't take me long to figure out who that was. Although I was surprised."

I chuckled despite my pain.

"I went outside looking for you. I recognized the RV down the hill. Peeked in the window and saw you trussed up like a pig for Sunday dinner with Lena Jay kneeling over you. So I ran back for the bear repellent. The only weapon I could think of." She looked at my groin. "I saw Ernie shoot you. Does it hurt?"

"It doesn't tickle."

"I'll bet."

I raised an eyebrow. "Kiss it and make it better?"

Karen scowled. "Still delirious, I see.

I shrugged. I'd tried.

"Oh!" Karen took off running towards the RV.

What the hell had gotten into the woman? Was my comment that egregious? "What are you doing?"

"I'll be right back!" Her feet slapped the ground. I chased after her.

She disappeared inside the RV. I heard shouts from Lena Jay and Ernie. She reappeared a few seconds later brandishing a sharp paring knife.

"You didn't—" I began.

"Slash their throats?"

"Well—"

"Nah." She whipped her eyes back to the RV's door. "Should I?"

"Let's call that Plan B," I suggested.

"Fine." She squeezed the knife's handle determinedly. "I'm gonna slash their tires." And Karen did. All four. The tires sank flat to the pavement.

"Good thinking." I snapped my fingers. "I just remembered something." I ran inside the RV.

"Ed? What the hell?"

Lena Jay and Ernie sat side by side, backs up against the mattress. They looked terrible. "Leave us alone, please!" Lena Jay begged. "Don't kill us. Not like you did Emily."

"Don't eat us!" Ernie added.

"What are they talking about?" Karen asked over my shoulder.

"I'll explain later." I started tossing the place, opening drawers and cabinets, looking under the seat cushions.

"Searching the place?" Karen poked her head in the minifridge and then the microwave "What are we looking for?"

I yanked open the glovebox in front of the passenger seat. "Ah-ha! Found them!"

Karen bounded up the narrow aisle. "What is it? A clue" Evidence?"

"Better." I held up my prize. "Cigarettes." I shook the box. "A whole carton."

19

We scurried back to our room. The night clerk paid us no attention, barely glancing up from his crossword puzzle, despite our disheveled appearances.

"Probably used to seeing ghosts this time of night." I said. I waved to the clerk as we veered towards the ancient elevator.

"Every time I step foot in this thing I feel like I'm stepping into a time machine."

"Trust me," I said. "Not the same thing at all."

Karen looked at me oddly. I was used to it.

We packed and left in a hurry. In under half an hour, we'd dressed, refilled our suitcases, checked out of The Stanley, and hauled ourselves and our belongings out to our pickup truck. Well, Samuel Hitchcock's pickup truck—on extended loan to us. How one of those plush Stanley Hotel bath towels ended up in my suitcase, I'll never know. But I figured if the hotel minded, they'd be billing Karen for it.

In the far corner of the dark parking lot, Lena Jay sat in the open side door of the RV, a big fat frown on her face. Ernie was struggling with the four flat tires by the glow from inside the RV. What he thought he was going to do about them I couldn't imagine. We smiled and waved as we passed.

"Adios." Karen shot them a one-finger salute.

"Damn." The pickup's tires squealed as I swerved past the exit and hit the side street.

"What?"

"I should've helped myself to some chocolate bars for the trip while I had the chance."

"I'll buy you some," promised Karen.

Traffic was light. The sky was dark. I turned on the headlamps and Karen gave me directions. When she wasn't shouting at me to take this turn or that, her nose was buried in a paperback novel. The Shining, to be precise. She'd picked a copy up in the hotel gift shop.

"I thought you hated horror?" I said.

"Shh! Trying to read here!" Karen snapped. She stuck her finger between two pages for a bookmark. "Besides, I don't hate *reading* horror. I hate *living* it."

"Difference noted." I lit a cigarette, took a puff, and drove on. They were Winstons but who was I to quibble with a free cigarette? Plus, Karen had long ago stopped nagging me about my smoking. I'd only had to compromise and keep my window cracked open a few inches. Noisy and wasn't doing my hair any good, but worth every bit of the inconvenience and discomfort.

As the minutes passed, the day grew brighter. My thoughts, on the other hand, grew darker. I had no idea what I was doing. What if I was wrong? What if Dr. Allison wasn't helping us but rather sending us off on a wild goose, rather Ken Dalton, chase?

And what did Emily Crenshaw's death have to do with Ken Dalton's disappearance? Had he murdered her believing that she was an alien, perhaps? The scientist could be delusional. Did he kill Crenshaw in self defense? I hoped not, if only for Karen's sake. She's be crushed by that. But her brother had been under tremendous strain, according to Marcia Allison.

I didn't believe in coincidences, especially a coincidence as big as this one. Ken Dalton frequents the Lil' Green Man Motor Court accompanied by Emily Crenshaw. She ends up dead behind the motel and he disappears. No, there was a deeper story there. Maybe Stephen King could figure it out—hell, the man could probably write the tale from beginning to end—but it was beyond my understanding. I needed to get to the bottom of it.

And Lena Jay and Ernie whatisname—a not-so-harmless pair of ARC agents. I studied the highway in the rearview mirror. Hopefully, we'd lost them for good.

My fingers danced atop the steering wheel. Why did I have the feeling that I was being used, manipulated? The eerie and uneasy suspicion that there was more to this picture than what fit in the frame.

A circuitous route led us east out of Estes Park, north, then west to Mummy Pass Creek. I checked the GPS. "We're getting closer."

Karen yawned. "About time." She cranked up the heater.

Endless blind switchbacks kept me on my toes. And the further we got, the smaller the roads became. Pavement turned to gravel then hard-packed dirt. Until the road we followed was nothing more than mudded ruts littered with sharp rocks. Mountains rose all around us. There were no other persons in sight.

I stopped the truck and killed the motor. Silence greeted us. Karen slid her paperback onto the dashboard and stared out the window. "I don't know, Ed. What would Ken be doing all the way out here?"

"Boy Scout jamboree?" I shoved my door open.

"Ken hates camping. Hates the outdoors." Karen slid out on her side and swung her arms in circles. "He wouldn't be caught dead out here."

"Let's hope you're right."

Karen shot me a look.

I moved to the rear of the pickup. "We'd better transfer everything we need to our backpacks." The big packs were part of the supplies we'd bought in Estes Park. "Lots of water." I scooped up some loose bottles, compliments of The Stanley. And three rolls of toilet paper, also compliments of the establishment.

Karen pulled items from her suitcase and shoved them into her pack. "You really think we're going to need all this? How far are we going, anyway?"

"All day hike to the campsite. We'll spend the night then—"

"Spend the night?" Karen dropped her pack. "Out here?!"

"Did I not mention that?"

"No, you know damn well you did not mention that!" Karen huffed. I couldn't blame the woman. The elevation must've been ten thousand feet give or take an inch. And things would only get worse.

I could only hope things eventually got better. If we did find Ken Dalton at the end of this hike, she'd thank me. If not...? Maybe murder me and bury my corpse out here in the wilderness where not even a coyote would ever find me.

"Better grab your sleeping bag," I instructed. "I'll carry the tent." I attached it to my pack with a bungee cord.

We bundled up, strapped our backpacks to our backsides, and headed up the trail. Karen's accompanying curses were like demented birdsong to my ears.

We followed a rugged trail through a subalpine terrain cutting its way through the Comanche Peak Wilderness and into the Rocky Mountain National Park. Alpine tundra let us know that this wasn't the tropics. I hadn't laid eyes on anything that looked like it might eat us but I did spot several marmot and a solitary black moose. Even Karen paused to marvel at the huge beast as it grazed at the edge of a small brilliant opal-blue pond.

"How high did you say we are, Ed?" Karen asked as we scrambled up a deep rift.

"Ten thousand feet, give or take."

"Damn, no wonder I'm out of breath." She laid a hand on her quaking chest. "I've never been so high in my whole life!"

"I've been higher," I said nonchalantly.

"Oh, yeah? How high?" she panted.

I gave her question some thought as we continued our climb. "Higher than a kite?" I saw no reason to provide an answer that might lead to her further mental confusion. She seemed to suffer enough as it was.

We reached the Mummy Pass Creek campground just in the nick of time. The sun was setting and the outdoor temperature plummeting. Karen had remained blissfully quiet the last few miles. Utter exhaustion can have that effect on a person. She tugged off her pack with a grunt and let it drop.

"Never again." She huffed and puffed and dropped to the cold ground.

"What luck," I said, shrugging off my own backpack. "Looks like we have the entire campground to ourselves."

"Fuck you, Ed." She threw herself out spreadeagled on the rough ground.

"I'll set up the tent." I unleashed it from my pack. "Maybe you could gather some firewood?"

"Ugh. Fine," she moaned, letting me know just how put upon she felt. Regardless, she scrambled to her feet and began desultorily gathering twigs and branches. "You do know we're supposed to have a park permit to camp here?"

"If a park ranger comes along, I'll be happy to file for one," I said, fumbling with the tent poles. Who knew assembling a little tent could be so complicated? "In the meantime, we're rapidly losing daylight."

"And body heat." She tossed a pile of kindling at my feet.

"That's the spirit," I replied, warming my hands over the blaze.

"Pretty sure campfires are illegal out here too," Karen just had to say. Anything to spoil the moment.

"Pretty sure freezing to one's death is also forbidden by law."

Fire blazing and Karen's temper hot, I doled out the baked beans. Seemed appropriate for a camping trip, plus, completely plant-based. I boiled water for her tea bags—compliments of The Stanley—and drank my beer—compliments of Karen's credit card which I'd employed at the convenience store some miles back in the small town of Glen Haven. We'd taken the opportunity to stock up on last-minute essentials.

"It is beautiful out here." Karen cupped her tea in the lid of her thermos and gazed at the stars.

"That it is." I listened to the fire crackle. "And no bears."

"Thanks for reminding me." Karen's eyes shot out into the inky forest, looking for signs of wildlife.

"And us with no bear repellent."

"Because I used it up saving your life." She helped herself to more hot water from the pan resting on one of the hot stones circling our cozy fire.

"That's a bit melodramatic."

"Ernie sent a bajillion volts through your crotch. They were talking about slicing you open!"

"I said thank you," I replied after taking a sip of beer and crushing the empty can underfoot.

"Yeah, but you never really explained what those two wanted with you."

"Sure I did. I told you they thought I might know something about Emily Crenshaw's death."

Karen frowned. "But that makes no sense."

"That's what I tried to tell them. The good news is that we haven't seen them since we left The Stanley."

Karen sat quietly. "Ed?"

"Yes?"

"What if this is a wild goose chase too?"

She'd verbalized the question I'd been asking myself these past hours. I had no answer. No good answer. "No guts, no gravy, right?"

"Seriously."

"Trust me," I replied. "Tomorrow all will become apparent. If a bear doesn't eat us. Or a wolf."

She glanced at the small blue half-dome tent, our headquarters for the night. The fabric quivered like it was afraid of the dark too. But I knew this was merely the wind. I hoped it was merely the wind.

"The tent looks awfully flimsy."

"Are you kidding me?" I said. "The poles are all aluminum and the tent itself is one hundred percent ripstop nylon." And I was confident, fairly confident, in my assembly thereof.

"Ripstop?" Karen stood and fingered the material skeptically. "Do the bears know that?" she asked sharply.

"Let's hope so." I sucked the last bit of life out of one of Ernie's Winston's and chewed on the butt. "What?" I said in response to Karen's look of disgust. "Pack it in, pack it out. You read the signs."

She crawled inside the tent.

I woke in the middle of the night to the feel of Karen's breath on my neck. She'd snuggled up against me in her sleep. Something moved outside. I couldn't tell what it was but it wasn't the wind whistling through the trees. This was something real. Some thing of substance. I caught a slight odor through the tent fabric but could not identify the scent. Whatever it was, it was large.

A minute later, it was gone and I slept. My dreams took me to places that did not exist anymore. And my thoughts were haunted with places and things I'd been trying not to think about for a very long time.

20

I crawled out of the tent on all fours. I smelled woodsmoke. And, if my nose didn't deceive me, instant coffee. "Good morning, Karen. Been up long?"

"Hey. Just long enough to get the fire started." Karen was seated cross-legged beside the campfire. The coffee jar, with a black plastic spoon sticking up inside, sat open beside her. She'd rolled up her sleeping bag and was using it for a seat cushion. I thought it was a good idea so I went back inside the tent and retrieved mine.

"If we were still at The Stanley, we could be getting maid service, not to mention room service," I mentioned wistfully.

"After what happened to you, I'd think you'd had enough of The Stanley. I know I have." She handed me a cup of hot coffee. "Just the way you like it," she said. "A sugary sludge."

"Thanks." I sidled up next to her and dropped onto my still warm sleeping bag. It wasn't fresh-brewed, fresh-ground coffee but it would do in a pinch.

"I'm freezing." Karen shivered despite the lengths to which she'd bundled herself up. Fleece-lined trousers, tee shirt, sweatshirt, hoodie, and a navy parka topped with a merino wool scarf. Purple fleece gloves protected her hands as best they could. The waterproof hiking boots did their job.

"Close to it, anyway," I replied, enjoying the first fall of sugar and coffee glide across my tongue and cascade down my throat. "Forty degrees Fahrenheit, at least. There's permafrost in these mountains." We looked up at the mountains. The mountains looked down on us. I didn't take it personally.

"Lovely." Karen drank her coffee, strong and black. She

pushed her feet nearer to the small flame.

Like her, I'd slept in my hiking clothes. Brown fleece-lined trousers with a zillion zippered pockets, black-and-white flannel shirt, orange parka—I had a fear of game hunters shooting at me —and a wool-trimmed trapper hat with a knitted brown moose on each side. Karen told me I looked like Elmer Fudd. I knew exactly who she meant. I'd learned a lot about America and the world watching Looney Tunes. As far as I'm concerned, it should be required watching in every elementary school. I've always felt the poor guy's been underestimated, like me. Even Bugs Bunny had a soft spot for the intrepid, if inept, hunter. "Don't worry, it'll warm up soon enough. Sleep well?"

"Considering I'm in the wilderness, with no mattress and no heat? Yeah. I've got to say, I've had worse nights," she admitted. She sounded surprised herself. "Must be all this clean mountain air."

"So you didn't hear anything during the night?"

She pinched her brows and looked at me. "No. Should I have?"

"No." I stuck my hand into the bowels of my backpack. I grabbed for the carton of cigarettes I'd placed there for safekeeping and came up empty. "You take my cigarettes?" My eyes shot accusingly at Karen and then scanned the clearing for evidence of her mischief. Had she tossed them?

"Don't look at me like that. I didn't touch your stupid cigarettes."

I frowned at her.

"Here. Have some cereal. Maybe it will satisfy your urge." She thrust the box at my midriff.

I now frowned at the box of Frosted Flakes. "Can I smoke it?"

"No, you can't—"

"It was a rhetorical question." I shoved my hand into the box and scooped up a handful of sugary flakes. I stuffed every bit in my mouth and chewed.

"What it was was a snide remark."

"Whaeffer," I mumbled and choked. Karen handed me the water bottle and I drank quickly.

"What's the plan?" Karen took the Frosted Flakes and spilled a pile into her lap. She plucked up each individual flake and popped them one at a time onto her tongue. Talk about fussy eaters.

"Let's look at the map." We had her phone but zero bars of reception so the device was practically useless. Except for photographing moose. I drew out the folding map—also courtesy of our shopping spree at the convenience store in Glen Haven—from the side pocket of my backpack and studied it. The first thing I noticed was the red mark. "Did you do this?"

"Doofwat?" Karen mumbled, spitting sugar flakes over our clothing and into the fire.

I jabbed my finger down on the map. "This. This mark. A red circle."

Karen coughed and cleared her throat. "A red circle? No, why would I do that? Where would I get a marker out here?" She ran her finger over the small red spot.

"Well," I said, "if you didn't do it and I didn't do it, then who did?" I thought about the sound I'd heard in the middle of the night and the sense I'd had that something or someone was prowling around our camp. A red dot appears magically on our map and my cigarettes magically disappear... I decided to keep these thoughts to myself. Karen would only become agitated.

"Are you sure it wasn't on the map when we bought it?"

"I suppose...but I looked at this map yesterday afternoon, several times, in fact. I didn't notice it then." But I noticed it immediately this morning. I didn't point this out. "You're right. Probably there the whole time."

"So what do we do?"

"We go there."

"Why?"

"Why not? You have a better idea? We can't sit here all day. And if we stay here too many days, we'll run out of food and water."

"I've got another dozen protein bars."

"A complete waste of money," I quipped. "You'd be better off eating the cardboard box they come in. It'd taste better too."

"Fine."

"I saw that."

"Saw what?"

"You rolled your eyes. In fact, you roll your eyes all the time." I wagged a finger at her. "You keep doing that and your eyeballs will loosen up completely. You'll never see normally again for the rest of your life. That's a fact."

She rolled her eyes at me.

Frustrated and needing something constructive to do, I began folding the map, methodically turning the creased pages this way and that. I got messed up halfway through the job and tried again. And failed again.

"Give me that!" Karen snatched the map out of my hands as I was about to throw it in the dying fire and folded it expertly.

"Show off." I stood. "We'd better grab all the food and water we can carry. It's a long hike."

"Where exactly are we going?"

"Mirror Lake. Some miles that way." I pointed north. At least, I thought it was north. Or was that west?

"What about all our other stuff? Our gear?"

"Leave it," I said. "We'll either be back or we won't."

"Thank you, Master Philosopher," Karen quipped. She tossed her sleeping bag, plus the coffee pot and utensils into the tent, and zipped up the flap.

We hit the trail. And the trail hit us back with everything it had. Steep ascents, perilous descents, sketchy trail markings and a hail storm that left us both bruised and wet.

A bright, yellow hot sun forced its way out of the dark clouds past midday and so did every other insect within a thousand square miles. My throbbing feet let me know they were not happy with the situation.

"Mosquitoes and wildflowers." Karen swatted all around her head madly.

"Got to take the good with the bad," I said, leading us up over a pile of nasty rocks. Half an hour later, we reached our destination. I halted.

"Wow." Karen came to a stop beside me and gaped in awe at Mirror Lake. Bright turquoise blue light reflected off its smooth surface. Ominous brown and gray rocky towers rose along the lake's western edge. We were the only people in sight. Okay, I use the word *people* loosely.

No Ken Dalton, no Marcia Allison. No Lena Jay or Ernie for that matter. No Elmer Fudd except for this poor imitation.

"So now what?" Karen demanded, as if reading my thoughts. "I don't see any red circles." She swung on me. "Or any X-marks-the-spots. It's getting late. Even if we start back now, we'll never make it back to our campsite before dark. And I do not want to be hiking that trail in the dark, Ed."

"Let's hope it doesn't come to that." I pulled out the map while Karen took a swig from our dwindling supply of water and munched on a vegan strawberry-flavored pea-protein bar. One down, eleven to go. She settled down on her haunches. "Sure you don't want one?"

"I'd rather eat dirt." I examined the map more closely. "I think we need to go that way." I pointed to the rocky cliffs.

"No way. I'm no mountain goat."

"The red marking is definitely over there." I waved my arm around vaguely. "Somewhere."

"Somewhere, Ed? Somewhere?" She leapt to her feet. "You drag us out here to the middle of nowhere? The literal middle of nowhere!" It was her turn to wave agitatedly and she did so with gusto. "And now you tell me it's out there somewhere!? Where, Ed? Where?"

I didn't know what to say.

"And where is Ken, Ed? Where's my brother? Because I don't see him! This whole misadventure is costing me thousands of dollars. Hell, by now, it's probably cost me my job." Tears sprang from her eyes. "And what do I get? What do I have to show for it? Nothing!" She threw her arms wide. "Not a goddam thing!" Her voice echoed off the cliffs and across the lake.

Karen sank to her knees and brought her hands to her face. I tiptoed over and let my fingers fall lightly on her shoulder. "Trust me," I said.

Karen lowered her hands and sniffled. She looked into my eyes and I held her gaze.

"One more time. Trust me." I extended my hand. She took it and I helped her up to her feet. "That's better."

"Sorry," she sniffed.

"Nothing to be sorry about. You're the client, after all. You've a right to express your feelings. And to expect results. And it's results you shall have."

Her brow dug furrows across her forehead.

"This way," I said with probably a lot more confidence than I felt. But I did feel something. Sensed something in the air. And it was definitely in the direction we now went, hand in hand.

We hiked along the edge of the lake, sometimes following a narrow deer trail, other times cutting through the unspoiled forest. Sometimes, I think I went backwards, and other times in circles, Karen either failed to notice or was too tired or kind to mention. Probably the former.

We slid along a rocky tower with vertical rifts running all the way to the top, hundreds of feet above us. We scampered carefully through piles of fallen rocks of every shape and size. A twenty-foot-tall jagged black slash caught my attention and I angled us towards it—following my nose as much as my eyes.

"What is it, Ed?" Karen squeezed between the rocks and stood beside me. "A mineshaft?" We faced a dark rectangular opening carved into the rock.

"Maybe." It did look like a mineshaft. Thick oak beams bordered the six-foot entrance. Everything looked centuries' old. Leaves, the dried dung of unknown critters, and other debris littered the ground. Beyond was nothing but blackness.

"What's it doing way out here?"

"Waiting for us?" I stepped inside. Karen followed, one hand clinging to my left shoulder. "Shine a light, would you?"

She pulled out her phone and pressed on the flashlight. "Doesn't look like this place has been used for ages."

"I wonder." I noted a quiver in her voice and I couldn't blame her for it. There was something very odd about finding this underground manmade structure so remote from the world. The light of the phone wasn't much but it was enough to see that the rock walls surrounding us had definitely been carved by the hand of man—or a very dexterous moose.

"Pass the phone this way." I grabbed her hand holding the phone by her wrist and angled the light at the ground. "Mmm."

"What is it?"

"The remains of a cigarette." I bent and retrieved the stub.

"So what? That just means some other hikers found this place before us. Probably took shelter here in a rainstorm or something." She kicked at the debris littering the ground. "I'm surprised we aren't seeing crumpled beer cans. And more graffiti. Can we go now? I'm cold." She turned to leave.

"Not so fast." I held Karen back. "Not just any cigarette, a Winston." I dangled the butt in front of her eyes. That was the smell that led me there.

"And?"

"And in we go. I relieved Ernie of a carton of Winstons from his and Lena Jay's RV, remember? And if you didn't throw away my cigarettes—"

"For the last time, I did not throw away your stupid cigarettes, Ed."

"Then this cigarette butt is a sign." I held it under her nose. "Telling us we've arrived. Just like the red marking on the map, and the GPS coordinates Doctor Allison slipped me back at the Lil' Green Man."

"And the ones in the tunnel?"

"And the ones in the tunnel," I said. "You see, everything points to here." I ran a hand along the cold stone wall curving around and above us. "And here we are."

"And you think Marcia Allison is responsible for all this? Why? Why go to all this trouble? All this cloak and dagger stuff?"

"Perhaps she wished to help us, lead us to Ken, but did not wish to risk the military authorities, such as General Grant, knowing that she was assisting us. She could get herself in trouble."

"I guess that makes sense."

"Then again, the map and the cigarette could be the work of some unknown person or persons."

"Great." Karen snorted. "Who is this mysterious person or persons who somehow managed to get hold of our map between the time we bought it and this morning?"

"I have no idea."

"The map and cigarettes have never been out of our sight."

"Except when we were sleeping."

"Are you suggesting some unknown person or persons snuck into our camp last night—in the middle of nowhere, I might point out—while we slept just to mark our fucking map and steal your cigarettes?"

"It's not outside the realm of possibilities."

"It's beyond the realm of common sense, Ed! You're saying this mysterious unknown person conveniently marked our next destination for us, and then left a cigarette butt on the ground outside some long-forgotten abandoned mine expecting us to discover it? I mean, it's a cigarette butt, Ed. The world's full of 'em! Who'd be stupid enough to plant a cigarette butt as a clue for us to find a million miles from nowhere and expect us to find it? Who, Ed? Who?"

"I couldn't say. But we found it, didn't we?"

"Yes, but—" Karen rubbed her hands across her face, back and forth, up and down, angles both obtuse and obscene. Smearing her nose, cheeks and chin this way and that like her face was fabricated out of soft rubber. I was beginning to worry she'd rub out her features. And her features were rather attractive—blue hair and all—surprising, considering how filled with anger her face presented at the moment.

Finally, she stopped moving. Her hands dropped limply to her sides. "Yeah, we did." She blinked. "We found it." She latched onto my sleeve. "You mean this time there really is a door? You're not making fun of me like in the tunnel at Estes Park?"

"No. And yes, this time there really is a door. And I'm willing to go out on a proverbial limb and say that we will find Ken inside." Who or what else, I could only imagine…

"Ed, I love you! I knew you could do it!" She threw her hands around my neck and jammed her lips into mine. Karen Dalton was a woman of contradictions.

"If we can find the door. Help me look."

"Right, right!" Karen fell off me and began digging feverishly at the ground.

I left her to her own devices and ran my hands along the sides of the rocky chamber. We stood about six feet in from the entrance. The cave curved slightly to the left then stopped abruptly at a wall of loose rock blocking further exploration. If there was a door in that direction, we'd never get to it. It would take a lot of hours and a lot of manpower to move all that rubble. I retraced my steps to the sound of Karen's furious scratching at the hard earth. What a strange woman.

I returned to the spot where I'd discovered the discarded cigarette butt, which I'd slipped into my pant pocket for safe keeping. No, I wasn't going to eat it. I may be quirky but I do have my standards. Besides, it wasn't even my brand.

I took a closer look at this section. Thick hand-carved beams spaced approximately four-feet apart flanked the sides. More braced the ceiling. Two of the wooden beams on the left side differed from the others. These two stood a mere three-feet apart. Was there a reason for this?

I pulled off a glove and ran my bare fingers along the edge where wood met rock. What I'd taken at first glance for a dark knot hole was an inset black metal button. I pushed it. Because that's what you do.

We experienced a slight tremor beneath our feet and heard the sound of stone on stone as a slab of rock slid to one side, revealing a seven-foot-tall gray metal door.

"Wow, just like in the movies," Karen gasped. She joined

me. "Now what? How do we get inside?"

"More importantly, perhaps," I replied. "What will we find inside?"

"Yeah, there is that." Karen took a step back. "I don't see any door knobs or handles or-or anything. Any ideas?"

I had a couple but I was not ready to show all my cards. "Remember the tunnel under the street in Estes Park?"

"Of course, why?"

"What did you do that time?"

"I banged on the wall." Karen frowned. "*Now* are you poking fun at me?"

"Go ahead," I urged. I mimicked knocking. "What have we got to lose?" When was this woman going to learn to trust me? "Knock."

Karen tilted her head dubiously and planted her hands on her hips. "This is no time for your jokes, Ed. We could be this close to finding Ken!" She pinched thumb and forefinger together. "This close."

"Knock."

"Fine. But if you're having fun at my expense..." Karen warned me with a stern look then raised her hand and sucked in a breath. She knocked tentatively.

"Again, like you mean it," I suggested.

Karen balled her hand into a fist and rapped hard, twice. She turned her fist to my face. "I warned you—"

We heard a faint whir and looked at each other. The steel door abruptly swung out and up like an overhead garage door, minus the clang and clunk.

21

"Look out!" I warned.

Karen jumped backwards as the heavy metal door swung for her jaw. She tumbled into my arms and knocked me in the jaw with the back of her head. I saw stars. And not the good kind, not the real ones. What is it they say? No good warning goes unpunished?

"What is this place?" She looked around, eyes filled with awe. "I feel like I don't belong here. Like I don't fit in."

"Welcome to my world," I said.

A rather anticlimactic pale-complexioned late-middle-aged man with brown hair and dark eyes greeted us. He was wearing plain gray cuffed trousers, a green-and-white holiday University of Hawaii sweatshirt complete with a row of Xmas trees over a row of white snowflakes—did he realize it was summer, or had he been in this underground cave system so long that he'd lost track of the seasons?—and brown loafers with tassels. I liked him already.

Not exactly some extraterrestrial killing-machine, then again, he was no Ken Dalton.

"Welcome." He smiled warmly. "Mister Turner? Miz Dalton? Doctor Allison said to expect you. Come."

The stranger spread a well-manicured, welcoming hand and stepped to one side. A row of overhead recessed lighting revealed a polished stone floor extending some thirty feet or so before it disappeared to our left. "I'm Allan Pflock. With two Ls." he added. Karen clung to me. Once we were inside, Pflock pushed a button on a handheld remote and the overhead door swung down. Sealing us inside.

"Is she here?" I asked as he led us around the corner where we discovered a chamber some forty-feet in circumference. An inverted gray-brown bowl hewn from solid rock.

"All in good time, Mister Turner. First, welcome to the Haven. I'm Allan Pflock. With two Ls."

"Didn't he just tell us that?" Karen whispered in my ear.

"Let's get you checked in and settled. Plenty of time to chat afterward."

"Checked in? Karen asked.

"Yes. I'm afraid living quarters are tight. Doctor Allison said the two of you would be comfortable sharing one room."

"Won't be the first time," I replied. "Does it come with free satellite TV?"

"Afraid not. No outside communication whatsoever, Mister Turner." Pflock crossed quietly to a six-foot-long gray metal desk, vintage a WWII war movie, pushed up against the wall. A monitor sat on the desk attached by black cables to a boxy computer unit on the floor. The room was otherwise empty. Not exactly the lobby of a Hilton. Not even a Motel 6.

The sole brown leatherette chair squeaked as Pflock sat and opened the bottom left drawer. He removed two silvery metallic bracelets and handed one to each of us. "Please slip these on for the duration of your visit."

"No, thanks. I don't do jewelry," I replied.

"Please. It's for your own safety. We can't be too careful, can we?"

"Of what?" Karen wanted to know, slipping hers over her hand and giving her wrist a trial shake. "Not bad."

Pflock pushed the desk drawer shut with his knee. "The bracelets allow access to your living quarters, the dining room, exercise facility, spa, and all other personal and shared spaces."

And no doubt denied us access to anything Pflock and whoever else was in charge did not want us to see or learn of.

"You'll find a map in your room." He stood. "Leave your packs. Someone will bring them to your room. Save you the trouble."

"It's no trouble," I replied. "We've carried them this far."

"Then you must be exhausted." He motioned for us to drop our backpacks.

After exchanging a glance at one another, we shed our packs, leaving them on the ground beside the desk. I didn't see what we'd gain by arguing with Pflock. If anything, we might be denied further entrance. And since we'd gone to all the trouble of coming this far, I had no intention of retreating.

"Come. Follow me," Pflock said.

Karen stepped in his path. "What about Ken?"

Pflock stepped around her. "All in good time." He raised his own bracelet to a metal box the size of an electric outlet screwed to the wall about four feet up from the ground. An aluminum door rolled up and we went in with Pflock in the lead.

I brushed my bracelet against the metal box as I passed. No response. I tried again, tapping my bracelet against the matching metal box on the inside of the door. Again no response. I doubted that Karen's would have done anything either.

Did this mean only Allan Pflock, with two Ls, had the ability to get in and out? Or did it mean Karen and I were having our access restricted?

Either way, that could be a problem.

Pflock waved his hand right, left, and forward as he gave us what sounded like a much-practiced and well-oiled friendly spiel in which he described the Haven, a secluded burrow where the country's top minds could escape from the pressures of everyday life. Seek out the company of other like minds or maintain a hermitlike existence. "It's all up to the individual. It's all about choice here," said Pflock.

Still, this did lead me to wonder...had it really been Ken Dalton's choice to come here? Or had his boss insisted or forced him to retreat to the Haven? Was he a prisoner of this place? Were we?

"Ten private quarters. Two conference rooms. Dining hall and kitchen are that way." He pointed down the right branch of a

WELCOME TO MY WORLD

corridor. "Library's through there." He pointed to a pair of doors as we passed them.

I noticed several computer stations inside. "So you do have computers," I noted. "Internet access."

He turned to face me. "No, no. We are on an internal LAN only. Like I said, no outside communication."

"What about scientists like Ken Dalton who wish to continue their work while here?"

"They bring whatever files they'd like with them. Thumb drives," Pflock explained. He stopped. "Here you are. Lucky seven," he quipped, pointing out the room number on the wall next to our arched metal doorway. He slid his own bracelet against the metal box on the wall and our door rolled upwards and disappeared in a slit in the door's head casing. "Home, sweet home. Cozy, isn't it?"

"Beats spending another night in our tent," I replied. "You should see it. Barely room to stretch our legs, right, Karen?" She nodded but I kept my attention on Pflock. If he'd seen our tent and campsite, he wasn't telling and I caught no sign of his trying to hide the information. Of course, that didn't mean he hadn't been the thing I'd heard traipsing around our campsite in the middle of the night and leaving us a trail of clues to follow.

"Are all the rooms alike?" asked Karen. A vaulted ceiling gave the impression that the room was larger than it actually was. A low-profile queen-sized bed sat center stage. Nightstands and fixed lamps stood on either side. Karen ran a tentative hand along the cranberry-colored bedspread.

"Yes. There's a small closet behind that door. The other leads to your private bath."

"Thank goodness for that," Karen said. "I'm dying for a bath."

"Sorry, by bath I meant shower."

"Close enough." Karen opened the door and sighed with pleasure. I caught a whiff of disinfectant. I'd never seen a woman look so happy at the sight of a toilet. She hated pooping in the woods. Her words, not mine.

"Make yourselves at home. Dinner is in…" He glanced at the stainless-steel banded watch around his wrist. "One hour. If you have any trouble finding the dining hall or need anything in the meantime—"

I cut him off. Pflock talked a lot but never really seemed to say anything. "I'm sure we'll manage." I walked him to the door. "Okay if we wander around?"

"Of course. Feel free."

"Mi nuclear bunker es su nuclear bunker?" I quipped.

"Ha-ha. Very funny." Pflock winked at Karen. "This one must keep you in stitches."

"More the other way around," I answered for her, thinking of the physical abuse I'd been suffering at her hands. I considered it a wonder I had no stitches. Shows the value of a thick skin.

"What about Ken?" Karen asked. "When will we see him?"

"He's quite busy at the moment. Asked not to be disturbed for any reason," Pflock answered. "But he's delighted that you're here, Miz Dalton. Believe me. You'll see him in due time."

"How did he know we were here?" I asked. We'd been with Pflock since our arrival. Pflock's only reply was an enigmatic smile.

Karen frowned and threw herself down on the bed. "Just like my dumb brother to make me wait." Her fists slammed into the mattress on either side of her. "And after scaring me practically to death with all this talk of aliens being out to get him and me spending the past week hunting high and low for him!" Her fists slammed the mattress a second time.

"Try to get some rest," I suggested. "Save your energy for your reunion." Sounded like it was going to be a doozy. That whole love-hate thing that people have going can be quite confusing, if entertaining, at times.

"You might want to lock your door when you do sleep," Pflock suggested, standing in the open doorway and waving goodbye. "There's been a murder."

"What!?" Karen jumped off the bed like it was on fire.

"Oh, dear." Allan Pflock's hand flitted to his mouth. "I

wasn't supposed to say anything. You didn't hear it from me." He zipped his lips then smiled and said goodbye.

The aluminum door rolled down and we were alone in our home, sweet bunker.

"What the hell, Ed? Who's murder?"

"How should I know?" I released her death grip from my neck. "We only just arrived."

Karen paced back and forth. She picked up a queen-size pillow and punched it over and over. "You don't suppose he means that Emily Crenshaw woman?" She savagely kicked the pillow through the bathroom door.

I shrugged. "Not likely. I mean, she died in Nevada. Would he even know about her death?"

"Doctor Allison could have told him," Karen replied. "He's obviously been in touch with her."

"True. But that still doesn't explain why he recommends us locking our door here."

Karen's eyes grew wide. "Ohmygod! It's not Ken, is it? Do you think he meant Ken? Ken's dead?" Her hands flew to her face. "The aliens got him!" She grabbed the remaining pillow off the bed.

"No, no." I grabbed Karen's hands and pulled them from the pillow she was struggling to rip apart. Who knew if we had any spares? And I like having a pillow when I sleep. "Calm yourself. Pflock said we'd be seeing your brother soon."

She sniffled. Where had those tears and all that mucous come from? The woman was practically a mucous machine at times.

"He most definitely did not say we'd be viewing your brother's cold corpse."

She slugged me in the gut while saying, "I hate you."

I doubled over in pain. I knew I should have stopped talking sooner. When I regained my breath, I said, "Still feel like taking a nap?"

"Are you kidding? I'm too wired to sleep. Sorry I hit you. Are you okay?" She patted my tummy like I was two years old.

Actually, it did make me feel a little better.

"I don't take it personally. What do you say we do a little exploring?"

"Are you sure it's okay?"

"You heard Pflock, he said feel free." I had a feeling there was a caveat or two attached to the phrase.

"Something about that man rubs me the wrong way."

"Me, too." I held my wristband to the metallic box at the wall and I was relieved to see our door obligingly roll itself up. I'd had some doubts about it. There was something very prisonlike about our situation.

The hallway was quiet and appeared empty. But that didn't mean hidden eyes weren't watching us. I would've bet they were. Maybe even snooping on us in our quarters. A theory I probably shouldn't mention to Karen. I would mention to her that we should be careful what we say and keep our voices to whisper level if what we had to say was important.

"Which way?" Karen wanted to know.

"We know what's back there." I indicated the direction we'd come in from. "So let's head that way." I motioned for her to follow me. We walked in silence for several minutes. All of the living quarter doors were down and without windows there was no way to know if anyone was currently inside any of the rooms.

A couple of the rooms we passed were fitted out as labs. But these sat unoccupied, as was the library. And no further sign of Allan Pflock. Weird.

"What do you make of what Pflock said?" she asked. "Do you think he was joking? About the murder, I mean?"

"Seems an odd think to make a joke of."

"No, duh. If we could only find Ken, we could ask him. Figure out what's really going on around here." She took a look down the next empty corridor. "Speaking of which, where is everybody? And don't say they've all been murdered."

"Okay." I gave the question some thought. "Hiding from a murderer?"

"You're right," came a familiar voice.

"Doctor Allison!" Karen cried, spinning around. "Where did you come from?"

"I just arrived. I hear Allan showed you to your quarters." The doctor was wearing a brown tweed pantsuit with a white blouse and low-heeled brown shoes.

"Yes. And without shoving cloth sacks over our heads first," I added in reference to Marcia Allison's previous form of welcome.

"You found the Haven."

"Thanks to you. And you alone?"

Dr. Allison left my question dangling. "I'm relieved you're here, Mister Turner." She placed a friendly hand on my shoulder and leaned closer. "I could really use your help."

"Oh?" I gazed at her hand. I half-expected it to morph into a black widow spider and bite me.

"There's been a murder," she confessed quietly.

"Yes, so we heard," I replied.

She appeared surprised.

"What we didn't hear was *who* was murdered," I said.

"Or how," Karen added.

Dr. Allison pursed her lips. "Come." Her heels clicked against the polished concrete floor as she marched us down the corridor. She stopped outside room 2. She raised her arm and pushed back the sleeve of her jacket. She tapped the metal box outside the door with a wrist bracelet identical to our own—in form if not in function. The aluminum door rattled upward. "It was Professor Pflock," she told us as we peered inside.

"Pflock?" Karen said. "How can that be?"

"We were speaking with the man not minutes ago," I explained. "If he was dead, he did a good job of imitating life."

"Yeah," Karen said, taking a look around the room. It did, indeed, appear identical to our own although the mattress was bare. "It was Pflock himself who told us—"

"Oh, sorry. I'm talking about Alan with one L," Dr. Allison explained. "He's in cold storage."

"Come again?" Karen said. "He definitely said there were

two Ls."

"In fact, he told us twice."

Dr. Allison managed a chuckle, which seemed in bad taste under the circumstances. "No, no. You don't understand. That *was* Allan with two Ls you spoke with. I'm talking about Alan with one L."

"There are two of them? Two Professor Pflocks?" I asked. Nothing in the room appeared out of place. No sign of blood or struggle.

"Alan with one L is, was, Allan with two Ls' hubby."

"I see."

Karen whistled softly. "Wow, that's horrible. The poor man. We had no idea."

"He seems to be holding up rather well under the circumstances," I said. "How was Alan with one L murdered?"

"Strangulation," Dr. Allison was quick to say. "Strangled right here in his bed. At least, it appears that way. I'm no physician. Ken is and that was his conclusion."

"When was Pflock killed?"

"Earlier today. We haven't determined an exact time of death. Allan with two Ls discovered the body. They were supposed to meet for breakfast and when Alan with one L didn't arrive, his husband came looking for him. Found him dead right there in their bed."

"And where is he now? The dead man, that is."

"Cold storage." Dr. Allison explained that there was a cold storage room between the labs and the kitchen. "It's used for food storage as well as anything of a scientific nature that requires a subfreezing temperature. I thought it best to tuck him away there."

The doctor explained that the Haven had been originally carved out of the mountain as a top-secret military facility decades earlier. What it had been used for, she'd never been told. "The military abandoned the facility and offered to lease it to LANL approximately forty years ago. Like I explained, we maintain it as a sort of working retreat. It's proven useful and convenient."

"I'd hardly call the location convenient," remarked Karen. "Not after what we went through to get here."

"No but it does keep the outside world at arms' length," Dr. Allison replied.

"Someone's arms managed to get inside," I couldn't help saying. "Alan with one L is proof of that."

"Unless that someone was already inside," suggested Karen.

"Yes," agreed Dr. Allison. "I suppose there is that."

"And the bedcovers?" I asked. "Was there any sign of a struggle or other traces or evidence? Anything that might point a finger at the killer? Or whether they came from within or without?"

"Nothing apparent. As for the blankets, we used them to wrap the body up before securing it in storage."

"Sure, what corpse wants to be cold?" Karen can be funny when she wants to.

"So much for preserving evidence," I remarked. "You probably should have left him and everything else in this room where you found them and notified the authorities."

"We are the authorities here, Mister Turner. We don't tolerate outsiders."

"But you do tolerate murderers?"

"You're a detective. I'm asking for your assistance. Are you going to help me or are you going to argue about rules and morality?"

"I am not sure how I can help you," I replied honestly. "Especially with any and all evidence destroyed."

"You could take a look at the body," suggested Karen.

I looked at her darkly. I do not enjoy eyeballing dead bodies unless they are served up hot on a warm plate, and are of one of the socially-acceptable meat or fish varieties.

"Good idea," agreed Dr. Allison. "Come, it's this way."

"Fine. But this is going to put me off ice cream for months, if not years."

22

"Any suspects? First and foremost among them being Allan with two Ls?" I suggested as Dr. Allison peeled back the blanket to reveal Alan with one L Pflock's upper torso. The three of us huddled in the aptly named cold storage room. A thin layer of rime covered the cranberry blanket. "Not that I'm an expert, but judging by those markings around his neck, strangulation seems the appropriate diagnosis."

"I don't see how Allan with two Ls could have done it. Several persons saw him this morning. Besides, he and Alan with one L were crazy in love."

"Love does strange things to people. Any discord between them?"

"Like I said, they adored one another. They'd been married over a decade. Recently celebrated their anniversary."

"No jealousy? Perhaps one of them had a not-so-secret lover?"

Dr. Allison shrugged and pulled the blanket back over the victim's head. "Not that I am aware. You might ask around."

"Speaking of around, where is everyone?" Karen asked.

"Our guests stick mostly to themselves. Working, meditating, reading."

"Strangling?" Karen suggested.

"The killer might have been an outsider. An intruder," I suggested. "If so, that would probably point to premeditation. We're a long way out in the middle of nowhere for a random breaking-and-entering gone bad.

"Pflock says no one's been in or out today except the two of you," said Dr. Allison. "Besides, the man was a respected biologist, who'd go out of their way to murder him?"

"Why didn't he put up a struggle?" I asked, taking a last look at the bundled corpse.

"He could have been sleeping when the killer struck," the doctor replied.

"And never woke up." I scratched my bristly chin. I hadn't shaved in days. "I've always thought it might be nice to die that way. Go to sleep and never wake up. But not like this." I fingered the edge of the blanket.

"Can we get out of here?" Karen had been giving herself a bear hug ever since we'd stepped inside the windowless, steel-clad, cold storage room. "I'm freezing. Not to mention, being around this stiff, no offense, is giving me the heebie-jeebies."

We stepped outside and Dr. Allison eased the heavy door shut. We discovered Allan Pflock with two Ls pouring himself a cup of brew from the drip coffee machine on the counter beside the stainless steel refrigerator. He reached into an overhead cupboard and pulled out a bottle of whiskey. He added a splash and then another before recapping the bottle and returning it to its place—a place I made note of.

"Pflock, there you are," said Dr. Allison. "How are you holding up?"

"Hello, Marcia." He sipped his beverage. "I've been better."

"I'm so sorry," Karen wrapped her arms around Pflock. "Why didn't you tell us?"

Pflock smiled sadly. "That the victim was my husband?" Tears welled up in his eyes. "I can barely believe it." His hand shook as he gulped his coffee and whiskey.

"Let me refill that for you." I gently took his cup and filled it with half coffee and half whiskey. I helped myself to a few ounces of whiskey using a Rocky Mountains National Park mug —featuring bold yellow-leafed fall aspens—I plucked from the mug tree standing on the corner of the countertop. The mug tree itself was carved and painted to resemble one of the ubiquitous Colorado quaking aspen trees.

"How many people are staying here now?"

"Twelve, counting yourselves, Marcia, and myself. Well, eleven now," answered Pflock.

"Support staff?"

"A cook, Sara Chronis. I've included her in the headcount. We're mostly responsible for our own rooms but she also handles any housekeeping chores that need doing."

"Like sweeping up dead bodies?"

Pflock chose to ignore my comment. Karen shot me a dirty look. I suppose I deserved it under the circumstances. Circumstance being that Pflock's hubby was the dead body serving as the butt of my remark. "And a maintenance worker on call."

"Is he here now?" I asked.

"No. Comes in once a week from Boulder," put in Dr. Allison. "He's not due again until Tuesday, right, Allan?"

"Yes, Marcia."

"No security?" I said.

"There's never been the need," Pflock replied.

"Until now," I said.

"Until now," Pflock agreed, wringing his hands.

Dr. Allison suggested we all go to dinner. Pflock excused himself. "Sorry, I'm not up to it. You understand." He carefully rinsed his empty mug in the sink and hooked it back on the mug tree. "Might I have a word with you, Marcia?" He dried his hands fussily on a University of Edinburgh tea towel hanging on the side of the fridge by way of a magnet. "I was thinking we might hold a memorial for—" Pflock's next words caught in his throat.

"Of course. I'll meet you in my office in a minute." To me and Karen, Marcia Allison said, "You two go ahead. I'll catch up with you in a few minutes."

We silently watched Pflock disappear.

"He's not staying in the room that his husband was strangled in, is he?" Karen asked.

"No, there are a couple of spare rooms at the moment. He's moved into number nine. What room did he give you?"

"Seven," Karen replied.

"You mentioned that Alan with one L was a biologist," I began.

"One of the best in his field," answered Dr. Allison.

"What about Allan with two?" I asked. "I assume he's a scientist of some sort?" She nodded. "What's his area?"

"He's an anthropologist. The Pflocks collaborated and published many interesting, if highly controversial, papers together. Perhaps you're familiar with their work?"

"I'm afraid not. Enlighten us."

"The Pflocks are strong proponents of the theory that extraterrestrials visited the earth tens of thousands, if not hundreds of thousands, of years ago." Dr. Allison studied our faces. Looking for what? Signs of disbelief?

Karen didn't disappoint. "Sounds crazy, if you ask me."

The doctor shrugged. "Read their papers. They make a strong case for such visitations. Including the theory that these aliens mated with early hominids, which led to the evolution of the Neanderthals. What about you, Mister Turner? Believe in aliens?"

"The stuff of fairytales," I replied. "You?"

"I'm a scientist," Dr. Allison replied. "I keep an open mind. If someone comes up with irrefutable evidence, I'll believe it. Until then..." She stuck her hands in her pockets. "It would be nice if the Pflocks' theories were true. Imagine, if we could find DNA evidence of extraterrestrial beings—maybe embedded with Neanderthal DNA—we could learn so much. A discovery like that would really open up new territory. Who knows, we might even be able to replicate one."

"An alien!?" Karen said. "Please, let's not open that Pandora's box of troubles. Diseases, germs, who knows what harm that could lead to."

"I agree," I said. "Humans have enough problems of their own. Why create new ones?"

"Leave the past in the past?" Dr. Allison said with a wan smile. "Is that what you're suggesting?"

Karen and I nodded.

"If only life was that easy."

Dr. Allison went one way and we went the other. But we did not go straight to the dining hall. We went to the library. I threw open the door. "Hardly the Duke Humfrey's Library at Oxford University." The Haven's library was nothing to write home about. A small trapezoidal room with metal shelves running along the edges, plus three desks lining one of the non-parallel sides, and a frumpy green sofa pushed up against the other.

I was thrilled to find the library deserted. I wasn't thrilled to find that none of the three impressive computers sitting on the three desks would allow me access to the Internet and the outside world. Whether it could if it wanted to was another matter entirely. "How are you at hacking?"

"Sorry," Karen replied, tapping uselessly at the computer to my right. "I don't even keep a password on my phone. What's the point, anyway? I mean, who cares? I don't." She paced.

"We might learn more about our companions. Something that might lead us to who killed Alan with one L."

"We might," admitted Karen. "I know it sounds terrible for me to say this, but I really don't care, Ed. It's not what we came here for. We came here to find Ken, remember?" She kicked the side of the sofa and threw herself down. "Find him and get out of here. I want to go home."

I pushed the computer keyboard aside. "You're right. Let's find Ken and go home." I extended my hand.

"You mean it?"

"Yes. And the first thing we do is get to dinner. Allison's probably wondering where we've disappeared to. Let's not make her send out a search party. Then we'll insist on seeing Ken. In the morning, I promise, we're out of here."

Karen took my hand and we went in search of the dining hall. Being in the company of the superior being that I am and not the world's worst detective, we discovered it in a matter of minutes. The scrumptious smells sending signals our way didn't hurt the process.

We collided with Marcia Allison at the entrance. "Just

arriving?" she asked.

"My fault," I said. "We got lost."

"The Haven can be a maze if you're not familiar with it." She opened the door and we followed her inside. A long white table with a tapered brushed-aluminum base stretched across the middle of the dining room. White swivel chairs with tan leather cushions on round bases surrounded the table. A half dozen faces looked at us with avid curiosity.

"Everyone," began Dr. Allison, "meet Ed Turner and Karen Dalton. They'll be staying with us for a time." She made the introductions. We were in the presence of a Doctor Robert Berlitz, Doctors Max and Katja Schuurman, Doctor Zultan Crobar, and Vishnu Pushpak who told us that, unlike his colleagues, he preferred to be called professor.

"Ed Turner, PI." I spread a wave across the table of eyes looking at us like a pair of new zebrafish plopped into a small fishbowl teeming with piranha.

"You're a principal investigator?" Prof. Pushpak commented. He spoke English well but with an Indian accent. He had black hair and dark, deep-set eyes. "May I inquire what school or lab you are affiliated with?"

Karen snickered.

I sent her a telepathic message letting her know what I thought about getting disrespected by a woman with a degree in poetry. Sadly, Karen Dalton was no more capable of receiving telepathic messages than I was capable of sending them.

"You may and it's not Harvard," I replied to the professor, taking note of his crisply-knotted crimson, black, and white Harvard necktie and matching enamel cufflinks. "It's the proverbial school of hard knocks."

Pushpak, a large man with bulging cheeks and bursting black beard, tugged at the lapel of his dinner jacket. The man dressed in a pinstriped charcoal suit, complete with vest. Here was a man who knew how to dress for dinner. Karen and I still wore our dirty and smelly hiking clothes, all the way down to the muddy hiking boots. "I don't understand."

He looked to Dr. Allison for answers and she gave him one. "Mister Turner is a *private* investigator, not a *principal* investigator. A detective."

"Are you now?" This from Katja Schuurman, a lovely woman with brown hair and sultry cat eyes framed with glasses. She wore blue jeans and a black-and-white fair isle sweater. "How unique." She twirled her fork and glanced at her husband who seemed disinterested.

"Marcia call you in to investigate our little murder?" demanded Robert Berlitz, seating at the head of the table to our left. "That's quick thinking."

A crescent of inch-long brown hair circled his skull. He was wearing an unzipped blue windbreaker over a flannel shirt and corduroys. He rested both elbows on the table, one on each side of his empty dinner plate. He had hooded blue eyes and a scarred complexion just visible under several days growth of whiskers on his cherubic face.

"No, Bobby," Dr. Allison said, pulling out a chair and plopping herself down near him.

"Merely a coincidence," I replied. "And is any murder little, sir? What branch of the military are you in, if I may ask?" I'd noticed the chain from what appeared to be dog tags round his neck.

Berlitz appeared taken aback. He pointed his spoon at me. "You're good, Turner. You're good. Air Force, retired." He drew himself up taller in his chair.

"And you, Karen Dalton," Crobar snapped. "Any relation to Ken Dalton?" Crobar had a large bald head that glistened under the overhead lights and sent out moonbeams as he swung it side to side. His handlebar moustache was bent and his face deadly sallow. He looked more dead than Alan with one L. Crobar had arrived to dinner in wrinkled black trousers and a JPL sweatshirt over a collared shirt. A gold tooth provided added character. Not that he needed it. His name alone provided plenty.

"I'm his sister." Karen sat. "Where is Ken? Shouldn't he be here?"

I took an empty chair beside her. Dr. Allison sat to my left. She shifted her chair and nuzzled up close.

"Held up in his office, I suppose," offered Max Schuurman, a man who had to be pushing the limits of seventy. And I meant age, not sit-ups. Was Katja his wife or his daughter? Like his wife or daughter, he spoke with a thick Danish accent. His tan tweed jacket had seen better days. His hair was thick and white. Black-framed bifocals clung to his bulbous nose like a bat hanging on for dear life. His jeans looked vintage but I was betting that he'd bought them new in the sixties.

"Can you blame him?" Pushpak said sharply. He seemed nervous as a bird in a cat shelter.

"What about Allan with two Ls?" Katja asked.

"He isn't feeling up to it," Dr. Allison explained. "Ah, Sara." She smiled at a beautiful under-thirty woman with long red hair and brilliant green eyes as she rolled a dining cart in from the kitchen. "Just in time. Who's ready for dinner?"

"And this is our Sara Chronis," stated Dr. Allison, always the hostess, "this is Ed Turner and Karen Dalton. They'll be spending the night."

"Sure, welcome aboard but did you hear about the—"

"We all know about the murder, Sara."

"Sorry."

"What's on the menu, Sara?" I asked.

"Bison," Sara announced cheerily.

Karen coughed.

"And rattlesnake." Smiling, Sara lifted covers from serving dishes. "With potatoes."

Karen blanched.

"Karen is a vegetarian," I explained.

"Vegan," Karen corrected.

"Hmm." Sara plopped a plump baked potato on Karen's plate. It rolled to the rim then off. Karen stabbed it with her fork and returned it to her plate.

"I'm sure I can cook you some fresh veggies. Will that do?" Sara asked.

"Thank you," replied Karen. "That would be lovely. If it's not too much trouble?"

"No trouble at all. That is why I'm here, after all. To keep you all happy and well fed."

Now that was a life's calling worth applauding.

"There may be some tofu in the freezer." Sara turned to go. "Anyone care for something to drink besides the wine?" She waved her hand in the direction of the four bottles standing in the center of the table. Two red, two white. One of each had popped their respective corks.

"Can I get a beer?"

"Of course, Mister Turner." She turned to Dr. Allison. "You too?"

Dr. Allison smiled. "You know me all too well."

Sara returned quickly with two open bottles of Stella Artois. We clinked our bottles together and drank.

Everyone else at the table was drinking the wine. I offered some to Karen. She opted for the red and, to my surprise, insisted I fill her wine glass to within a quarter-inch of the oh-shit-I've-spilled-it mark.

"Can I get a cola also?" I asked Sara. "Room temp, if you've got one."

"I do. Be right back." Sara winked at me, flashed her derriere, and disappeared into the kitchen.

We helped ourselves to roasted bison, deep-fried rattlesnake, and baked potatoes. Not a green vegetable in sight. All we needed now was something steamed. And out it came, a bowl overflowing with steamed broccoli, cauliflower, and carrots. Karen was in heaven.

Sara laid a brick of tofu atop Karen's plate. "I sauteed the tofu with onion and chives. Hope you like it." She handed me a lukewarm can of soda.

"Thanks." Karen picked at her food.

Sara joined us at the table and helped herself to the spread. She also poured herself a small glass of white wine.

I ate everything on my plate and helped myself to seconds.

I drank down half my beer and tipped in some cola. "What? Don't knock it till you've tried it," I replied to the looks of horror that fell on me from around the table.

To my surprise, Katja asked for my can of soda. I handed it across.

"Thanks." She poured some into her burgundy. "It may not be beer but what the hell, right, Mister Turner?" She winked in my direction and raised her wine glass. "Skol."

I joined her in the toast. So did everybody else although we were the only two mixing our drinks.

"That's utterly disgusting," Zultan Crobar shook his head. His eyes twitched. With an accompanying splat and rattle, he fell headfirst into his half-eaten bison steak.

23

"Zultan!" Dr. Allison leapt, tipping over her chair. She ran to Zultan and grabbed his shoulders. She pulled him up with effort. "Zultan! Are you alright?"

Zultan Crobar's face had looked better, seeing how it was now smeared with baked potato and bison meat juice.

Sara ran to the assistance, waving a napkin. "Zultan?" She peeled back an eyeball. "He's dead."

"She's right," I said, gazing curiously at the spectacle.

"Dead? Are you sure, Ed?" Karen asked.

"I know dead."

Dr. Allison flipped over Zultan Crobar's wrist and felt for a pulse. She shook her head in the negative. "Nothing."

"Where's Ken?" Katja said, her voice quavering. "He's a doctor. Somebody call Ken for chrissakes!"

"Take it easy, dear." Max patted Katja's hand and offered her his wineglass. I was definitely leaning in the direction of her being his wife, his much younger wife. "Not even the greatest physician in the world can save a man once he's dead."

"I'm afraid Max is right," barked a man bursting into the dining hall.

"Ken!" cried Karen. She raced to her brother. Ken Dalton gave his sister a half-smile and a quick hug. "Where the hell have you been?"

"Later." Ken pulled her hands off him. He hurried to the slumped body of Zultan Crobar. He checked his pulse at the wrist and neck and peered into his eyes. "Shit."

Katja burst into tears. The others gaped at the dead man.

"Is he?" Karen brought her hands to her lips.

"Poisoned, I'd say, judging by the coloration around his lips," replied Ken Dalton. Karen's brother was a medium-sized man with medium-brown skin and dark hair. The family resemblance was clear despite his lack of bright blue tresses. He was dressed in frumpy denim jeans, a long-sleeved black Henley shirt buttoned to the hilt, and blue sneakers.

"Was it something he ate?" Dr. Allison asked.

"Like an allergy to bison?" suggested Max Schuurman.

"Rattlesnake venom?" ventured Katja Schuurman.

I didn't know if he'd had an allergic reaction to the exotic meat, but I knew for certain he'd never be eating it again. And I'd never heard of a fried rattlesnake biting anybody from the afterlife.

"But he's barely touched his food," Karen noticed.

"Poor Crobar," Bobby Berlitz said. "He was a good man. Isn't there anything you can do for him, Dalton?"

"It's out of my hands now." Ken sagged into an empty chair and pushed his hands through his hair with enough force to move a mountain. "Besides, I'm not a practicing physician. Never have been."

"Really, Marcia, we have got to telephone the authorities," Max Schuurman insisted.

"Of course."

"What do we do in the meantime?" Pushpak stood in the far corner of the room, cradling his wineglass, as if he feared that whatever had killed Crobar might be contagious.

"Cold storage?" I suggested.

"Ken?" Dr. Allison asked. "What do you think?"

"Fine. I don't care. Do whatever the hell you want. It's too late now. It's all too late." He buried his face in his hands.

Karen hurried to her brother. She knelt beside him and draped her arm across his back and whispered soothing words.

"Lend me a hand, Doctor Berlitz?" I begged. The ex-military man looked fit enough to lend assistance in the task at hand. "You too, Professor Pushpak?"

"Not me." Pushpak waved his free hand. His eyes bulged

with horror. "I'm not touching it-him."

"Just me and you then, Turner," Bobby Berlitz said gruffly. He hoisted himself from his chair and grabbed Crobar's left arm. I grabbed the other arm and we dragged him out of his seat.

"I can help." Sara grabbed Zultan Crobar's legs and easily lifted them to her hips.

"Thanks," I said.

We manhandled the corpse out of the dining hall. We followed Sara's directions through the kitchen, down a short corridor, and into the windowless cold storage room.

"I hope you don't mind stashing another body in here," I said, meaning my question for Sara as we edged our way past frozen fruits, vegetables, meats, and bread products. My breath came out in puffy white clouds. I hate the cold. Then again, I hate the heat. Give me good old thermal equilibrium anytime. "Not very appetizing."

"Meat's meat," Berlitz said.

"Is that the official military position?" quipped Sara. Of the three of us, she was breathing the easiest. She led the way, dragging Crobar's corpse down the narrow path between the wooden pallets and metal shelves by the ankles. Berlitz and I held the rest of him suspended in midair. I noticed something in a quart-sized glass jar that resembled pigs' feet. Someone's science experiment or tomorrow night's dinner?

"It's *my* position," Berlitz said testily. He boot-kicked a blanket lying in the path that Sara and I had simply stepped across.

"Wait!" I hollered.

"What is it, Turner?" Berlitz demanded.

I set down my share of the body, forcing him to do the same. Crobar's feet thudded to the ground as Sara released her hold on his ankles.

"Stop dawdling, Turner! Let's speed it up. Damn thing's heavy and I'm freezing my ass off in here." Berlitz glared at me.

"The blanket." I picked it up. "Isn't this—"

Sara shouted up ahead. "He's gone!"

Berlitz and I shot our heads around. "Who's gone?" Berlitz was first to ask.

"Alan." Sara looked shaken. "He's not there."

"What do you mean he's not there?" Berlitz barreled over Crobar's unmoving body and shoved his way down the narrow path. "I'll be damned!"

I joined them in looking at the crumpled row of boxes where the weight of Alan with one L had recently made itself known. "He was there less than an hour ago. I saw him myself."

"Corpses don't get up and walk away," Berlitz's jaw worked quickly side to side.

"Maybe he wasn't really dead?" I suggested. "Only in a deep coma perhaps?"

Berlitz frowned. "Sure or maybe came back as some shit ass zombie or something. Come on, Turner, stop talking nonsense. I saw the man with my own two eyes. I know a dead man when I meet one. Sara, what do you have to say? You keep your damn food here. What do you know about this?"

Sara threw up her hands. "Nothing. I swear! I haven't been here all day. Everything I need for the day, I keep in the freezer box in the kitchen. We only use this for long-term storage and bulk supplies. It's you researchers who are in here more than me. In and out at all hours. With all your chemicals and such."

"You accusing *me* of having something to do with Pflock's disappearing corpse?" Berlitz's face grew bigger and redder.

"No," Sara said, keeping her voice even. "I'm not suggesting anything. Simply stating a fact."

"If I might interrupt, I'd like to suggest we pick Crobar up off the floor where we left him."

"Good idea,' Berlitz said. "Freezing my ass of here. Let's get him settled. Then we'll figure this out." Looking Sara in the eye, he said, "And we *will* get this figured out."

"Screw you!" Sara blew past Berlitz and out the cold storage room door.

"Bitch," swore Berlitz.

For a second, I feared that in her anger at Berlitz she'd close and padlock the door behind her with me stuck inside with the ill-tempered ex-military man. But she left the door ajar and I heard her angry pounding steps fade into the distance. Berlitz and I manhandled the awkward corpse to the rear and placed him where I'd last seen Alan with one L Pflock lying in eternal repose.

I situated the blanket atop him, not sure what good it would do. It wouldn't keep his reanimated body from rising and walking out of here like Pflock. Secondly, it wouldn't prevent anybody from discovering him. Thirdly, it sure as hell wasn't going to keep him warm and cozy.

Shutting the door to the cold storage room behind me on my way out, I couldn't help wondering if Pflock was going to disappear too.

24

"Sara, where'd everybody go?"

Sara Chronis paused from clearing the dining table and collecting the dinner dishes. "I don't know about that jerk Berlitz —I haven't seen him since I stormed out of the freezer." She blushed. "Sorry about that, by the way."

"No apology necessary. Everyone's on edge. In Bobby Berlitz's case, I'm sure it's also ingrained in his personality."

"I'd like to ingrain a broomstick right up his tight—" A plate exploded into several shards the instant she threw it down in the plastic tub on the cart. "Damn. Again, sorry." She picked out the pieces and threw them in the trash.

"Can I help?"

"No, I got this." Her fingers tickled mine for a moment then fell away. "To answer your question, everybody else went to their quarters. After what happened to Zultan, nobody was interested in sticking around. All this food wasted," she moaned, tossing bits of bison and rattlesnake into the plastic bag-lined trash bin hanging off the side of the rolling food cart. "Chocolate torte for dessert too."

"Homemade?"

"*Haven made*," Sara quipped.

"The next best thing."

Sara smiled at me. "Would you like some, Mister Turner?"

"First, call me Ed. Please. Second, I'd love a slice." Guilt took over as I thought about poor Karen, finally reunited with her brother but under some of the worst possible circumstances. How could I eat torte at a time like this? "Third," I said, caving. "Better make that to go."

"You got it. Be right back." True to her word, Sara returned in moments. I spent the moments she was gone inspecting the late Zultan Crobar's chair and spot at the table. Nothing suspicious stood out. And the efficient Sara Chronis had already cleared his dishes, utensils, and glass. Should I be suspicious of that fact?

She handed me a square of chocolate torte so large that it dwarfed the plate and could've served as third base at an MLB-sanctioned ballgame.

"Thanks." My plate weighed as much as a giant cane toad and looked far tastier. I'd seen a giant cane toad specimen once at the LA Zoo. Close up. Now that thing looked like an amphibious creature from an outer space sci-fi film.

"My pleasure. Consider this one of my last acts as chef cum housemaid cum mommy to this bunch of children."

"Childish, are they?"

"Look Mister Turner, Ed, these people may have all the pieces of paper and fancy degrees in the world but what they don't have is smarts. And they all act like spoiled little monsters. I've had enough."

"Been here long?"

"About two years." Sara wiped her hands down her green slacks. "After I finish clearing up, I'm out of here."

"I can't say I blame you." I motioned to the head of the table. "I see you removed Crobar's dishes."

She shook her head. "Yes and no. Despite what these idiots think, do, and say, I'm smart enough to know there could be evidence, of what I don't know, or fingerprints, something that might point to who or what killed Zultan. I used a napkin to pick each piece up."

"Smart."

"Thanks. I only wish I'd had the chance to do the same with Alan with one L's room and things."

"But you didn't?"

"The others packed him up and cleaned up his quarters before I even learned what happened." She planted her hands on her hips. "Never even asked me if I was okay with them dumping the body in the same place I keep our food stores."

"Not the most sensitive bunch?"

"Only when it comes to themselves and their precious work. Nothing and nobody else seems to matter."

"What is the nature of their work?"

"Hell if I know. I mean, I hear snatches of this and that, like during mealtimes, but mostly they keep me out of the loop and shut up whenever I'm within earshot. Not that I give a damn. They're all *loopy*, if you ask me." She circled her index finger around her ear in the universally-accepted gesture for morons.

"Ken Dalton included?"

"What do you mean?"

"I'm wondering if he seems as loopy to you. I'd love to hear your opinion of the man."

"Hmm." Sara thought a moment. "Keeps to himself mostly. He's been in and out of here the last couple of years. Barely speaks to me. Seems high strung, higher each time he comes. Reminds me of a tea kettle about to blow its top, if you know what I mean?"

"I think I do." A new thought came to mind. "Tell me, did anyone here have a beef with Zultan?"

"Enough to poison him? I don't think so. One thing I've learned is that there's a lot of politics among these egghead types. A lot of positioning for power and prestige in their precious world of academia. But not to the level that you poison your competition. And nobody here at Haven was really in competition with one another anyway. Everybody here has his or her own area of expertise. I believe they were working together as a team. With a common goal."

"But you don't know what that goal is?"

"Not a clue. You're a detective, Ed. If you find out before I leave—which with luck will be in the next hour or so—how about filling me in? Not that I care much."

I promised Sara I would. "Sorry to see you go."

"It's a small world, Ed." Sara gave me a peck on the cheek.

"I placed everything Zultan touched in plastic bags. They are on the prep counter in the kitchen, if you'd care to check them out."

"Later. Right now, I'd better go see how my client is doing."

"Client?" Sara stabbed a dessert fork into the middle of my torte. "You'll need that."

"Karen Dalton hired me to locate her brother Ken."

Sara's brow wrinkled, which did nothing to diminish her good looks. "I didn't know he was missing."

"Not from your perspective but from hers." I explained how Ken had telephoned Karen in an agitated state a week or so ago claiming that aliens were out to kill him.

"Wow. See what I mean? All these people are nuts!"

"So you aren't a believer? In aliens?"

"Little green men and grays that come to earth because they don't have cows on their own planet to mutilate, so they've got to drive six bajillion miles here just for the pleasure? No." Sara pulled on a long bunch of her flame red hair. "No ETs, no Big Foot and no Loch Ness monster."

"Good for you." I hoisted my plate. "Smells heavenly." A thick dusting of white powdered sugar layered the top. "Thanks again for this."

"When you finish that slice, feel free to come back for more. Like I said, there's plenty. Help yourself."

"I might."

She flicked her damp towel over her shoulder. "Mind if I ask you something, Ed?"

"Shoot."

"You mentioned Karen is your client."

"Yes, that's right."

"I just wondered because at first I thought you two were a couple."

"We're a couple, alright. A couple of what, I couldn't say."

Sara laughed.

I carried my slab of chocolate torte to Ken's quarters, room three, according to Sara.

A laugh and a slab of chocolate torte. I was batting a

thousand. Although I couldn't say the same for Zultan Crobar... He'd struck out.

25

Karen and Ken Dalton sat side by side on the edge of his rumpled bed. Both faces showed dismay and fatigue. And a whole lot of frustration. It was very warm in the room compared to the others I'd been inside. The blanket lay on the floor. The room was a cluttered mess. A foul smell filled the room.

"Don't look at me," snapped Karen seeing the look of disgust on my face.

"What is that horrid smell?" I waved my hand in front of my nose. "Burning elephant dung incense? Gross. I'm losing my appetite. Almost," I admitted, jamming my fork into the tip of my chocolate torte and savoring that wonderful first bite. Thick and chocolatey and flourless. Perfection. I ran my avaricious tongue across my lips to scrape up every last speck of powdered sugar.

"May as well be." Using Ken as a prop, Karen hauled herself to her feet. "It's my idiot brother. He's burning hair. Says it keeps the aliens at bay!"

"Hair? Whose hair?" I cut another bite's worth, offered it to the Daltons who each declined, thankfully. I shoveled it into my mouth before either could change their mind.

"His, Crobar's, Alan with one L Pflock's, and now mine!" Karen grabbed what was left of her tresses and spun around.

"Yikes!" I couldn't help blurting. I choked on my torte. A jagged line of hair showed where a clump of hair had been clumsily removed from the back of Karen's head.

"Yeah, yikes. It's in there." She pointed to the bathroom. "Smoldering in the sink." She clipped Ken in the ear. "Moron. Ask next time." A pair of guilty-looking scissors rested against the base of the lamp.

"Cheer up, Karen. At least we've found him. Alive and in one piece, I might add." Although I wasn't sure how long he was going to remain in one piece given Karen's current frame of mind and penchant for outbursts of violence.

I slowly circled Ken's quarters, balancing my plate and eating as I went. He'd crammed his space with scientific equipment. Most of which I couldn't identify and had no idea what the pieces might do or be capable of. I picked up one unfamiliar device off his dresser. "What's this?"

"I call it an exoviter."

I set my empty plate on the nightstand. I fingered the metal device and looked at it from all angles. Not unlike a gun or rather a child's version of a spacegun—an item I might find for sale in one of the vendor stalls in LA's Toy District. A long aluminum cylinder with a glassy yellow opening at the business end, and a white plastic grip. A small battery pack clung to the rear of the grip. "What's it do?"

"It's an alien detector," Ken said. He took the exoviter from me. "At least, I think it is. I've been working on it forever. This is V fifteen."

"An alien detector?" Karen snorted. "Really, Ken, you've come up with some dumb ideas before, but this?" She snatched the exoviter out of her brother's hands and waved it around the room. "First burning hair and now alien detectors?"

"Careful with that," I urged.

Karen chuckled. "What? Are you afraid of this stupid toy, Ed?"

I shrugged. "Hey, what do I know? It could shoot out an electrical discharge. Like that nasty taser of Ernie's." I rubbed my groin. I did not have fond memories of that moment. "Or emit deadly radiation." I reached for the exoviter. "Let's not take unnecessary risks."

"Give it to me." Ken extended his hands and Karen reluctantly returned him his device. "I'm sure it's perfectly harmless. To humans that is."

"You know what I found under his bed?" Karen asked me.

"Dust bunnies?"

"No."

"Little green extraterrestrial dust bunnies?"

Ken laid the so-called exoviter on the floor at his feet.

"An Ouija board and a crystal ball," Karen answered, rolling her eyes.

"Seriously?"

"I didn't know what else to do," bemoaned Ken. "Nothing's working." He was looking at me as he spoke. "At this point, I'll try anything."

"Have you tried having your head examined, dummy?" Karen asked.

I should've known by now that I could count on her to ask the tough questions. I moved closer for a peek under the bed and my right foot landed on the exoviter. We all heard the crunch so there was no use denying it'd been my fault. "Oops." I picked it up. The tube was bent and the grip cracked. "Sorry about that."

Ken sighed. "Probably wouldn't have done any good anyway."

"That's the spirit," I replied, patting him on the back. I dropped to my knees and pulled out the crystal ball. Using my palm, I wiped off a thin layer of dust resting atop it. "What do you do with this?" I peered into the glass.

"Probably use it as a bowling ball to knock over these mystery aliens," joked Karen.

"It's *alien*. Singular."

"You told me *aliens*," Karen shot back.

"No, I told you *alien*."

"No, when you called me, you definitely told me *aliens* were trying to kill you."

"I said *alien*—"

"Alien, aliens," I interrupted the debate. "Tomato, potato. Let's try to stay focused, kids, two people are dead." I balanced the crystal ball in the palm of my hand. "What's it do?"

"I had a theory that I might be able to communicate with

it."

"His alien," Karen said in case I hadn't understood. But I had.

"Use a crystal ball to communicate with your alien?" I'm sure I've heard dumber things but I couldn't think of a single one at the moment. Like all those idiotic tales from folks claiming to have spotted flying saucers and a colorful assortment of other UFOs. Why did they always report flashing lights, blinking lights, colored lights, strobe lights—a cornucopia of lights!?

Why on earth, and I use the term loosely, would any respectable alien fly all this way to this little ball of dirt and magma and then start flashing all their damn lights, which was a sure way to get spotted by Earthlings and self-aware mynah birds, unless they did want to get spotted by the indigenous species? Why not use some Star Trekian cloaking mechanism? Why flash their lights? Were they signaling to other flying saucers in the area that they were about to pass them?

And don't get me started on alien abductions. Why abduct some beet farmer or country school teacher? Why not a king or a president? Better yet, a billionaire you can hold for princely ransom of gold and other rare metals and minerals. Maybe some World Series tickets too. If I was going to abduct an earthling, that's what I'd be holding out for, especially if the Dodgers win their division.

Ken snatched the crystal ball from me. "It was just a theory."

"And the Ouija board?" Karen demanded. "Trying to communicate with old dead Aunt Alien?"

"Now, now, Karen. Let's not be too hard on your brother. He's been under a lot of stress. And there have been two deaths all in the space of one day."

The only magic an Ouija board possessed was its ability to magically take money out of the pockets of those silly enough to purchase one of the board games—and I do mean *games*. There are far better ways to talk to the dead. And what happens if you get a spirit who's a lousy speller? What good is an Ouija board then?

Karen frowned. "What about me? What about us, Ed? We've been under a hell of a lot of stress too. And we came all this way just to find you." She shoved her brother, kneecap against kneecap, but not so hard as to cause either any pain.

"I didn't ask you to," mumbled Ken, rubbing his knee.

"Didn't ask me to? You sure as hell did. You called me telling me aliens were trying to kill you and then disappeared!"

"Alien," Ken made the mistake of correcting. I held my breath but Karen merely growled at him.

"Did you think I wasn't going to come looking for you?"

"You shouldn't have." Dark circles ringed Ken's eyes—making his eyeballs look a bit like twin Jupiters—and his skin sagged. He plodded to the bathroom and splashed his face with cold water. The sizzling hair smoked in the sink bowl. He stepped back in the room.

"Tell me about this alien, Ken," I demanded.

"Well..." Ken glanced at his sister as if afraid she'd strike him again.

"Go ahead," I urged, gently. I warned Karen with a look. She threw herself into the lone lattice-backed wooden chair.

"I can't be certain," Ken began, his eyes focused on the wall. "The military could be lying to me but I am convinced that there is only the one alien. At least, I've never seen any evidence of more. And it's hostile. Out for my blood."

"A hostile alien out for your blood?" Karen snorted. She crossed her right leg over her left and frantically kicked the air. "Why would it want you? I mean, I'm mad enough to kill you, but why would this theoretical extraterrestrial being be mad at you? You steal his flying saucer?" She was on a roll. "Take it for a joy ride? Put a dent in its fender?"

"Karen—" I cautioned.

Ken turned to face us. "I guess you'd be mad as hell too, if somebody kept you locked up for eighty years."

"Eighty years?" Karen's eyes bugged out. "You weren't even alive eighty years ago, Ken. None of us here in this room were! So why's this ET blaming you for his troubles? You didn't lock him up!"

"I have no idea." Ken explained that he was recruited by the LANL while working at JPL. His story meandered this way and that. Bottomline was that he'd met Marcia Allison at the LANL. She introduced him to General Grant and General Grant introduced him to the alien, a creature they called Mirabilis. He'd been held in Air Force custody since the late 1940s. Only a close-knit, close-lipped group of senior military officers and civilian insiders were ever let in on the secret. Not even President Truman or any president since had been made aware of the extraterrestrial's presence. His existence was as secret as it got.

"Mirabilis had been relatively docile and quiescent. Over the years, other researchers had made some progress in communicating with him. Hand gestures mostly but he seemed to understand up to a point. Appeared to be cooperating with us. To a degree, at least. He was held in a containment chamber. All of a sudden though, not long after I was introduced to him..." Ken fell into a wordless silence. "He grew upset. Agitated. He began to fight us. Make demands we couldn't meet. Finally..."

"Yes?"

"He tried to escape. Fortunately, the military was able to subdue him. At least, temporarily. He's escaped again."

"And murdered Emily Crenshaw?"

"Yes. And I had the feeling that he was lurking. Hanging around. Following me."

"Stalking you," Karen whispered in a chilled voice.

"Waiting for his opportunity to murder you," I said.

"That's right." Ken glared at me defiantly as if daring me to dispute him.

Silence filled the room for a minute.

"How would you describe this alien?" I asked.

"About your height but far more stout."

"Human looking?" Karen found herself asking. I wondered if she was starting to believe.

"Yes, in a Troglodyte sort of way, if you know what I

mean?"

"Explain."

"His hands are huge." Ken spread his own rather small hands. "Big, muscle-bound shoulders. An enormous nose. A stooped posture. Head twenty percent larger than the average human skull with matte black eyes."

"Sounds like the missing link," wisecracked Karen.

Little did the woman know how right she was. Sort of.

"You never learned to speak with him?"

"Not really. No one did. Either he didn't understand us or we didn't understand him or he just didn't give a damn about talking to us."

"Except to give you his name," I cut in.

"Nah, Mirabilis? That was a moniker some researcher stuck on it in the early days of its capture."

"But why Mirabilis?" I knew it meant miracle in Greek. Was there some connection?

"I don't know," said Ken. That's the name I was told and that's the name I used. The creature does seem to respond to it. Guess he got used to it. A better name would be Satan as far as I'm concerned."

Ken considered a moment. "When Mirabilis did speak it was sort of like birdsong, cooing. Musical, if you get my meaning. But nothing that made sense to us. That's why I was called in. The team was hoping I could connect with Mirabilis somehow. Eighty years of study and they'd hit a brick wall. Then I show up and all hell breaks loose!"

"That is interesting," I said. "You mention his capture. Do you know where he was captured?"

"I asked. I was told it didn't concern me or my work. Does it matter?"

"I suppose not," I admitted.

"What matters now is that Mirabilis is stopped. Before he kills again."

"Why not report this to the authorities? They caught him once. They can catch him again."

Ken shook his head in the negative. "I don't think so. I believe the alien has been biding his time, playing with us. Who knows? Maybe he'd been injured when he fell to earth and was recovering very slowly. Maybe he's healed now." Ken threw up his hands. "Whatever the hell happened and why, there's no telling. But he's out for blood now and I don't think anything or anybody can stop him."

"That includes you," Karen said. "Forget about Mirabilis. Not your problem."

"Sorry, I have to try, Karen."

"But sorcery and magic and hoodoo voodoo?" This from sister Karen.

"Science wasn't getting me anywhere. All my training. All my years conducting carefully constructed experiments. All for nothing," Ken said gloomily. "I was desperate. Thought I'd try magic, voodoo, anything."

"Pseudoscience?" Karen said with disbelief. "You? You're a scientist. And a well-respected one—at least up until now," she remarked, driving the knife blade in a little deeper. The woman really didn't have much of a filter.

Ken responded with an indifferent shrug. "Maybe it is pseudoscience. But who's to say? What do you think I should try, sis? Reading it some poetry? Some Keats? Or how about some Tennison?"

I suppressed a grin. Ken could give as well as he got.

While Karen spluttered and wracked her brain for a pithy reply, Ken continued. "Up until accepting my current position and meeting Mirabilis, I'd have said creatures from outer space were the stuff of science fiction. Turns out, I couldn't have been more wrong." Ken inspected the busted exoviter and hurled it into the bathroom. The exoviter crashed to a halt on the floor. "When Mirabilis murdered Emily...that changed everything. There was no going back. I loved her." His chest shuddered. "I'm a scientist, not a murderer, but it's kill or be killed right, Ed?"

"Yes." I couldn't deny his logic. Ironclad.

"So I tried to kill him first."

Karen gasped.

"What did you do?" I had to know. This could be vital to everyone's future.

"They'd a special cage built for Mirabilis. That's how we transport him from place to place by truck or air. For his sake and ours. Based on our limited knowledge and understanding of his physical body, I rigged this one with a high-powered magnetic field, overriding the existing fail safes. I really thought it would do the trick. Tear him apart atom by atom."

A gruesome image. "But it didn't." I knew I was saying the obvious.

"No, in fact, it only mad him mad. Mad enough to break out of the cage—something he'd never even attempted once all these years in captivity—busted the steel bars like they were sticks of butter. And disappeared."

"And now he wants you dead, Ken," Karen said. "Nice going. See what you get for poking a stick in the hornets' nest?"

"If Mirabilis wants you dead," I had to ask, "why aren't you?"

Ken and Karen looked at me in confusion. "Dead, that is. After all, Alan with one L is dead, as is Zultan Crobar. I'm assuming you believe Mirabilis murdered both men. Plus, Emily."

"I'm sure of it. Although I don't know exactly why."

"It's not like he's eating them," I heard myself saying.

"Gross, Ed!" Karen replied.

"What? I mean, if he'd been lunching on the men, wouldn't we have at the very least found some remnants? Bones?"

"Unbelievable," Karen said. "You see what I've had to put up with all because of you?" She looked at her brother accusingly.

"To answer your question, Ed." Ken stood. "Why am I not dead? I don't know. Lucky, I guess." He revealed that Mirabilis had made several attempts on his life. An explosion in his lab, a car accident in which his driver was killed, and a third in which he found brodifacoum in his oatmeal.

"Rat poison?" I mentally squirmed. That'd be an ugly way

to go. The nasty substance interferes with the blood's ability to form clots. Left untreated, you'd die of internal bleeding. Even inhaling the powder can lead to severe and potentially deadly complications. Personally, I'd rather eat fresh strawberries or, heaven forbid, peaches. "What saved you?"

"I thought the bowl looked and smelled funny. So I sent it to the lab to have it tested. Everybody poked fun at me but nobody was laughing when the test came back positive for the poison."

"And Emily Crenshaw?"

"Yeah, Emily." Ken wrung his hands. "What about her?"

"You knew about Emily's murder?"

"Yes. She was supposed to meet me at the Lil' Green Man. She was already dead when I arrived."

"You were there? At the motel?" Karen pounced. "Why didn't you make your presence known?"

"I couldn't! Not with Mirabilis on the loose."

Karen shook her head.

"What was Emily Crenshaw's involvement in all this?" I asked. "We know she worked for the ARC."

"Yes, she was an alien hunter. I privately reached out to the organization for help with Mirabilis and they sent her. Marcia and the general would be pissed if they knew."

"What about Lena Jay and her companion Ernie?" I didn't know their last names.

"Who?"

"Not important."

"You reached out to a goofy alien hunter? One of those conspiracy nuts?" Karen said. "What? Weren't the ghostbusters available?"

"Funny, Karen. Put yourself in my shoes."

"I'd like to put my shoe up your butthole!"

"Let's let your brother talk, Karen."

She stuck out her pink tongue but kept her mouth shut—quite a feat when you think about it.

"At first, Emily came on to me. I'm not an idiot. I knew

right away that she was only trying to snoop around. See if she could get me to spill any secrets. Apparently, she heard we were involved in a top secret project and suspected it involved the existence of extraterrestrials. Came on to me at a bar one night."

"If you knew what she was up to and that she was only using you, why didn't you stop her in her tracks?" asked his sister.

"I was desperate and lonely. Pathetic, right?"

"How did she know about you?"

"I've no idea. She never said. Then again, people like those in the ARC and all the other UFO-chasing groups are always suspecting the government and the military are involved in some secret project or another. Emily was right even if she was guessing and didn't know exactly how. We met a few times. I needed somebody to talk to. Somebody outside the program. We became close."

"Understandable." I skimmed the pages of one of Ken's spiral notebooks lying atop a four-drawer cabinet. Lots of notes, lots more crazy rantings. The man was clearly under a tremendous strain. How much of what he was going through was real? How much was fantasy? Illusion?

"Later, when Mirabilis escaped and I realized the danger, I called Emily...Emily." Ken broke into tears. "It's my fault she's dead."

"If it makes it any easier for you," I said. "Just remember, someone killed her but it wasn't you."

"Yeah," he sniffed. "But it might as well have been. Pflock and Crobar too."

"What were their roles in your work?"

Ken released a heartfelt sigh. "I really shouldn't be saying more. They could send me to prison. For life. Talk to Marcia."

"I intend to."

"Me, too," Karen said stiffly. "And so should you, Ken. Tell her you quit. Immediately. Quit and walk out of here. Come home with me."

He smiled wanly. "I wish it was that easy."

"It is," Karen replied.

"You think the military will sit back and watch me go?"

"What can they do?" Karen said. "Nobody can stop you. It's a free country."

Ken chuckled but clearly not because what she said was funny.

Sara Chronis burst through the open doorway. "I can't get out. I'm locked in."

26

"Sorry," Sara said, looking abashed. A red backpack sat on the ground at her feet. "I didn't mean to interrupt."

"No problem, Sara," Ken said." You say you can't get out?"

Sara raised her arm and wriggled her metal bracelet. "Nope. I don't know what's going on. Damn thing's not working. That's never happened before."

Ken crunched his brows together while he fondled his own metal bracelet. "Why didn't you use the key?"

"It wasn't on the hook. So I thought I'd come look for assistance. I heard the voices in here and came down."

"Did you try the back door?" Ken asked. "Or the manual override?"

"No. Why would I?"

"I'll go check it out with you," I offered. What was all this about a back door?

"Thanks." Sara shouldered her pack.

I followed and, although I'd offered to go alone, Ken and Karen tagged along. A small army moving along the narrow corridor.

The doorway leading to the antechamber stood wide open. I gazed up at the overhead door. I tapped my bracelet against the metal pad. The door shivered to life and started to descend. I hit the pad again and the door reversed course and retreated to its slot in the ceiling. "This door seems to be working fine. Maybe it's your wristband, Sara."

"Maybe," Sara agreed but she appeared worried. "Let's see." She tried it against the metal pad. Once again, the inner door went up, went down. "Works fine here, at least." She frowned. So did I.

Ken opened the inner door once more and popped into the antechamber. The desk was unattended. The computer screen peered at us blankly. I assumed Allan with two Ls was resting in his quarters. Crying over his recent loss.

We marched to what I now understood to be the Haven's back entrance. I tapped the metal pad. Nothing. I tried again. More nothing. "You try, Ken."

He did and got the same result as me.

"This is weird," Sara said, tapping her bracelet too.

"Let me," Karen barged past us and slammed her metal bracelet against the sensor pad. "Shit." She banged it again and again.

"You're going to break it," complained Ken.

"It's already broken!" snapped Karen.

"Let's try the manual override you were speaking of, Ken. This it?" I pointed to a red button on the side of the pad.

"Yes, that cuts the electronic circuit and allows you to haul the door up over there. Pull the pulley release, then turn the crank."

He pointed to the front right corner of the door where I saw a pulley half-hidden behind the steel rail. I pulled the black handle and the pulley shot loose and whipped me across the face. I howled. The crank spun uselessly on its sprocket.

"You okay, Ed?" Karen and Sara chorused. Both women appeared at my side. Karen made ugly eyes at Sara.

"Yeah, fine. Surprised me, that's all." I stepped back and rubbed my cheek.

"That's a nasty welt," Sara commented. "Let me get you some ice for that."

"I'd rather have a couple cubes of ice floating in a tumbler of bourbon," I managed to reply. "That might make me feel better." I gave my cheek a final rub then manned up, such as it was.

"So the cable is broken too." Ken banged his fist against the door. It rattled but refused to budge.

"It appears so," I said. "Somebody's cut it."

"Or *something*," Ken said.

"What's that supposed to mean?" asked Sara.

"That means we're all trapped here." Karen stated the obvious.

"No need to panic," I replied, although Karen was clearly already in the beginnings of panic mode. "Perhaps Doctor Allison knows of a solution to our problem. Any idea where she is, Ken?"

"Probably in her quarters. It's this way." He waved us on.

We regrouped and our little army marched back the way we had come. Ken led us to room eight and came to a stop. "This is her room." The door was shut. He rapped on the door.

A drowsy looking Marcia Allison opened her door. She was dressed in a calf-length fluffy green robe with a gray trim collar. A black sleep mask pushed up on her forehead. "What's going on?" she asked, cinching her belt and eying us all curiously.

"I can't get out," Sara said. "My wrist bracelet isn't working. Nobody's is."

We chorused our agreement.

"Impossible," said Marcia Allison. "We've a failsafe system in place. An override." She pushed past us to the door on green slippered feet. "Why do you want out, anyway, Sara? Where are you going at this hour?"

"Home. I've had enough."

"Home?" Dr. Allison eyed Sara darkly. "We'll talk about that later. First things first." She shoved her feet into a pair of matching furry slippers tucked halfway under the bed. "What happened to your face, Ed?"

"A steel cable mistook me for a whipping post."

Her brow edged upward but she offered no follow-up questions. Apparently I wasn't worth worrying about.

The three of us formed a line behind Dr. Allison as she led on. We followed like sheep as she plodded, arms swinging, down the corridor and turned left down a second gently curving corridor.

"I'm confused," Karen said. "Aren't we going in the wrong direction?"

"Me too. Where are we going?" I called. "The entrance is in the other direction."

She swung her head around without missing a step. "What are you talking about, Turner?"

"The entrance." I pointed over my shoulder. "It's that way."

She rolled her eyes. "I know my way around my own facility. Enough talking."

Ken whispered in my ear. "You talking about the secondary door we just came from?"

"Secondary door?" Karen asked for the both of us.

"Yeah. The big overhead thing we checked out before waking Marcia. Hello?" I nodded and he continued. "We don't use that one much. I mean it doesn't really lead anywhere except out to the lake. That's all any of us utilize it for."

"Yes, Ed," Sara added. "That's why I didn't bother to check it out to see if it was working. It's not connected to any roads and we don't have vehicles out there even if it did. Hell, you'd have to walk out. Not a pretty thought. It's a pretty lake, though. I go there myself sometimes when I need to get some fresh air. Have a little me time. I could show it to you sometime, if you like?"

Karen cleared her throat and glared at Sara. "I thought you were leaving?"

Sara shrugged.

We slammed to a halt facing a dull heavy metal gray door I'd never seen before. It was marked EXIT in blocky black letters.

Dr. Allison pushed up the sleeve of her robe and impatiently tapped the metal security device on the wall with her bracelet. "Shit." She tapped again.

Nothing. She clamped her hand over the thick steel handle and gave it a yank. More nothing.

"So this door leads outside?" I asked Ken.

"Up the stairs to the parking lot."

"Parking lot?"

"Yeah, I mean, we call it a parking lot. It's nothing more

than a clearing in the woods where we leave our vehicles," Ken explained. "There's a primitive road, if you can call it a road, that leads out of here."

"It meanders through the mountains and connects to the main road, such as it is," furthered Sara.

"And all the roads around in these mountains are pretty much snow-covered and impassable a good part of the year," finished Ken.

"A parking lot? And a road?" Karen threw her hands in the air. "We must've hiked fifty miles to get to this place!"

"Why would you do that?" Sara wondered aloud.

"I'm wondering that myself," I said. I was definitely feeling used, and abused, and confused.

Dr. Allison pointed at a board bracketed to the wall. Six hooks drilled into it held an assortment of keys. One hook stood out because it was empty. "Where's the key?" she asked no one and everyone. Nobody knew.

"It was gone when I got here," Sara explained.

"I haven't seen it," said Ken. "I can't remember when I last even looked for it."

Dr. Allison shoved her sleeve down to her wrist. "Sara, we know your bracelet doesn't work. The rest of you try."

We took turns placing our bracelets against the metal pad. The results were unequivocal. Dr. Allison shooed us away. "Why are we wasting time on this? Out of my way." She yanked the cover off the metal box. "What the hell?"

I peered over her shoulder. "What's the trouble?"

"Somebody's cut the wires and jammed the manual override. She tugged at a short metal bar. "I should be able to release the electronic lock with this." She tugged some more, grunting her frustration.

We were not getting in or out via this door.

"You tried the lake door?" Dr. Allison asked Sara. Sara nodded her head yes.

"We all did," Ken added.

"I want to see this. Let's go." And she did.

We dutifully marched to the entrance to the cave that Karen and I had first come in to the Haven via. Dr. Allison's metal bracelet was identical to ours and worked just as well—which is to say, not at all.

Dr. Allison studied the interior. "Again?"

"Mechanical override is busted too." Ken gave the useless crank a spin. Whi-iir!

"Sabotage?" Dr. Allison asked. Her fingers toyed with the sliced cable.

"It could be," I suggested. "The question is why. Who wants to keep us here at the Haven?"

"Hello, do you even have to ask the question, Ed?" Karen said. "The killer, of course."

"Mirabilis," Ken said with a quiver in his voice.

"Who?" asked Sara.

"Nobody," snapped Dr. Allison glaring death at Ken Dalton. She pulled in a breath. "This is all some glitch. These things happen. So let's not start with wild conjecture, people. Allan has a remote that opens this door. That might still work."

I doubted it but saw no point in bursting everyone's balloons at this point so I said, "That's right, I remember now. He used it when we arrived, remember, Karen?"

"Yeah, that's right." She brightened.

Dr. Allison began walking at a brisk clip and we all hastened to keep up. "He's probably in his quarters."

And that's where she led us. She banged her fist on his door so hard it shook in trepidation. So much for respecting his period of mourning. "Allan? Allan, are you in there?" Bang-bang! "It's me, Marcia. Open the damn door." She gave him an entire half a second to comply. When the door failed to open as commanded, she tapped her bracelet against the metal pad. The door rose. Ta-da!

Some things in the universe still operated correctly and as expected.

"Empty." Dr. Allison stormed to the middle of the room. The bedclothes were rumpled, the pillow indented, the bathroom door stood ajar. "Shit." She spun in a slow circle. "Where are you Allan?" She yanked her sleep mask down around her neck.

"Now what?" Karen asked.

"We split up," Dr. Allison suggested. "He's got to be here somewhere."

"Unless he locked us in and fled," Ken replied.

"Why the hell would he do that?" Dr. Allison's face brightened in anger.

"Because he's Mirabilis," Ken was quick to answer.

"Are you sure?" asked Karen.

"I'm only suggesting—"

"Who is this Mirabilis?" Sara demanded.

"Nobody!" snapped Dr. Allison, struggling to maintain control. "Doctor Dalton has been under tremendous stress, haven't you, Ken?"

"Yes, but—"

"We will split up and we will find Pflock. We will straighten everything out."

"There's still the matter of two murders," I reminded her.

"Yes, Mister Turner, I'm well aware of that." She threw her arms in the air, splitting her robe wide open and revealing pale green pajamas. "We all are."

"I'll check my kitchen and storage areas," Sara said. Without waiting for approval, she stalked off.

"I'll check with the others," Ken said. "Ask if they've seen Pflock. He might be with one of them."

"I'll go with you," Karen said. Was she afraid she'd lose her brother again if she didn't stick close?

"Before you do anything, Ken, I'd like a word with you. In private. My office."

Ken frowned. "Fine." He thrust his hands in his pockets.

"Guess I'll check with Pushpak, Berlitz and the Schuurmans. Maybe Pflock's with one of them, like you suggested." I tapped Karen on the forearm. "Why don't you come with me?"

"But—"

"Go ahead," urged Ken. "Holler if you find Pflock."

"You can bet on it," Karen said.

We hustled down the corridor and ran into Sara Chronis hurrying in our direction. She appeared agitated.

"What is it?" I demanded.

"You want the good news or the bad news?"

Karen moaned and pressed her palms to her ears. "Whatever it is, I don't think I want to hear this. Good or bad."

"Go ahead," I said. "Out with it, Sara."

Sara nodded and swallowed hard. "Okay. First, I didn't find Allan with two Ls."

"Is that the good news or the bad news?"

"None of the above." She stared into my eyes. "The good news is that I thought I'd check on Zultan's corpse. I mean, after Alan with one L disappeared, I wanted to be sure the same hadn't happened to Zultan—what with everything weird going on around here."

"Don't tell me...you mean he's missing?" Karen gaped, wide-eyed. The old covering the ears trick was just plain useless.

"No, no, he's there, alright."

"That's a relief," Karen's hands fell to her side.

"Yeah." Sarah moved her lips around uneasily. "Except he's also been relieved of his head."

Karen screamed.

"Calm down, calm down," I begged. Whatever pitch she was transmitting in pierced my eardrums and sliced deep into my medulla oblongata. Cranial nerves nine through twelve went into a sympathetic vibratory state and I felt a bad headache coming on.

"Shh." Sara threw her arms around Karen, saving me the chore.

"I need to see this," I said to Sara.

"Well, I don't," Karen said with a shudder.

"I'll go with you," Sara offered.

We left Karen in the otherwise empty library. "Lock the

door," I told her.

"There is no locking mechanism." Karen rattled the door handle.

"Then shove a chair in front of it," I insisted. "Sara and I will be right back," I promised. "Don't let anyone in while we're gone."

"Even Ken?" Her eyes were red from crying.

I thought for a moment. "Even Ken."

"But—"

I stopped her with a finger. "But Sara and I will be back in five minutes. Tops."

Sara and I scurried to the cold storage room. Zultan Crobar's corpse stretched across a pile of cardboard boxes. His head, as Sara had announced, was missing in action.

"I don't get it," Sara perched her hands on her hips. Her breath came out in white ribbons. "Why would somebody chop his head off?"

"They really butchered him too." His head appeared to have been hacked off. "What do you think? A meat cleaver?"

"That'd be my guess. I keep one in the kitchen."

I tossed the blanket back over the remaining ninety percent of Zultan Crobar's corpse. "Let's see if your knife's still there."

It wasn't.

"The cleaver's gone. I keep it right here." Her hand gripped the edge of a steel drawer filled with knives, ladles, and other kitchenware.

"Do you recall the last time you saw it?"

"Sure, a few hours ago. I used it to cut up the bison."

"And when you were finished?"

"I washed it and put back in the drawer." Sara slammed the drawer shut. "I need to tell you something, Ed."

"Oh?"

"Yes." Sara sighed. "Look, I probably shouldn't say anything..."

"But?"

"But with everything going on here..." She twisted her neck side to side.

"You know something about all this, Sara? Is there something you're not telling me?"

"I'm not who you think I am." She took my hand. "I'm not what I appear to be."

I pulled my hand away and stepped back. "What are you?"

27

"CIA."

"Culinary Institute of America?" I asked. She had baked an excellent chocolate torte.

"Central Intelligence Agency."

"I see," I said, although I didn't. "And the others here don't know this?"

"No. And please don't tell them."

"Mum's the word." I metaphorically zipped my lips.

She hoisted herself up onto the prep counter and sat. "I'm working undercover."

"Not even Doctor Allison is aware of who you really are?"

"Nobody and I mean nobody, all the way up to General Grant."

"What's the general got to do with this?"

"Hell if I know. That's why I was sent. The CIA would very much like to know what the Haven Sent and air force are up to."

"Haven Sent?"

She cracked a smile. "Agency code name for Grant, Allison and the tight-knit group involved in...well, whatever the hell it is they are involved in. My job was to infiltrate the org and see what I can learn." Sara swore. "And I don't mind admitting, much to my boss's annoyance, I haven't been able to learn much in two years. Two years of playing cook-housekeeper to these brats." She cocked her head, looked at me funny. "Ken mentioned something or someone named Mirabilis?"

"Yes, yes, I believe he did." I rubbed the back of my neck.

"What is it? Who is it?" Sara locked eyes with me.

"Honestly, I'm not sure." That was sort of honest and sort

of true. All in all, not so bad of me. Besides, what did I know about this woman? Nothing. Not even if she was honest herself, telling me the truth. "I don't suppose you have some ID on you, do you? Identifying you as an agent of the CIA?"

"You suppose right." Sara folded her arms. "Guess you'll have to take my word for it."

"I guess I will. You've been here two years and haven't learned anything?"

"Bits and pieces but not enough to build a picture of anything concrete, if you know what I mean."

"I do." My eyes swept the kitchen. "You mentioned I might have more chocolate torte?"

She grinned and slid her butt off the counter. "In the fridge, I'll cut you a slice." While Sara prepared me a second plate, I considered my options. Should I tell Sara about Mirabilis? It wasn't like anybody had sworn me to secrecy.

Where did my duty lie, except for with Karen Dalton? And as far as that went, I'd done my job, done what she'd hired me to do. If I went home now, who could blame me? There'd been no way either of us could have foreseen what that job was going to lead to...this mess. This deadly mess.

"Thanks." I took the proffered fork and dug into my torte. "You know, if you told me you were a graduate of the Culinary Institute of America, I'd believe you." I lifted my plate to my nose. "This is that good."

"Thanks, Ed."

"You've been here a hell of a lot longer than me," I said between bites. "What do you make of the sudden two murders?"

Sara slid a fork from the drawer and helped herself to a bite of my torte. "Hey, this is pretty good." She licked her lips. "I don't have a fucking clue, Ed." She pointed her fork at my face. "Maybe one of the scientists finally cracked and has gone all Jack the Ripper."

"Possible." But not likely.

"Maybe you'll see something I haven't. You and your client arriving certainly seems to have started something."

I frowned. "I hope this isn't our fault. I would hate to think we'd been the catalyst for two deaths." I dropped my empty plate in the sink, my back to Sara. "What do you think of all the stories one hears down the years about the military hiding flying saucers and extraterrestrials?"

"At lovely vacation spots like Area Fifty-one and the Wright-Patterson Air Force Base?" Sara laughed. "The CIA's been chasing those rumors forever. If it's true, the air force is a damn sight better at hiding the truth from the CIA than the Agency is at rooting it out. Then again," she added, throwing her hands in the air, "I'm a lowly field agent. The Agency might, hell, probably does, have knowledge of all sorts of things to which I am not privy. Why? You believe in little green men, Ed?"

"I remember when little green plastic army men were all the rage," I replied, evading the question and hoping she wouldn't notice. "Why were you trying to leave tonight? If you are CIA, shouldn't you be sticking around? Saving everyone's lives and finding the culprit?"

Sara rinsed my plate and our two forks and set them on a towel beside the sink basin to air dry. "I couldn't communicate with the Agency inside. I tried to leave because I wanted to report, make them aware of what was going on and how the situation was rapidly escalating. I would have come back."

"That's good to know. I might need your help."

"Ditto."

"We'd best get back to Karen," I said, realizing we'd been gone more than the five minutes I'd promised her.

"Why don't you handle that, Ed? I'd like to keep looking for Allan with two Ls—not to mention Zultan's missing head." And the sooner we're able to get out of here, the better."

"For all of us," I agreed. She went her way and I went mine.

The library door stood open. And empty. Where the hell had Karen gone?

I wandered down the corridor and turned the corner. "Karen, there you are!" She stood staring into an open doorway. "What are you doing here? I told you to stay put. Don't you realize how much danger you could be in out here all alone? Karen?"

She turned, her face pale, eyes wide. Her splayed arms moved spastically. Her mouth opened and closed over and over but no words came out. Only a horrible little squeak, like the death throes of a mouse with its neck caught in a wicked little trap.

The sound of my feet clattering as I hurried up the corridor echoed off the narrow walls. "Karen? What is it?"

She slowly raised her arm and pointed a shaky hand.

A somber sigh fell over my lips, splashed my shoes. Inside room four, Bobby Berlitz lay atop his bed. He wasn't asleep and he wasn't moving. He was just lying there, arms at his sides, head propped up on two pillows, toes pointed at the ceiling. Dressed in the same outfit he'd worn to dinner, the blue windbreaker over the blue flannel shirt, and corduroys. Black shoes. All in all, he looked just like he had the last time I'd seen him. Except...

28

Except now Robert "Bobby" Berlitz was dead, clearly dead. With a big clumsy ET etched in blood on his forehead. His blue eyes stared lifelessly at us staring at him.

"Oh, Ed."

I took Karen's ice cold hand. She fell into my arms.

I folded her in close to my chest. "It's okay, it's okay," I said over and over. Despite how ridiculous I sounded even to myself, my soft words seemed to placate her. I noticed her heart slow to a more normal rhythm.

"Let's get away from here." I pulled the door shut. Looking at Berlitz wasn't helping things. Even I found the sight of those primitive initials carved into his forehead unsettling.

Karen sniffled and followed, never letting go of me. We returned to the library. I sat her down on the sofa and handed her a glass of water in a paper cup from the water cooler standing in the corner.

She drank.

"You okay? Better now?"

"Yeah, yeah, I guess." She pushed her hair off her glistening forehead.

"Good. Can you tell me what happened back there?"

Her shoulders bounced up and down. "Nothing. I mean, I don't know. I waited and waited. Seemed like forever."

"Sorry."

"When you didn't come back, I got worried something might have happened to you. I decided to go looking for you." She picked at her fingernails. "Did you find Allan with two Ls?"

"No. No sign of him." I patted her knee. "Continue."

"Right. I went looking for you and Sara and—" Once again, Karen stopped before she'd really said anything as another thought came to her. "Where is Sara, anyway? She okay?"

"Yes, she's fine," I fought to remain patient. "She's still looking for Allan with two Ls." I grabbed both her hands. "Now, tell me what happened to Berlitz."

"I-I don't know, Ed. I noticed the door was ajar as I walked by. I stopped to say hello because I wondered if you might be inside. Nobody answered, so I knocked. The door fell open and… and there he was."

There he was alright.

"No sign of a struggle again either."

"Who would do such a thing?" she asked.

"Those initials are a message. I'm sure of it," I told her. "What that message is and who it's intended for, I can't be sure."

"But it was the alien, wasn't it? This Mirabilis that Ken was telling us about. He's real, isn't he?"

"Either that," I replied, pulling her to her feet, "or somebody wants us to believe he is."

"You mean someone might be faking the whole thing? But why? Who'd want to go around murdering people and making everyone think it was some berserk alien?"

"I couldn't say." I pulled her to the door. "As for why, that's easy. To take the blame off themselves."

"Where are we going?"

"We need to find everyone. Gather them together. The way things are moving, no one is safe, especially not alone."

"Yeah."

We ran up the corridor. Ken's room was unoccupied.

"Do you know where your brother is?"

"No. I saw him go with Doctor Allison, just like you did. Maybe they're still in her office. Where is it?"

"I have no idea. Let's try the next room." That was room five. No one answered. I slid my wrist bracelet against the metal box and the door invited us inside for a look. Apparently, only the door to the outside world no longer worked. I stepped into the dimly lit space, the only light spilling in from the corridor. "No one's home."

"Who's room is this?" Karen scooted in beside me.

I turned on the bedside light. A cold brass incense burner filled with ash sat on the nightstand. The lower open shelf of the nightstand held a half-dozen psychiatry textbooks. A two-inch thick hardcover with the title Progressive Interventional Psychiatry sat open within reach of the bed. I bent and studied the other titles, all heavy-duty scientific psychiatric tomes, one of which bore Pushpak's name on the spine. "I didn't realize Pushpak was a psychiatrist. Interesting."

"If you say so." Her hand rested on my shoulder. "I'm more interested in knowing where the guy is."

"At least he's not lying dead on his bedspread with ET's initials carved into his forehead like a Halloween pumpkin." Three murders and apparently three very different means of death, four if I counted Emily Crenshaw. Was that supposed to mean something? If it did, I was flummoxed as to what.

Karen frowned. "Thanks, not, for that lovely imagery, Ed."

"I try." I peeked under the bed. "Not here."

"He's not in the bathroom either," Karen told me.

I dusted off my knees. "Who's left?"

Karen furrowed her brow. "I haven't seen Max and Katja since dinner. Have you?"

"No but I remember someone mentioning they are bunking in room six. So the Schuurmans are next. Let's go."

Leaving Pushpak's door open, we started for room six. While that was numerically the next room, Pushpak residing in room five, there seemed to have been no rhyme or reason given to the assigning of numbers to the rooms at the Haven. After two twists and one wrong turn, we stumbled on room six. Karen and I gave each other a look—a look that said "Do we really want to do this? Do we really want to know what's behind room six's door?"

"Go ahead," urged Karen. "Knock."

I did and Max Schuurman greeted us. His tan tweed jacket

draped over the side chair. Up close, I could see the big pores of his fleshy nose and realized just how big his teeth were too. He cradled a glass of scotch protectively in his hands.

"What is it?" he demanded.

"We're looking for Allan with two Ls," I answered.

"And Doctor Pushpak," added Karen.

"Yes, have you seen either man?"

"Not since supper, such as it was."

"Yes, what a pity Crobar had to fall dead into his dinner plate at the table and spoil everyone's evening," Karen snapped.

"Where's Mrs. Schuurman?"

"Showering, why? And why all the questions?"

"There've been three murders, aren't you concerned, if not for the safety of everyone, then for your own?"

"And your wife's," put in Karen.

Max Schuurman appeared puzzled. "You say there's been a third murder? Whose?"

"I'm afraid Doctor Berlitz has been exterminated," I replied.

"That's a quaint way of putting it," came a sultry female voice with a sexy Danish accent.

We all turned our heads. Katja Schuurman stood half out the bathroom door with a fluffy green towel covering her from chest to upper thighs. Water dripped from her hair to the floor. Exhibit A, now confirmed as Max Schuurman's wife. That was one mystery solved. At that point, I was willing to take any victory no matter how small.

"Put some clothes on, woman," muttered her husband.

She ignored him. "You say Bobby has been murdered?" Katja Schuurman used her left hand to hold her towel shut, leaving the upper portion of her white breasts exposed. Her right hand held a black hair brush. "What was it? Poison too?"

"I've no idea what the cause of death is yet," I admitted. "Maybe Ken can tell us." I shot his sister a look. "When we find him."

"Dalton's missing too?" Max asked.

"No, he's with Doctor Allison," Karen explained. "We found Berlitz lying dead on his bed. Somebody carved the initials ET into his forehead. You two know anything about that?" she pressed.

"No," blurted Max Schuurman, he took a quick gulp of courage. "Why the hell should we?"

"No reason," I answered. "I'd like everyone to gather in one place, the dining room or the library perhaps. Someplace secure. I think it would be best if we all stay in one place until we can get this sorted out."

"Don't worry about us," Max strode to his tweed jacket and reached into the inside pocket. "We've both got guns."

"You're armed?" Karen stared at the weapon, a nasty black semi-automatic he pointed at the ceiling.

"Put that thing away, dear." Katja snatched the weapon from her husband. Her towel slid to her waist. "Oops." She slowly pulled the towel upward, her eyes signaling mine. Why was she looking at me?

I turned my eyes on her husband. "I'd still prefer we all remain together until we find the person responsible for these murders."

"Person?" Max refilled his glass from the bottle on the dresser. "You mean alien, don't you?"

"Now, Max," began Katja.

"What? This is no time to be holding secrets. Haven't you heard, Mister Turner? We've an alien here with us. And I do believe he's about had enough of our company and our hospitality."

"Max does have a point." Katja laid a damp hand on her husband's shoulder. She was so close I could smell her coconut and almond shampoo. "I'd hate to be next."

"Let's hope there is no next," I replied.

29

For a library I was hearing a lot of noise. Everyone—those of us left alive—was yelling to be heard. The din was unbearable.

"This is untenable, Marcia!" Spittle flew from Max Schuurman's mouth as he berated Doctor Allison for their current troubles.

"Now, dear," Katja tried to placate her husband. I had a feeling this was part of her normal marital duties. She'd swapped her bath towel for a tight-fitting pair of blue jeans and a cowl-necked white sweater, and slip-on white sneakers. "Marcia's doing her best."

"Doing her best to get us killed!" Max replied. He held a bottle of scotch he'd carried from their quarters close to his chest. It seemed the man did have at least one redeeming quality.

"Excuse me," I cut in. "Is that for everybody?"

"What?" He looked confused.

I tapped the side of the bottle with my fingertip.

He sighed as if heavily put upon. He shoved the bottle into my hands. "Here, help yourself."

I did. I poured a generous serving into a mug. "Anybody? No?" It looked like Max and I were drinking alone. I took a sip and fluttered my eyes. Max was no cheapskate. This was the good stuff. I drank some more and set the bottle on the black plastic tray—less chance of Max Schuurman monopolizing the booze that way.

Karen tapped me on the shoulder. "Do you really think this is a good time to be drinking, Ed?"

"Three people dead and locked in with this unruly bunch and a potential killer?" I offered her my half-empty mug. "Can you think of a better time?"

She frowned but that didn't stop her from imbibing. "What are we going to do?"

I waved Ken over. "Did you have a chance to look at Crobar?"

"Yeah, I looked." Ken appeared twice as worn out as he had when we'd first crossed paths, and he'd looked awful then. His eyelids drooped to his knees and the eyes themselves were bloodshot. By the smell of his breath, he'd been doing some drinking too.

"And?" Sara stood beside one of the bookcases whispering with Allan with two Ls.

"And he's dead. What the hell else can I say, Mister Turner? Examining corpses is not my bailiwick. This isn't an alien crime scene investigations TV show."

"Calm down, Ken," Karen said. "Ed's trying to help us."

"I know. Sorry, Ed." He pushed his cheeks with his palms. "This is all so creepy."

"Scary is what I'd call it," replied his sister. "There's a murderer out there." She looked over our shoulders at the barricaded library door.

"And the only person not accounted for, alive or dead, appears to be Pushpak," I stated.

"Vishnu?" Katja Schuurman called. "That's right, where is the man?"

"Anyone seen Vishnu?" Dr. Allison shouted.

No one had.

"Could he be the murderer?" Karen whispered to both her brother and me.

"Or the murderer's latest victim," was my answer. "What about Allan with two Ls, Ken?"

"What about him?"

"I heard you tell Marcia that you were the one who found him. Is that right?"

"Yeah, so?"

"Where? What was he up to?"

"He wasn't up to anything. I found him in his old room."

"The room he shared with his husband?" Karen asked all goggle-eyed.

"Yep. Lying in bed in a fetal position, tears streaming down his face."

"Did you ask him about the remote control device for the exit?"

"Sure. He says he lost it. He said the last time he remembered using the device was when he let the two of you inside. He said he must have misplaced it."

"And you believe him?" Karen wondered.

"He sounded sincere."

"Still." Karen slitted her eyes at Allan with two Ls, standing across the library. "I wonder...maybe he's an alien. An accomplice of that Mirabilis creep."

"If only I had my exoviter." Ken looked at me accusingly. "Maybe we could find out."

"I said I was sorry," I replied.

"There is another possibility," Karen said.

"What's that?" I asked.

"Maybe Mirabilis has fled and locked us inside," offered Karen.

"Good point. That is a possibility." I refilled my mug. "Another is that the creature is here."

"You mean here in this room?" Karen turned her gaze on those of us remaining, Allison, Sara, Allan with two Ls, and the Schuurmans. And then there was the MIA Vishnu Pushpak.

"What? Invisible or something?"

"Maybe," I acknowledged. "We can't rule it out, can we?"

"Not a comfortable thought, Ed," Karen scolded me.

"Then again, maybe Mirabilis isn't here in the library with us but is hiding someplace else inside Haven." I took a slow drink. "And if this alien is here, where is it hiding?" And what did it want? And what was it waiting for? I might have added. "Where could one hide in Haven, alien or not? Any ideas, Ken?"

Ken appeared surprised at the question. "Hell, I don't

know. This place has been here forever. The military dug this bunker out. Most of it was closed off permanently. We only use a small portion of what the air force once utilized. The tip of the iceberg. Rumor has it this underground system once extended miles. There's even a spot where I'm told they dumped radioactive waste."

Karen glared at her brother. "Isn't that dangerous? Should we even be here?"

Ken shrugged indifferently. "I'm told it's safe."

Karen snorted. "Oh, that makes it okay then, the military says it's safe. I feel so much better now." She waved her fist in her brother's face. "If I wake up with radiation poisoning, you are so dead!"

The others gasped.

"Sorry," Karen blushed, realizing she probably shouldn't have uttered the D word threat under current circumstances.

Sara joined us. "Excuse me, I heard you talking. I've searched everywhere. I haven't seen any sign of Professor Pushpak. And, like Doctor Dalton said, the military welded shut most of the corridors years ago. Prior to turning the facility over to JPL. They're still sealed, as far as I can tell, Ed."

"Sara's right," put in Dr. Allison. She gave Sara a funny look.

"Vishnu seems to have disappeared in a puff of smoke," Katja Schuurman said.

"Say, you didn't bump him off, did you, Ken?" Max said with a twinkle of trouble in his eyes.

"What's that supposed to mean?" Karen said angrily in her brother's defense.

"Didn't Ken tell you? He's been trying to communicate with—" He cast a wary eye at Dr. Allison. "A certain someone using a crystal ball of all things!" He laughed. "Pushpak argued with him about it. Told him he needed help. Psychiatric help." Max tapped his fingers on the side of his skull.

"That's enough, Max," warned Dr. Allison. "We're a team here, remember?"

"Yes, a team. A team being exterminated by a bloodthirsty

alien from another planet!"

"Excuse me?" Sara took a step back as if Max's words had physically pushed her. "A what?" She glanced at everyone. For their parts, everyone looked guilty.

"Nothing." Dr. Allison wedged herself between Max and Sara. "Max is drunk. Aren't you, Max?"

He snorted. "Not drunk enough. In fact—"

"Sara!" snapped Dr. Allison.

"What?"

"Did you check the boiler room?"

Sara frowned. "Actually, no."

"Did anybody?" Dr. Allison asked us all. Heads shook no.

"What would Pushpak be doing in the boiler room, for chrissakes, Marcia?" Max Schuurman asked.

"He might be taking some initiative," Dr. Allison replied. "Checking out the electrical equipment. Looking for a blown fuse or a malfunction."

Max grumbled.

"Fine, I'll take a look," said Sara.

"No, Ed, why don't you go?" suggested Dr. Allison. "After all, you're the detective. You're the one most equipped to handle the situation."

I heard murmurs of agreement—none of those murmurs of agreement came from me, I might point out. I almost asked the Schuurmans' for one of their guns in case I encountered trouble. But I'd probably be more dangerous to myself—such as shooting myself in the toe—and I doubted how effective one or even half a dozen of their bullets would be on Mirabilis. "Leave it to me," I said, seeing I had no good options.

"I'll show you the way." Sara headed for the library door and pulled away the chairs blocking egress.

"No, thanks, Sara." I turned to Karen's brother. "I think Ken should show me."

"Me?" His hands fluttered to his chest.

"You know the way, don't you?"

"Sure."

"Ed—" Sara pulled me aside. "What are you doing? It could be dangerous out there."

"Yes." I nodded towards the others. "But it could be dangerous here too. Stay and keep an eye on them."

"Okay. Be careful."

"I intend to be."

Karen pushed herself between us and grabbed my neck. She whispered in my ear. "If you see any aliens, don't try to be a hero. Run," she urged. "Run like hell." I promised her I would—a tiny white lie. "And don't let anything happen to my brother."

She turned to Ken and warned him with her finger. "And you, don't let anything happen to my...to Ed."

We squeezed out the door and into the quiet corridor. No sight nor sound of murderous extraterrestrials. Hell, not even a marauding Viking stirring things up.

"Which way?" I asked Ken.

"Follow me."

A couple minutes later I found myself in a compact laundry room staring at an idle white washer and dryer. A green hamper filled with a mix of dirty clothes sat atop the washer. The horrible chemical scent of laundry detergent filled the air.

"This is the door," Ken tapped on a gray metal door to the right of the laundry sink. A sign indicated this led to the boiler room. "Ready?" I nodded and Ken turned the knob. The door was unlocked.

The inside was no larger than my apartment closet. "This is the boiler room?" I gazed at the empty space. "Where is everything?"

Ken grinned and hit the light switch, illuminating a strip light above our heads. "You're standing on it."

"What?"

He motioned for me to step back. When I did, he grabbed a recessed handle in the floor and pulled. A hinged hatch clanged open. I peered downward. Light spilled into the hole revealing a metal ladder bolted to the wall. I calculated the floor to be approximately sixteen feet below.

"Odd place to put a boiler room," I remarked.

"I hear it's bigger than it looks. Never been down there myself." Ken's voice reverberated below. Thrumming and dripping sounds rose from the depths. "This is the maintenance guy's domain."

I leaned over the hatch. "Hello? Anybody there? Pushpak? It's me, Ed Turner."

"Looks like nobody's home, Ed," Ken said, sounding uneasy and relieved at the same time.

"You may be correct with regard to Pushpak but knowing the alien like you do, would you expect it to answer?"

"Actually, no." Ken frowned. "Do you want to go back? Get the others for some backup?"

Of course I did! But some things or people or extraterrestrials or monsters from the past, one had to face alone. Or in the company of a Ken Dalton. "You can go back, if you want to, Ken—and I don't blame you if you do—but there's only one way for me...and that's downward." Hmm, maybe I could have phrased that better because it sure as hell didn't sound heroic. John Wayne or Clark Gable could have summed the situation up so much better.

And down we went.

30

Electric pumps, air handlers, electrical boxes, water pumps, an emergency backup generator, and more—all twisted around the black iron pipes as thick around as two of my legs bracketed to the floor on thick braces—filled the cramped space. A handful of black pipes half the size of the big ones disappeared into the tall ceiling. Sending and receiving water and waste, I suspected. Sprinklers hung from more one-inch pipes crisscrossing the ceiling. The only thing not filling the space was Vishnu Pushpak...or Mirabilis.

I coughed. "Enough dust here to coat the surface of the moon."

"Yeah." Ken tiptoed across the floor and examined a stack of boxes in the far corner. A pair of fluorescent light fixtures provided our illumination. "A whole lot of nothing."

"Tell me more about Mirabilis," I said as I poked at the circuit panel, wondering if its malfunctioning could have led to our current entrapment.

"There isn't much more to tell. He doesn't talk and barely attempts to communicate with us. It's been hell trying to learn anything of him or from him in eighty years. And to be honest with you, I haven't had any more luck than all the others who came before me."

"Sure you have," I replied. A glance at the backup generator led me to believe it was in order.

"Why do you say that?"

"You seem to have provoked him enough that he wants you dead."

"Gee, thanks."

"You also mentioned you transport him to and fro in a special cage, as you call it."

"Yeah, more of a container or capsule really. It's not like he's a circus attraction."

"I should hope not."

"It's a self-contained box with bolt-down furniture. No windows. He can't see out. Nobody can see in. Totally secure."

"Where is it now?"

"Topside, in the truck. He's never given us any trouble so we lead him on foot from there or wherever we want him to go."

"So he's aware of the location of your vehicles."

"Good point. You don't think he's driven away in our truck, do you, Ed?"

I could only shrug. "Stranger things can and do happen. But I wouldn't worry. I don't suppose anybody's ever taught him to drive a car, right?"

"No, thank god for that. Could you imagine Mirabilis out on the road, driving solo?"

I could.

"You call him a he, why?"

Ken shrugged. "Easier than saying *it* all the time. Plus, me and everyone else get the feeling that *it* is a male. I'm not sure that makes any sense, though. Mirabilis may not have any sexual differentiation in our human sense."

"Good point."

"Vishnu has a lot of theories about that. We can't test any of them out seeing as how we only have the one alien specimen."

"Another good point." I slid behind an air handler the size of a garden shed bolted up against the far wall. Concrete blocks lined the wall. I squinted. Almost no light reached this far back. "What's this?"

"Huh?"

"I spotted something back here."

"What is it? Not Pushpak's headless corpse, I hope."

"No, no. It's another door."

"Another door?" Ken squeezed in behind me.

"Not a door really. A hatch about three-foot square. A metal panel bolted to the wall." I sucked in my stomach and pushed in between the air handler and the wall. I fingered the hatch. No dust. I counted eight screws.

"Too bad we don't have a screwdriver," Ken said behind me.

I gripped the head of the nearest screw and it came loose in my hand. I yanked it out completely. "No need." It was tedious and my fingers were sore by the time I was done but I managed to free all the screws.

"That was easy," remarked Ken.

"Too easy, maybe?" I said over my shoulder. Meaning it might have been opened recently.

Ken frowned. "You're right."

I yanked the loose hatch out of its frame and set it on the ground. I saw blackness and more blackness and smelled a faint hint of oil. "Any idea where this goes?"

"Straight to hell would be my guess."

I stuck my head inside. Nothing and no one bit it off. Always a good start. "Do you have a phone or, better yet, a flashlight?" Not for the first time, I remembered mine and Karen's gear lying back at our campsite. More remained in the pickup truck. I assumed it was secure. Not a lot of hikers around to pilfer the stuff and not many black bears are in the market for a pup tent.

"No but I know where to get one." Ken patted me on the shoulder. "Hang tight. I'll be right back."

I listened to the sound of Ken Dalton scampering up the ladder and the following noises of his steps fading into the distance. I shut my eyes and strained to listen for sounds of something, anything. All I heard was nothing.

I didn't realize how dry my mouth had become. My heart thumped against my chest. I swallowed, wet my lips, and clamped my hands to the vertical sides of the hatchway.

"Waylo?" I whispered. I pictured the sound of the word traveling like a silent sparkling comet down the length of the black hole. "Waylo?" I asked again after getting no reply. "Is that you? It's me, Eidh," I said, using my given name.

The lights in the boiler room blinked out and I heard the what sounded like the hatch between the laundry room and the boiler room slamming down.

What little light there had been in the boiler room now ceased to exist.

Something or someone whispered to me from inside the narrow metal-lined tunnel. Was that laughter? Were they laughing at me? Taunting me? Could it be Waylo? After all these years? That was the sort of thing he'd do. He was forever teasing me, taunting me.

"Waylo?" I tried again.

Nothing. I breathed easier. Something might be down there but it wasn't Waylo. No, my brother was dead. Long dead.

I chided myself. I should have known better. I did know better.

If there was a mystery in this obscure tube, I would find it. The sound I'd heard might have been nothing more than mindless machinery or simple-minded mice.

I hitched myself up and slithered inside the black tube. I inched forward, crawling as best I could on my elbows and knees. My spine scraped the rivets along the top.

I coughed as dust caught in my lungs and paused to catch my breath. I wasn't a contortionist and this crawling around in complete darkness was a royal pain.

Suddenly it was not dark. A liquid ball of hot yellow fire hurtled towards me. A silent fireball of death and mayhem. Bringing back old memories, memories I'd been trying to bury, of destruction, of desolation, of being stranded. Marooned in a land that did not want me. A world where I did not belong.

I tried to twist away. But it all happened too fast. The heat grew intense. No space to turn around and no time to even if there had been. The fireball was upon me. I shut my eyes and held my breath.

The world became a hot yellow ball. And I was in the middle of it. I pushed backwards, using all my strength. And I do mean all of it. This was not the time to hold back. I was alone now and if I wanted to survive, there was only one way I was going to.

So I did it.

I flew backwards, bouncing off the walls of the metal ductwork. I popped out. My back slammed into the sturdy aluminum-sided air handler. I tumbled to the hard concrete floor. My ribs took the brunt of the blow. Legs and arms all twisted up and wedged against the wall. Fire poured over me. I pushed through. The boiler room was bathed in dripping yellow fire. The snap and crackle of burning metal, rubber and plastic created a din.

A horrible scent stuffed itself up my nostrils. I suspected it was me. I held my hands over my eyes and searched for the metal ladder. My only hope for escape. I caught sight of it shimmering some yards away and stumbled over the pipes towards it. Overhead, the fire sprinklers finally flicked on and rained down on me. But the intensity of the flames was too great for the sprinklers to do any good. Their efforts would do nothing to put out this flame. Wouldn't even slow it down.

I clamped my hands over the hot metal ladder and shot upwards. The hatch exploded on impact with my head and flew off, banging into the clothes dryer.

I coughed and shuddered. My seared hands pulsed with pain. My knees were quaking. That was a hell of a lot more energy than I had expended in ages.

Then I blinked because someone was standing in front of me.

31

"Ed!?"

"Karen!" We fell into each other's arms.

"What the hell happened?" she cried.

"Slight mishap." I coughed and waved my hand in front of my nose but the horrible smell remained, clinging to me like a noxious parasite.

"What happened to your hair?"

"Huh?"

"Your hair, it's all gone!"

"It is?" I ran my fingers across the top of my head and then traced the line of my eyebrows, at least, the line of where my eyebrows would be if I still had any. I didn't. Only charred stubble. "Eyelashes too?"

"'Fraid so." Karen gently touched my head. "Does it hurt?"

"Nah." I dusted off my tattered clothing, surprised that I had any clothes left on my skin at all. My shirt and slacks were charred messes and the heels of my hiking boots had melted, which was making standing and walking difficult. Balance isn't one of my strong suits at the best of times in this human package.

She picked up the dented metal hatch. It had left a long jagged gouge in the clothes dryer.

"I hope they don't send me the bill for that," I quipped between coughs.

Karen sat the hatch on the floor and peered into the hole. Warm air whooshed out. "The flames look like they're dying down."

"That's good. Could spell trouble if the fire spread

throughout the Haven."

"What exactly happened? And how is it that you're okay? I mean, I'm glad, very glad that you are but…"

"But?"

"But shouldn't you be dead?" She stared at me. Thank god there was no mirror because I definitely did not want to see me at the moment. I could only imagine. "And the hatch." She toed the busted hinges. "Look at these hinges. That's thick steel. The hatch too. How the hell did you manage to escape?"

I smiled. "You know what they say, fear and danger can do strange and miraculous things. Give a person superhuman strength. Right?" I wobbled to the laundry sink. I turned on the cold water spigot, cupped my hands under the stream of icy water and splashed my face. "Ahh…"

"But-But that's just it." Karen's voice trailed away.

I grabbed a dirty towel from the laundry basket—nearly burnt to a crisp. Beggars can't be choosers.

"What's it?" I asked, toweling myself off.

"For a minute there…as you came popping up from down-down there…" She pointed at the hole leading to the boiler room. "You-I don't know how to say this."

"Spit it out, Karen." I tossed the towel to the floor.

"You didn't look *human*."

Oh. Oops. I thought quickly.

"You know how it is. That same fear and anger probably got caught all up in your head too. The mind," I said, tapping the side of my skull and cringing at the feel of burnt-down-to-nothing hair, "can play tricks on you."

"But Ed. This was no trick."

Something went boom below us. The floor shook. Shrill fire alarms echoed in the distance.

"Maybe we should leave. It might not be safe here." I took her by the arm and pulled her away from the laundry room. "What are you doing here, anyway? I thought I told you and everyone else to remain in the library."

"The general showed up with two men-in-black guys."

"General Grant?"

"The one and only."

"How'd he know about the trouble? I thought there was no way to communicate with the outside world?"

"I don't think he did. He seemed surprised to find us all holed up in the library. He's interviewing everybody now. I snuck out to look for you and Ken."

"I'm glad you did." I planted my hands on her shoulders and squeezed.

"Ed, really, what happened? And that hatch back there?" She looked over her shoulder. "It was a bent and twisted mess."

I laughed off her concern with a joke. "Much like me, some might say."

"I'm serious, Ed." She yanked my arms and I stopped. "What was that thing?"

"Thing?"

"Yeah. For a minute you looked totally different. And I mean *totally*, Ed. You looked like-like a Troglodyte!"

"I assure you, I am no Troglodyte," I replied with a frown on my face.

"Sorry. But you-you changed." She blinked twice. "At least, I think you did."

"Like I said." I patted her head. What a lucky girl, she had hair! I mean, it was blue, but it was hair. "Must be the stress and strain, Karen. I keep telling you, the mind can do funny things to one's perception. Now let's get out of here. Where's Ken?"

"Fine. But I'm not letting you get away with-with whatever the hell it is you're getting away with." She waved her finger at me. "We will speak of this again. And I will get to the bottom of this."

She came to a screeching halt. "Wait! Ken! Where is he? Ohmygod, he wasn't down there with you, was he?" Horror filled her eyes and she turned to run back the way we'd come.

"No, no. Relax." I held on to her. "Ken was gone before the-the event. He went to get a flashlight. You haven't seen him?

"No, I thought he was with you."

"Let's pick up the pace." And we did.

It wasn't hard to find the others. We only had to follow the sounds of shouting. That led to the library. General Grant and Dr. Allison were exchanging sharp words. Sara, the Schuurmans, and Allan with two Ls were wrapped up in their own conversation. Grant's two men in black stood stoically behind the general.

"You!" shouted General Grant, turning on his heel and glaring at me like everything was all my fault.

"General." I nodded.

"What happened to you?" Sara ran to my side.

"You know all those PSAs about smoking being hazardous to your health?"

"Yeah…"

"Turns out they're true. Who knew?"

"Ed was almost killed," Karen explained as Sara turned to her for a more rational explanation. Although I thought I'd explained myself rather well. "Burnt to death in a fire."

"Fire? Where?" demanded the general, a man used to getting answers.

"Down in the boiler room," I replied.

"Is it out?"

"Let's call it contained," was my answer. I didn't believe we or the greater facility had anything to worry about. Surprisingly, we still had power. There must've been a battery reserve somewhere else that had luckily remained unscathed. Leave it to the military to build in backup to the backup.

"That explains the fire alarm," Dr. Allison replied. "Allan, would you mind shutting the damn thing off?"

He said he would and departed.

"Any idea what caused the fire?" Sara asked me.

"Or who?" suggested Max.

"I don't like this." General Grant paced. "What about our asset?" His eyes met Dr. Allison's. "Is it secure?"

"Asset my ass! We're talking about Mirabilis, General!" shouted Max Schuurman. "Say it, Mirabilis! Your precious asset."

He snorted, his fingers forming air quotes. "More like a killing machine." Max whipped out his gun and waved it around. "Next time I meet him, I'm going to be greeting him with this." He leveled the Glock at the glass coffee pot and fired.

BAM!

Karen threw her arm over her eyes as glass shards bounced off us all.

"Put that thing away! Are you crazy, Max?" General Grant motioned to his two aides. They moved in tandem and quickly disarmed him. One of the two thrust the gun in his pocket.

Should I mention that the lovely Katja Schuurman was likely also armed? Nah, let the general discover that fact for himself, if indeed he ever did.

Dr. Allison frowned heavily. "In answer to your question, General, I hope so." She turned to me. "Is there anything you can add to this discussion, Ed? Through the library window, we all saw Ken go running past moments before we heard the fire alarm."

"Where is he now?" I inquired. I breathed a sigh of relief as the fire alarm suddenly ceased.

"We haven't seen him since he ran by," Katja Schuurman said.

"So he's fled," suggested Max. "Maybe he's working with Mirabilis—"

"Hey!" Karen cried indignantly.

"Doctor, I'm warning you!" General Grant leveled a finger at Max Schuurman. "Keep your mouth shut."

Max waved the general off. "Warn all you want. Like it or not, there's a bigger threat here than you, General. And it's a little too late to be coy. Three murders, an attempted fourth." He pointed at me, marking me intended victim number four. He wasn't wrong. "Now that I think about it, maybe Ken isn't just working with Mirabilis. Maybe, just maybe, he is Mirabilis."

Karen jumped him. Katja raised a brow in amusement as Sara and I pulled Karen off Max. He wiped blood from his lip with the back of the hand. "You crazy bitch. What's wrong with you?

You an alien too?"

General Grant slammed his palms down on the reading table. "What if Max is right? How do we know that...Mirabilis, there, I've said it, god help me, isn't like a chameleon or that he can't transfer his mind into the brain of one of us?"

"Take over our bodies?" Katja said.

"Control us." Max dabbed at his busted lip. "Yeah. That could explain a lot."

"General," Sara began, "what exactly is this Mirabilis?"

"Who are you?" the general demanded.

"She's employed here at the Haven," Dr. Allison explained.

"She cooks and cleans for us," Max added.

"Well, then off you go, young lady. We don't need any cooking or cleaning at this time. And you can, you *will*, forget you heard anything."

He had no idea how wrong he was.

General Grant made shooing movements with his hand. When Sara refused to budge, he made similar movements to his men in black and they escorted her out the library door by her elbows.

"Fine. I'm going to go look for Ken," Sara said.

"Stay out of this!" General Grant ordered. But I knew his words were wasted on Sara. She'd never listen.

"How did you get inside the Haven, General?" I wanted to know.

"What kind of imbecilic question is that, Turner?" General Grant smirked. "Same way I always do."

"The main entrance?"

"Why is this man even here, Doctor Allison?" the general barked.

"I thought he might be of some use given the current situation."

"Useless is more like it." The general strode to me and pulled himself up to his full height, which wasn't exactly awe-inspiring seeing as he was only an inch or two taller than me. "As for the entrance, why the hell was it standing wide open?

Somebody want to explain that to me? What the hell kind of security is that? That your doing, Turner?"

"I told you, General," Dr. Allison cut in. "We were locked in. All of us, Ed included. We were trying to figure out an exit strategy when you showed up."

"And now the door is wide open and Dalton is missing," Max summed up. Karen turned on him and he ducked behind his wife.

General Grant huffed. "I want him found," he told his two men in black. "And if there is any sign of Mirabilis, detain him. But under no circumstances harm him."

I had a hunch that if they did stumble on Mirabilis it wasn't harming the alien they were going to have to worry about, it was managing to keep themselves for getting harmed or killed by our alien visitor that would be key to their survival.

"Yessir, General," they barked in unison and made a quick exit.

32

Karen and I exited the library. We weren't wanted anyway and both of us were sick of listening to the others squabbling and doing their best to assign blame to one another for all their troubles, the three recent murders included.

We returned to our quarters, where I changed clothes. We loaded up our backpacks and headed out.

"Are you sure about this, Ed?" Karen shouldered her pack.

"Better to go now while the others are busy with each other. What if the general insists we stay?"

"You have a point." Karen led the charge.

The exit Dr. Allison had led us to earlier hung ajar. No longer locked in, we followed a tunnel leading to a shaft, leading to a metal stairway, leading to the surface, and, finally, a well-defined trail. Pinprick stars filled the night sky. The moon lit up the clouds in shades of gray and deep purple hanging over the distant peaks. Not a flying saucer in sight. I shivered in the dry cold air.

Some yards away, under the shelter of fir, pine, and spruce trees, I counted a black Humvee with a heavy-duty winch bolted to its front, two Jeeps, a military halftrack, and, the black sheep of the bunch, a light-blue metallic Toyota Corolla four-door.

Karen's fingers dug into my forearm.

"What's wrong?"

"I think there's somebody in that car." She pointed at the Toyota. "See?"

"I'll check it out." I started to move. Karen held on.

"Not without me, you're not."

"Fine."

We walked slowly over, listening to our feet crunching over sticks and leaves. Might as well have been brittle white bones. That was the kind of night it was and the sort of mood I was in.

The dead eyes of Vishnu Pushpak smiled at us, his face smooshed against the driver's side window. His body slumped over the steering wheel.

"Gross," Karen said, sloughing her backpack.

I peeked inside.

"What do you see?"

"A bullet hole. In his chest. That's odd."

"Odd how?" She pressed her face to the window and gasped.

"A bullet hole?" I surveyed our surroundings. All appeared quiet. Not the proverbial creature was stirring. "Not very original, wouldn't you say? Very...human."

"Maybe not," Karen agreed. "But it will still kill you dead."

"True."

Karen rubbed her arms for warmth which made me want to do the same.

"I wonder if the general knows."

Karen pulled a face. "I wonder if he or one of his goons pulled the trigger."

"Good point. What's all that?" We hadn't been up from the underground more than five minutes and suddenly Karen Dalton's phone was going crazy, ping ping pinging to announce about one hundred and ninety-nine incoming calls and texts. Breaking the silence. Disturbing the dead.

"Sorry, let me check." She dug into her rear pocket and extracted her phone. The glow from its screen lit up her face.

While she wrestled with her phone, I pulled open the driver's side door and took a closer look at Pushpak's corpse. He didn't complain when I search his pockets. I came up empty. A key ring holding four additional keys hung in the ignition but Pushpak wasn't going anywhere. Leastwise, not under his own power. In his next car trip, he'd be the passenger, not the driver.

With Karen occupied, I edged out of the Toyota and walked to the dark edge of the woods. I stuck my hands down my front pockets. "Waylo?" The woods didn't answer. Karen's curses, exclamations, and laments provided background. "Anything important?" I asked, returning.

"Bullshit telemarketers, one from my landlady complaining about Amazon and Dash deliveries piling up outside my door. Crap."

"What?"

"My boss telling me I'm fired."

"Why?"

She shrugged uncaringly. "Probably because I've been missing so much damn work. I know I missed my deadline on the Macaffee job."

"Sorry."

"What are you going to do? I'll get another job."

"Involving poetry, maybe?"

"Such as?"

"Poet laureate of California?"

"Yeah, more likely writing pithy phrases for Hallmark cards."

"That's the spirit. You see, there is a future in poetry."

"I was joking."

"Right. Sorry."

"Oh, shit," Karen cut in as the texts and phone messages kept invading her phone. "It's Ken."

I leaned over the phone screen.

"What does he say?"

Karen read, "Had to go to keep you all safe. Gone to Ed. Will fix this. Forgive me. Go home." She shoved the phone back in her pocket.

"Gone to Ed? I'm Ed. What the hell is that supposed to mean?"

Karen bit her lip. A moment later she snapped her fingers. "Of course!"

"What?"

"Ed. It means Edinburgh. He always called it Ed for short."

"I'm not that short."

"Ha-ha. He's heading to Scotland."

"Are you shitting me? What for?"

"No idea." She shot her chin out at me. "So?"

"What?" I have a tough enough time with the English language, body language is a whole other vocabulary I have yet to master.

"So are you coming to Scotland with me to save my brother or am I going alone?"

"He told you to go home."

"You think I'm going to listen to my dumb brother?" She crossed her arms. "So are you in or are you out?"

"I told you I hate to fly."

"Right, I remember. Did you know that Edinburgh is famous for its whiskey." She playfully poked me in the chest. "In fact, one summer I visited Ken when he was in grad school there —"

"Ken went to school in Edinburgh?"

"University of Edinburgh, I told you before. Anyway, we took a whiskey walk."

"What, pray tell, is a whiskey walk?" It sounded intriguing but I did my best not to let it show.

"Just what it sounds like. You walk around with a group of people and sample whiskey at all the distilleries in Old Town. Sounds fun, right?"

"There are worse ways to pass the time," I admitted. Like a walking tour of vegan eateries. "Why would Ken be returning there now?"

"I have no idea. I don't know why my brother does anything, to tell you the truth. But we've got to go, right? See where the trail leads? Save my brother?"

I feared it was going to lead to death. Hell, it already had. Just ask Vishnu Pushpak. Okay, so the professor couldn't answer, one look at him spoke volumes.

Not to mention, it was not out of the realm of possibility

that Ken had led me into a trap, knowingly or not. A trap which might have led to my death.

"I googled Edinburgh some before my trip that time. Did you know Edinburgh has more UFO sightings than anywhere else in the UK? And that just about half the people living there believe aliens have been visiting them? Incredible, no?"

"Incredible, yes." If anything, it said more about the mental state of Edinburgh's denizens than it did the veracity of the burg being a hotspot ET destination.

"Hey, maybe it's where Mirabilis lives!"

"What? Sharing a houseboat with the Loch Ness Monster?"

"Sure, maybe it's his pet sea monster from outer space."

I frowned at her. "I was joking." Sometimes, like now, I really worried about the woman.

"Whatever. So are we going or what?"

"Promise me one thing."

"What's that?"

"That you'll let me get drunk on the plane." I'd demand smoking privileges too but I knew that was beyond her power to grant.

"Deal."

We shook on it.

"Should we report the body?" Karen indicated Pushpak still resting quietly behind the wheel of the Toyota. The door hung open like a broken wing.

"No, it will only slow us down. Either the general knows about this already or he'll learn soon enough. Hell, the general or his men may even be responsible. Pushpak can wait."

"What if a bear eats him?"

"Bears gotta eat."

"That's a horrible thing to say!"

"Not if you're a bear." Karen's look said it all. "Fine." I slammed the door shut. There'd be no bear feast this night. I scampered from vehicle to vehicle.

"What are you doing now?"

"Securing us transportation." I yanked open the door of the

Humvee. Damn, the driver's side door was heavy. And thick as my mattress. "This'll do."

"Seriously, Ed? I'll bet this gas-guzzling phallic symbol of misplaced manhood belongs to the general."

"All the better. Besides, it's the only vehicle with keys. Unless you want to ask Pushpak to move over?"

"No, thank you."

"Then hop in."

Karen crossed to the other side of the black mechanical monster. With a struggle, she climbed up and in. "What about Samuel's pickup truck?" Karen asked.

"We'll send someone to pick it up and haul it down to Nevada for him."

"If you say so." Karen buckled up. "But what about your brand new Flying Saucer Diner mug?"

"What about it?" I started the engine and slipped into reverse. This vehicle was massive. We could probably scale a mountain with it. Maybe get three miles to the gallon doing so but it would be worth every drop!

"You left it inside the pickup."

"Shit on a stick!" The woman was annoyingly right. I'd left my new mug. I'd also left the remainder of my carton of Ernie's Winston's at our campsite but had no intention of making the arduous hike back for those. Cigarettes were cheap, not as cheap as they used to be back in the day, but cheap enough. And I could always add their cost to Karen Dalton's bill. But my coffee mug…

"Fine." I steered along the primitive road. The vehicle might have been built to stop light artillery but I found every little bump jarring and unbearable. I listened to my teeth rattle. "I suppose we can afford a small detour." Sometimes you just have to give in, especially times when it means postponing a horrible transatlantic airplane flight.

33

I watched as Karen returned from the restroom to her tiny, cramped seat. Did the airlines design their seats for little green men with no elbows? The things certainly weren't fit for humans. "Here, I brought you a slice of carrot cake. Flight attendant said he had some extra from business class. Wasn't that sweet of him?"

I backed away as far as I could—which wasn't far considering we were sitting in narrow coach seats at an altitude of forty thousand feet or so. The jet engines off our wing ceaselessly gulped enormous quantities of air in one end and shot them out the other.

I waved my hand to ward her off. "Carrot cake?" I eyed the thick slice with suspicion. White frosting coated the top. Sure, that wasn't so bad. In fact, it was good. But bits of carrot blended with the cake. "Who ruins a perfectly good cake with carrot? A-A vegetable?"

"Fine. I'll eat it myself."

I shrugged indifferently. What I wanted was a cigarette. I cradled my bourbon. At least Karen had kept her word. I was working on bourbon number four. How much longer was this insufferable flight going to last?

I flung off my hood. We'd picked up some fresh clothes in Denver before hitting the airport. We'd left Samuel's pickup truck in the long-term parking garage and told him where to find it. I told him to send us the bill for parking and shipping, unless he chose to make the trip up and collect the vehicle himself. Along with the thank-you note for letting us borrow his truck, I included a bottle of duty-free bourbon. I also asked him to ship the Tesla Roadster to LA and to charge the transportation to Karen Dalton.

Despite the warmth of the cabin, Karen was dressed in blue jeans over a pair of black leggings, a green flannel shirt and black fleece vest. I'd bought a pair of fleece-lined tan corduroys and a thick green pullover hoodie promoting the Colorado Rockies— the major league baseball team, not the mountain range. Not my favorite team but they'd do in a pinch hitter.

We'd ditched the general's Humvee when we recovered Samuel's pickup truck and what it held of our belongings. Whatever we'd left behind at our campsite was now bear and coyote property because that's the way finders-keepers works. At least I had my slick new mug back. It was safely stuffed away between my socks and underwear in my carry-on up in the overhead bin.

"What I don't get," Karen said moments later, nibbling her cake and gazing out the window. "Why go through all this? Why drag us half across the country and all the way out to the Rocky Mountains?" She swiped at a crumb of carrot hanging on to her chin. "And if this person or alien thing really wanted my brother dead, why not kill him and be done with it like he did the others, instead of going through all this trouble? And this is a hell of a lot of trouble."

"Because Mirabilis wanted us here. Me, at least," I answered.

"You? Why you, Ed? What's so special about you? I mean, no offense, you're sort of a nice guy and all but—and don't take this the wrong way" she added, grabbing a fold of my shirt up in her hand, "you're nothing special."

"Is there a right way to take that?"

"Sorry." Pink colored her cheeks. "I haven't been myself since this whole crazy thing started. Everything seems surreal." She carefully set the empty plate on her seatback tray. "I miss my old life. My old reality."

"Reality is a figment of your imagination," I told her.

"I'm beginning to believe that."

Karen cleared her throat. Served her right if she had a carrot stuck in her craw. "Speaking of aliens..." She glanced at our nearest seatmate, snoozing across the aisle. "Do you really believe this alien exists?"

"Don't you?"

"I believe what I can see."

"Oh? Do you believe in, say, love?"

Karen frowned. "You know what I mean."

"New topic."

"Okay." She appeared relieved.

"How did you find me?" I demanded.

"What do you mean?"

"I mean, why choose me out of all the private investigators in LA? Why didn't you go with one of the large firms, for instance? The city's filled with them."

"Why? I don't know. Ken called, which shook me to the bones, you know? I had to do something after that. I couldn't just go on with my life pretending everything was okay. I was worried. Couldn't sleep. I heard about you and just figured—"

"But how?" I interrupted. "How did you hear about me?"

"How?" She scratched behind her ear. "I'm not sure. Let me think." Her eyes brightened. "I remember now. It was a flyer."

"A flyer?"

"Yeah, you know, an advertisement for Ed Turner, Private Investigator, All Inquiries Welcome."

"There's no such thing. I've never made a flyer."

"Sure you did. I remember. I remember some kid handing them out on the street outside our office. I took one. I always do. I mean, I feel bad saying no whenever somebody's handing out a flyer. I don't want to hurt their feelings. Doesn't matter what it's for or whether I'm really interested or not. I took one once for a six and under dance class. I'm not six. And I can't dance."

I held up a hand. "Stop. What did this kid look like?"

Karen shrugged. "Heck, I don't remember. Just some kid in baggy jeans and an oversized tee shirt. And a skullcap."

"So you wouldn't recognize him if you saw him again?"

She was quick to answer. "Not a chance. Why? What does it matter?"

"I don't know that it does." I didn't know what mattered and what didn't. I couldn't wait to land in Edinburgh, Scotland. Get my feet on solid ground. Could I purchase cigarettes in the airport? Did they sell Camels?

After that? The future would unfold itself.

Yet whatever was going on and who or whatever was behind it all, had to be stopped. And, like it or not, I seemed to be the one up to bat next.

I only hoped I did not strike out.

The jet hit the ground hard. At least, it felt that way to me. Karen seemed to take the landing in stride. Flying in super-economy coach, with our seats next to the aft restrooms, we were the last to deboard.

I rolled the suitcase one-handed between the crowd. Our only other luggage was our backpacks. We slung them over our shoulders and marched stiffly through customs.

And into the arms of General Grant and Dr. Marcia Allison.

"Shit." Karen stamped her feet.

"I'll second that emotion," I said, studying the doctor's and general's anxious and stern faces. On the plus side, there was no sign of the general's two extra shadows. "So, you beat us here. Must be nice having an entire air force at your disposal."

"Sure as hell is." General Grant smirked. "And don't you forget it." He was dressed up in full uniform on this occasion. No doubt this was intended to intimidate us.

"Where are Tweedle Dee and Tweedle Dumber?" I asked.

The general refused to answer me.

"Enough. Where's your brother, Karen? Where's Ken?" Dr. Allison's hair was tucked under a gray wool cap. She wore a dark gray business suit and black leather boots. Deep red lipstick gave her the look of a freshly-fed vampire.

"Who?" Karen said defiantly.

"Let's walk." Dr. Allison grabbed Karen's arm and started pulling her down the concourse.

"Hey!" Karen complained.

General Grant reached for me.

"I wouldn't do that, General," I said softly.

We stared each other down as Dr. Allison and Karen grew smaller in the distance. I walked quickly to catch up to them. I was not letting Karen out of my sight. The general felt the same way about me because he matched me step for step.

We hit the exit door all together. Karen's phone chose that moment to reconnect with the outside world. Ping ping ping. A cascade of missed calls and texts.

Karen cast her eyes on me as she instinctively reached for her device.

"Is that Ken? Where is he? Give me that!" Marcia Allison snatched Karen's phone from her hands.

"Hey, you can't do that!" Karen lunged for her phone. Dr. Allison held it high over her head. An on-duty cop threw his eyes on us and glared suspiciously. General Grant waved to him and he backed off.

Dr. Allison's fingers twiddled with the phone. She looked at General Grant in triumph. "He's in Bonnybridge. Let's go. Get in the car."

A pinstripe-suited driver threw open the door of an unmarked black limousine parked in the No Parking Zone. The general and Dr. Allison hustled us inside. The driver carelessly tossed our suitcase and backpacks in the voluminous trunk. I prayed my new mug was safe in its nest of socks and underwear.

"Looks like we're going for a ride," I said, settling into the plush black leather backseat. "First class, too."

Karen and I rubbed shoulders in the rear seat. General Grant and Dr. Allison boxed us in like a pair of bookends.

"What's Bonnybridge?" Karen asked. "I thought we were going to Edinburgh."

"The town of Bonnybridge is purportedly the UFO capital of the world," I explained. "Think of it as Roswell and the Bermuda Triangle all tangled up in one or, as I like to think of it, one big ball of baloney. Bonnybridge residents regularly report hundreds of UFO sightings every year."

"What? Is it something in their drinking water?" joked Karen.

"They call it the Falkirk Triangle, so named for the imaginary triangle, and I do mean imaginary, lines connecting the towns of Bonnybridge, Falkirk to the east, and Stirling to the north." I watched the airport disappear behind us.

"I've heard of Roswell and the Bermuda Triangle, everybody has," Karen said. "But I've never even heard of the Falkirk Triangle or Bonnybridge. What's so special about them?"

"Believers claim the Falkirk Triangle is a passage into another dimension. If you believe the believers, there is a thinning, a weakening, of the interstitial spaces between multiverses and worlds that is more fragile and tenuous at the Falkirk Triangle, more so than anywhere on Earth. Believers claim it's the ideal place for aliens from other dimensions to slip in and slip out without a lot of fuss and bother. And when you're travelling lightyears, who wants to carry a lot of baggage and be bothered with airport security lines?"

"That's insane," Karen said.

"You sure?" Dr. Allison finally spoke up.

"Don't tell me you believe?" Karen replied.

"I've seen some things," Dr. Allison said.

"Must you, Marcia," snapped the general.

"That cat's out of the bag, General. Besides, we're all friends. Let's cooperate. What do you two say?"

"I say if we're abducted by aliens en route, I want a last smoke before they dissect me and stick a probe up my butt," I said.

"And I want to know what your plans are for Ken," Karen snapped. "What are you two doing here, anyway? Why can't you leave him alone?"

"Unfinished business," General Grant said softly. He tapped the driver on the shoulder. "What's going on? Why are you slowing down? I want to get there before dark."

"Can't sir. Sheep in the road and that camper van ahead."

The general leaned towards the middle of the car and swore as he looked out the windscreen.

Sure enough, a decrepit red-and-white camper van bounced along ahead of us a car's length away.

"Go around it!" General Grant ordered.

"But, sir, I'd have to go off the road and—"

"I don't care if you have to go off the fucking planet!" shrilled the general. "Do it, dammit!"

"Yessir." The driver nodded, frowned, and steered off the road. We all bounced in the air. The general's head hit the car's ceiling.

The camper van did the same, cutting off the pavement ahead of us, tenaciously jumping in front of the limo, inches from our front bumper.

"Shit!" Our driver swore and veered back onto the main road. Sheep cluttered the road and he slammed on the brakes. We all bounced into each other on the backseat, banging like bowling pins charged up with too much kinetic energy but with no place to go and spend it. Two sheep, startled looks on their wooly faces, shot into the air. The limo skidded into a shallow ditch running along a farmland, its nose digging into the mud. The two sheep landed in a heap near the front left tire.

"Driver! What are you doing?" screamed General Grant.

"Sorry, sir! I couldn't help it!" His hands slammed the steering wheel in frustration. Two big brown dead sheep stared at him with lifeless eyes filled with accusation.

"Are you okay, Karen?" I asked.

"Yeah. I think so. A little beaten up."

I was feeling that way myself. Glancing through the rear window, I was shocked to see two familiar faces running towards our stranded vehicle.

Dr. Allison carefully adjusted her clothing. "Get us out of here, driver," she ordered.

"Yes'm." He shoved open his door only to have it shoved back in his face by Ernie.

"Everybody out! The alien's ours!" screamed Lena Jay, her

face a mottled red, her eyes quivering.

Lena Jay was dressed in a knee-length lime green coat. A green headband kept her frazzled hair out of her crazed face. She and Ernie wore heavy hiking boots. Maybe they'd just returned from trail walking on the moon. Ernie was dressed in a blue bib overalls with a kangaroo pouch in the front and a Shining tee shirt. A black hat topped his head.

"And keep your hands up where I can see them!" Lena Jay yanked the back door open and waved her stun gun in General Grant's face. "You first, fatso!"

General Grant swore and lunged for Lena Jay. I knew that was going to end badly. And it did, she blasted him in the face with her stun gun. The general went down screaming.

Ernie was even more dangerous. He was armed with a pistol. He pointed this at Dr. Allison. "Can I shoot her?" he asked Lena Jay.

"Save you ammo for this one." She was pointing at me. "Come on, Ed. You too, girlie."

Karen and I stepped over General Grant's writhing form sprawled half across the seat. The other half of him sprawled over the cold hard ground. Ernie kept his gun on me and Karen. He led us to the camper van. He shoved us inside and locked the door. Through the camper window, we watched as Ernie climbed in behind the wheel. Lena Jay rode shotgun.

"What's happening?" Karen said. "Where are they taking us?"

Out the window, I watched as Dr. Allison kicked General Grant out of the limo. The limo driver, standing beside the beached vehicle, hollered at her. She roughly grabbed the heavy iron jack from his hands and smashed it into the side of his skull. He went down like a bag of bones.

The camper van shot forward. Karen and I were thrown backward, slamming into the rear door of the camper. As we raced away, I watched as, with Dr. Allison at the wheel, the limo's rear wheels spun and spun, kicking up mud and grass. As General Grant pushed himself up unsteadily to his knees, the car's tires finally found their grip. The limo shot violently backwards, taking out a trio of curious sheep who'd come to watch the show. The show was now over for them.

But not for us, I realized, as Dr. Allison barreled relentlessly after us. And I did not think for a minute that she was coming to rescue us.

34

The sky darkened. Day was at end. Summer was nearly at end. Were we nearly at our end too?

The beat-up camper van raced onward into a purple and bluish storm, the likes of which neither Karen nor I had ever seen before. The huge storm had popped out of nowhere. Flaming lightning shot through the air and stabbed the earth repeatedly.

Karen rummaged frantically through the flimsy camper van's even flimsier kitchenette drawers.

"What are you looking for?" I asked from the relative comfort of a one-inch thick orange plaid cushioned bench seat.

"I don't know!" Karen sounded harried. "Something. Anything. A weapon. An exoviter!"

I couldn't help chuckling. But I stopped quickly when Karen gave me the stink eye.

"Are you going to help me?" she cried. "Or are you just gonna sit there doing nothing while those-those maniacs drive us to our doom!?"

"I could break open the door, I suppose." I gave it a look. Flimsy by the looks of it. "Or one of the windows," I suggested. We'd already tried to open the rear door from the inside and, although we were able to unlock it, a chain and padlock on the outside kept us on the inside. I was pretty confident I could break us out. "But we must be going sixty miles per hour. That'll be tough on the knees when we hit the pavement." I rubbed my knees thoughtfully.

Karen slammed the drawer shut. "Nothing!"

I patted the space beside me. Out the window, a white

triangular road sign, featuring the black silhouettes of a mama and baby alien, flew by. We were nearing Bonnybridge.

Karen sat. "This stinks." She frowned. "What are Lena Jay and Ernie doing here? And how did they get here, anyway?"

"Flying saucer? Venus express shuttle?"

"Not helping, Ed."

"They say humor can get you through anything. Did you know that Norman Cousins believed that laughter could cure your ills?"

We bounced in tandem as the camper van dove in and out of a pothole at speed.

"Never heard of him."

"You've never heard of Norman Cousins? Back in the late seventies, he wrote a book titled Anatomy of an Illness as Perceived by the Patient: Reflections on Healing and Regeneration."

"Sheesh. Kinda long, isn't it? Is that the title or the whole book?"

"Very funny. He once became quite ill. In a nutshell, he was hospitalized but felt the hospital conditions and treatment were worse than any potential cure the facility and doctors might offer. He checked himself out of the hospital and into a hotel. Watched comedies, like old Marx Brothers movies and the Candid Camera TV show. Read funny novels and a variety of humor books."

"And?"

"And laughed himself back to health."

"Bogus."

"The New England Journal of Medicine wrote of his experience. An entirely new field of scientific study was born: psychoneuroimmunology."

She looked at me closely. "How do you know all this stuff?"

"I like to read."

"Sure, when you're not smoking and drinking."

"On the contrary, I sometimes do all three at once."

She laughed.

"See? I made you laugh. Don't you feel better?"

"Right. Maybe you should have been a doctor instead of a private detective. How old are you, anyway?"

"Age is unimportant," I replied. "We're either alive or we are dead. Nothing else in between matters."

"Yeah. Unfortunately, I fear we may soon be the latter."

"Not if I can help it." I patted her knee. "There's something you should know," I began. Actually, there were a million things she should know but I figured it best to start with just the one.

"Don't," she said. "Don't spoil things." She squeezed my hand. "Let's let things be what they are for now."

"For now," I agreed. I sensed a deceleration in our speed and straightened. "Something's happening."

The camper van slowed to a stop.

"What is it?"

"Shh," I whispered. "No talking. I believe Act Three is about to begin." I could only hope this wouldn't spell curtains for us, but Karen Dalton, in particular.

We heard a chain rattle. The camper van door flew outward. Ernie threatened us with his pistol. Lena Jay yanked Karen from the van and out into the hammering rain. I followed.

Hands over my eyes, I spotted the watery outline of a farmhouse in the distance, shimmering like a mirage.

"Walk!" demanded Lena Jay. Rain pelted us. The ground under our feet was soft and gooey, making walking a struggle.

Dr. Allison popped up out of nowhere. The cacophony of the thunder and rain drowning out the sound of her approaching in the limo. She wielded the long black limousine like a weapon. At the last second, the long car jumped in a water-filled pothole and she only managed to clip Ernie in the elbow rather than run him down in cold blood as it looked like she'd meant to do. The gun sailed from his hand and tumbled butt over barrel, landing somewhere unseen in the muck.

Ernie screamed. Lena Jay screamed. Karen screamed. Okay, everybody but me screamed. I did holler. I hollered for Karen to run. And she did.

Marcia Allison flew from the car and launched herself at Lena Jay with her arms extended like claws of death. Her body shimmered for a moment. Was I the only one who noticed? I pictured a squat pterosaur with long, ugly claws capable of slashing a person to shreds. I pushed Karen forward, towards the safety of the farmhouse. I hoped.

Lena Jay jabbed Dr. Allison in the neck with a stun gun in each hand. Marcia Allison did not go down.

Just as I feared...

"What's going on?" Karen screamed as she turned around to look. "What the hell is happening!?"

"Don't stop! Keep moving!" I shoved her forward in the dark.

Dr. Marcia Allison was no longer Marcia Allison. What had caused this letting down of the guard? Anger, the jolt of the stun guns, the storm, a sudden change of heart, or just deciding to give up all pretense because pretense no longer mattered?

No, this was no longer Marcia Allison. The creature before me, battling Lena Jay like she was a Toy District ragdoll, was Mirabilis, otherwise and in other times and places called Waylo...my brother.

The one who'd been missing and whom I had assumed dead all those years ago.

Karen fell to her knees. With a cry and a quick glance backward, she quickly scrambled to her feet and stumbled forward. Mirabilis/Waylo snatched Lena Jay by the neck and hurled her brutally through the air. The pseudo-Venusian screamed and flailed madly, uselessly, and landed in a barren field across the road.

Waylo wasn't letting Lena Jay off so easily as she writhed in the muck and weeds. He leapt across the road and with a snarl of triumph loud enough to be heard over the roar of the storm, he ripped her head from her body. He roared and snatched Lena Jay's hair in his fist. He swung his arm and flung her head away like a sack of trash.

I'd seen enough. I had to save Karen from a similar fate. I

WELCOME TO MY WORLD

surged ahead, towards the farmhouse. I grabbed Karen as I ran. I lifted her off her feet. She screamed in my ear as I carried her to the farmhouse. I put my shoulder to the door and smashed through. Wood splinters flew. The unexpected warmth of a blazing fire in a tall stone hearth caught us both by surprise.

Another surprise waited for us inside.

"Ken!" shrieked Karen. She pounded her fist into my shoulder. "Let me down."

I set her on a braided rug spread across the stone floor. I pulled the door closed as best I could but the wind and rain had no trouble working their way past the broken wood slats that still hung on bent iron hinges. The fire in the hearth danced—a Highland jig?

"Karen?" Ken looked up from a massive kneehole desk squatting across the front room. He'd had his nose buried in a book. Various pieces of laboratory equipment filled the desk. "Ed? What are you doing here? I told you to go home. You shouldn't be here." Sweat drained from his pores. He looked like he hadn't slept since leaving Colorado.

"You ran away. Left us to die!" Karen said accusingly.

This looked like a brother-sister moment. I turned to the fire and spread my hands, absorbing the warmth through my fingers and face. A glass of bourbon would have made the moment perfection... Except that Waylo was out there. What was he doing? What was taking him so long?

"No! No, it wasn't like that! I swear!" Ken ran from behind the desk. "I left because I didn't want you to die. It's me Mirabilis wants. I hoped that by leaving I'd be drawing it away. And it worked, didn't it? You're still alive."

"Jerk." Karen slugged him in the upper arm. I was happy to see I wasn't the only one she doled out her particular form of affection on.

Ken rubbed his arm. "I came to see old Professor Campbell. You remember Professor Campbell, don't you, Karen?"

"Sure, sorta. He seemed nice. And normal. He had us over for tea."

"So why come all this way to see him?" I couldn't help asking.

"I thought perhaps he was the one person who would believe me. The one person who would be willing to help me." Ken suddenly startled. "Are you two alone? Where's Marcia?" His eyes rose to the ceiling. "And where is Mirabilis? Is he out there? Have you seen him?"

"We intended to come alone." I explained about Dr. Allison and General Grant greeting us at the Edinburgh airport. I did not explain to him that Marcia Allison and Mirabilis were one and the same. No time for that now. I then told him about ARC agents Lena Jay and Ernie and their roles in our current situation. I nodded my chin over my shoulder. "They're all out there somewhere."

I continued to wonder what was keeping Waylo from joining us? Was he taunting me? Was he playing with me? Like he had when he'd led me and Karen in a circuitous route to the Haven? Was he biding his time? Why? He seemed to have everything and everyone he wanted, right where he wanted. I glanced uneasily out the broken front door.

"Ken, why are we here?" Karen insisted.

"These beings, extraterrestrials, extra-multi-universal beings, whatever the hell you want to call them." Ken shot his trembling hands through his hair and over his head. "They slip through a seam, or seams, between dimensions or universes or whatever. Professor Campbell tried to explain it to me years ago. Of course, at that time, I didn't believe him." Ken chuckled. "I thought he was bonkers. Brilliant but bonkers. Little did I know." He sighed wearily.

The poor man sounded tired. And more than a bit mad. I meant that in a welcome-to-the-asylum sort of way, not the I'm-so-mad-the-Dodgers-lost-in-the-playoffs sort of way.

Karen squeezed her brother's hands. "You're cold."

Ken shrugged off her concern. "I'm okay." He managed a small smile. "I'm glad you are too. You too, Ed. Sorry to leave you like that."

WELCOME TO MY WORLD

"No harm done," I answered. A bit of an understatement. "Hair grows back."

"Yeah. About that?" He looked perplexed. "What happened to your eyebrows and eyelashes?"

I lowered my hood.

"Oh, uh, your head too?"

"It's a long cautionary tale," I said. "Best told another day. We have bigger, more important things to worry about right now."

"Yeah," Ken agreed. "We sure do. Come. Look."

We followed him around to the other side of the desk.

"What are we looking at?" A dozen or so metal boxes of various sizes and shapes connected by ethernet and USB cables to a powerful-looking desktop computer. From there, cords and cabled tumbled from the desk and led to something that looked like an eight-foot robot mushroom.

"The professor built it. He calls this setup his seam ripper."

My brow flew up. "Seam ripper?"

"Professor Campbell claims that with this device," Ken patted the top of the computer monitor, "he can force open the seam between universes...or dimensions."

I whistled softly. "Does it work?"

"We're about to find out." Ken's hands reached out and fingers began punching buttons and spinning dials.

"Where is the professor?" Karen wanted to know.

"He's in hospital. He suffered a near-fatal heart attack before he could finish explaining how all this stuff works," Ken said, without stopping or even slowing down while the storm battered the house.

"How this stuff works! You mean, you're not even sure what you're doing?" Karen's voice rose in pitch. "And why are you doing this?"

"Isn't it obvious?" Ken said. The robotic mushroom several yards away crackled and glowed. "To get rid of Mirabilis, of course."

"You intend to send him back. Through the seam," I stated.

"You got it, Ed."

"Is that a Tesla coil?"

"Yeah. Highly modified though. Capable of quite a lot more." He gulped. "I hope."

"I'll bet." But would it work as intended or was all this a giant farce? A fantasy of Professor Campbell's mind?

"Will it work?" Karen asked the question I had left unasked.

"It's got to," Ken said. "If not, we'll probably all die." His eyes scanned the computer screen as his fingers flew across the keyboard. "Unless either of you've got a better idea?"

"I have an idea." Marcia Allison smiled.

Nobody smiled back.

35

"Marcia!" Ken looked up in surprise. Then he frowned. "I was hoping Mirabilis would appear. That he'd followed me."

"Hello, Ken." Her clothes were soaked through. She'd lost her cap and her hair hung limp to her shoulders. "Ed, Karen. Care to tell Ken, Ed? He seems a man in need of...enlightenment."

I drew a breath in then let it out very, very slowly. "Karen, Ken. Meet Mirabilis." We'd been preoccupied and hadn't heard him enter.

Marcia/Mirabilis smiled an evil smile.

"What?" Ken drew back a step, his back pressed against the wall.

There was no stopping now, so I continued. "The alien you know as Mirabilis, the woman you think is Doctor Allison, I know *him* as Waylo...my brother."

"Your b-brother?" Karen swept her gaze from me to Waylo and back again. "Ed? What are you saying? Is this another one of your jokes?"

"No." I shook my head sadly. "No joke. I wish it was." I reached for her hand. She pulled away from me. I should have expected that. "Doctor Allison is dead, isn't she? You murdered her and replicated her. Took her place."

"No!" Karen gasped. "Replicated her? How is that even possible?"

"Our kind have the ability to mimic others," I said.

"Amazing." Ken glanced up. "So you killed Marcia? And the others? Why?"

"For this moment," he answered matter-of-factly.

"To get my attention. To draw me here. To this place."

The place where it had all started. We'd come through the seam all those years ago. Then our vessel had been damaged as we shot across the Atlantic. Our engine failed and down we went, much to the chagrin of the residents of New Mexico in general, and Roswell in particular, who now had us to thank for their booming Alien HQ-based economy.

"Yes." Waylo shook himself, sending a shower of droplets across the room. "Hello, my brother."

"Waylo," I said steadily. "I thought you were dead."

"Left me for dead is more like it," Waylo hissed.

Behind me, Karen groaned. Ken clicked away furiously at his keyboard. Would it help?

"No. I didn't do that. I was injured myself. There was nothing I could do, Waylo."

He smiled a wicked smile. "You could have rescued me, saved me from captivity amongst these impudent monkeys!"

I slowly shook my head. "I couldn't even save myself." I wasn't sure I could now either. My brother had always been the smarter and the stronger of the two of us. When we crashed, we'd both been seriously injured, tried to hide ourselves. We'd been caught. I'd escaped. I'd left Waylo because I believed he had died en route to Wright-Patterson.

"Lies! You always were jealous of me. Now you get what is due you." Waylo was in a talkative mood. Enjoying himself. He explained how, as he recovered, he sensed my presence out there in this world, and started scheming using his power to lure me, reel me in. All the way to Falkirk. "Where we'd first arrived on this planet, before everything went terribly wrong. And you abandoned me."

"I told you I couldn't help you. I couldn't even help myself. I really thought you were dead."

"Ed, what the hell is going on?!" Karen hollered.

Waylo turned his gaze on Karen. "All those years, trapped like a lab specimen, I dreamed of freedom as much as I dreamed of your death." He pointed at me. "Finally, when that one came," he pointed at Ken who was still hunched over the computer, "I found my chance. I'd caught a taste of you in the city of Los Angeles. Karen Dalton," he said, turning his cold eyes on her once more, "you did your job well. You made quite a successful puppet. You brought me my brother. Thank you." He bowed his head.

"Fuck you!" she replied defiantly. She glanced at me. "I mean, sorry, Ed, I know this guy-girl-alien thing is your brother but still nobody talks to me like that and—"

The amped-up Tesla coil jumped and glowed orange, then purple, bathing us all in its violet light.

"I've hated you for so long, Eidh," Waylo told me. "Part of me would like to see you caged for the next hundred years. Poked and prodded by these imbeciles." He rubbed his hands together. "But the bigger part of me can't wait for you to die." With that, Marcia Allison's body morphed, no longer the body of the lovely but stern woman she'd once been. Her forehead shifted, face contorted and twisted, body shrunk, widened, and filled out. What had Karen said? Looked quite like a Troglodyte, that was the word she'd used. And it fit. Even in his natural form, I barely recognized my brother. He was more beast than Pazu—the given name of our species. "Time to go, brother."

No, I couldn't stop the uncomfortable thought from racing around inside my head. The thought that reminded me unkindly that I'd never beaten my brother at anything. Now the game was staying alive. Would he win this game, too?

I couldn't let him. Karen's life was at stake here. And her brother's. Waylo wouldn't let either of them live after all they knew and had witnessed.

I braced myself, shimmered. Let down my guard. Thank god, there was no mirror. I wasn't in the mood to gaze on a Troglodyte.

Karen screamed. "What the hell was that! What *are* you?"

I had revealed my true self. She may not have a cat but I did and I'd let this one out of the bag.

"Ed, what are you? Where are you from?"

"Venus?" I quipped, although I wasn't sure even Norman

Cousin's theory of laughter as the best cure could save us now.

"Is that a question?" She gasped, backed up, and tripped over her own feet.

"It's not an answer," I admitted.

"YOU MURDERED MY LENA!" Wild-eyed Ernie, left arm hanging limp and useless, jumped into the room. He held his gun in his right hand. His jaw was bruised and blood spilled from his mouth. Mud caked his clothing. He waved the gun at me.

"No, it wasn't Ed! It was him!" Karen shouted, pointing to the beast in the doctor's tattered clothing.

"No, no." Ernie looked confused. "Where's the doc?"

"That's the doc," Karen explained. "That thing is Doctor Allison!"

Waylo shrugged his shoulders.

Ernie wiped water dripping in his eyes with the back of his hand. "You're an alien. You're really a fucking alien!"

"Boo!" Waylo grinned and took a small step towards the alien hunter.

"The seams open! The professor was right!" Ken's cry cut the air. "It's open!" A long tube of twisting purple and red energy snaked in the air around us. The fire snapped out in the fireplace. Wind and rain hurled through the open door. The rain sizzled against the pulsing and spinning seam of energy

"Time to say goodbye, brother." Waylo sprinted across the room towards me. Before I could so much as blink, he barreled into me and lifted me off my feet. I locked my arm around his neck and squeezed. He dragged me towards the seam, waiting like a hungry python for its prey. He meant to toss me into it.

My fingers dug into his hard flesh.

Ernie came unfrozen and fired off a round of shots. The bullets didn't stop Waylo, didn't even stun him. But they did distract him. He dropped me and pounced on the poor alien hunter. Ernie screamed, fired off his remaining rounds, then threw up his hands to defend himself. Waylo ripped the gun from his hand. He ripped off Ernie's arm at the shoulder and bellowed triumphantly. Ernie slumped to the ground, his life force fading.

Karen cried in the corner, horrified and unable to help.

I threw myself at Waylo, hitting him in the knees, bringing him down. The pulsing and thrumming energy seam swung over our heads. Waylo ducked and we wrestled in a tangle of arms and legs on the ground. Smashing and breaking everything in our path, furniture, lamps, and the professor's Delftfield pottery collection. I feared we'd wreck Professor Campbell's seam ripper—our only hope, if I was unable to stop him.

Waylo broke free of my grasp. He kicked me savagely in the face as I struggled for breath on my back on the floor. His strong hands found my neck. He squeezed. I felt myself slipping away. My big brother always beat me at everything. I would die and he would live. He beat me again…

"No! No! Please!" shouted Karen. "Stop! Please stop!"

"Hey! Hey, Mirabilis! Over here!" Ken climbed awkwardly on top of the desk. He waved his arms. The Tesla coil sputtered and hissed in the background. The floor shook violently.

Waylo roared and pulled me to my knees. He dragged me toward the seam. I kicked my legs and swung my arms. My fists hit nothing, only air. The seam jumped over my head. Waylo let go and reached for Karen. She screamed.

"What?" I looked at Ken. What was he up to? Whatever it was he intended, it couldn't be good. "No, Ken, don't!"

"Ken!" Karen cried. She ducked from under my brother's outstretched arms as the bright pulsing seam veered towards them. Its fierce light burned my eyes.

I crawled blindly across the floor and reached Waylo's thick muscled calf. I dug in my fingers. He swatted at me but I refused to let go. "Enough!" shrieked Waylo. "Die my little brother!" He hoisted me off my feet and lurched towards the ever-moving seam. My doom.

Ken launched himself off the desk. He slammed into Waylo hard. Waylo's inhuman eyes grew wide, with surprise and anger.

His fingers slipped and he lost his grip. I fell to the ground as Ken and Waylo tumbled together. The Tesla coil coruscated like a hungry monster at feeding time. The seam grew, swept over the struggling pair like a rogue wave, and caught them with looks of horror and surprise on their faces.

"Karen!" Ken cried.

And then they were no longer there. We were alone in the room.

"They're gone," Karen cried in horror. "We have to save Ken!"

I pulled her back from the shimmering, writhing, and glowing violet seam. "It's too late. I'm afraid they are both dead."

"But the seam? You said you can go through it!" Her eyes pleaded with me for this to be true.

"Yes, but not like that. Not unprotected. I'm sorry, Karen." I hung my head. "I've failed you." In some way, I felt I'd failed my brother as well. Maybe I had.

I plodded slowly to the desk and shut down the computer. The Tesla coil burped, blinked, and then went silent and dark. A deathly hush now filled the room.

"Ernie!" Karen raced to the alien hunter lying prone on the hearth rug. A pool of blood spread from his empty shoulder socket. His dismembered arm sat beside the hearth growing cold. "He's dead."

I extended my hand and helped Karen to her feet. I was back to my normal self. My normal human-*ish* self that is. "Yes and, in spite of everything, including him shooting me in my man parts with his stun gun, I'm sorry about that. Ernie didn't deserve to die this way. Lena Jay either."

None of the humans killed by my brother had deserved their deaths, despite what some might have done to him in the name of their science. Vishnu Pushpak, Zultan Crobar, Alan with one L Pflock, Bobby Berlitz, Marcia Allison—the Haven hadn't provided much of a haven for them, had it? And now Lena Jay, Ernie, and Ken Dalton were gone.

Life had been cruel to Waylo and he had been cruel to life.

"But we aren't dead. We'd better go before someone takes notice of all this. We don't want to be here when the authorities show up."

"No," Karen said, taking a last look around the room, taking in her last images of her brother. "No, we don't."

"He saved your life, you know."

"I know." Karen sniffed. Tears filled her eyes. "So did you. Thanks."

"Don't thank me yet," I joked. "You haven't seen my bill."

36

A light rain continued to fall but neither of us were in a mood to care. Clouds hid the stars. That didn't bother me either. There was nothing out here worth seeing.

"I hate to say it," began Karen, "but Lena Jay's headless corpse is lying around out there somewhere."

"Unless she's off haunting the locals already," I said with a smile. Lena Jay wasn't all bad. Nobody was really. It was all a matter of perspective.

Karen grabbed my arm. "Somebody's moving around over there," she whispered. She stopped and pointed at the limo. The driver's door hung open and the soft glow from the overhead light revealed a dark figure rummaging inside.

"Wait here. I'll check it out."

"Like hell I will." Karen clung to my side.

As we approached, Sara Chronis unfolded herself from the limo holding a damp, closed umbrella. The car's glovebox hung open. "Hello, Ed." She hugged me warmly and smiled at Karen. Karen might have looked like she was smiling back. But I knew that smile. And it was not a friendly one. "Still in one piece. Glad to see it." She touched the stubble of my left eyebrow. "Starting to grow back."

I ran a finger over my right eyebrow. "Hey, you're right."

"What are you doing here?" Karen demanded.

"Following General Grant and Doctor Allison. Where they go, I go." Sara Chronis was dressed in a long black raincoat and black slacks paired with leather boots. A white scarf wrapped itself around her neck.

Karen cocked her head. "A bit over the top for a cook slash

housekeeper."

"Karen." I looked at Sara, who nodded. "Sara is a CIA agent."

Karen snorted. "Right. Give me a break."

"Ed's right." Sara reached into her pocket and flashed her ID.

"Shit," Karen said.

"My boss doesn't like that the general and the doctor are keeping secrets from the Agency. He sent me here to keep an eye on them. And to see if I can learn who or what this Mirabilis is."

"I really couldn't say," I said, giving Karen a warning look.

"What happened here, Ed? We found General Grant and his driver sprawled in the road a ways back."

"Are they okay?" The driver, in particular, had taken quite a blow to the head.

"Yeah. The general's in the Royal Infirmary in Edinburgh getting checked out and giving everyone grief. His driver needed surgery but he'll live."

"Glad to hear it."

"So where's Doctor Allison?" Sara looked off towards the farmhouse. "Inside?"

"Yes and no."

"What's that supposed to mean?"

I explained as the three of us returned to the farmhouse. I didn't explain everything—not everything needed knowing—but I explained enough to satisfy the agent.

Sara glanced at Ernie. "Poor guy." She inspected his empty gun. "So you're telling me this monster alien did this?"

"Lena Jay's corpse is out there somewhere." I didn't know if anyone would ever find the true human remains of Dr. Marcia Allison.

"What about Lena Jay and Ernie?" wondered Karen. "What about all this?"

"Not to worry." Sara walked to the desk and inspected the computer curiously. Then she paused beside the giant modified Tesla coil. She touched it. "Ow! Fucking thing's hot as hell!"

"I'm not surprised," I said. "Hell is what it leads to."

"Huh?"

"Not important. Can we go now?" Karen looked ill. It had been a tough day. A tough couple of weeks. And now her brother was gone forever.

"Sure. I'll clean up this mess," offered Sara. "Cleaning up is what I do, remember?"

"What if the local authorities get wind of this? Or the press?" Karen wondered.

Sara smiled. "We'll blame it on the aliens, right, Ed?"

"Right. Good idea," I said. "Believers will believe it."

"Yep," Sara said. She settled herself behind the desk and pulled out her phone. "And the skeptics will claim a government coverup."

"And they'll both be right." Karen and I started through the broken front door. "Wait. I'll be right back." Sara glanced up from the computer as I hurried over to the mantle and pulled down a dusty bottle of Glenfiddich I'd spotted there earlier.

Karen scolded me with her eyes.

"What?" I said. "To quote the late great actress Ava Gardner 'I wish to live to one hundred and fifty years old, but the day I die, I wish it to be with a cigarette in one hand and a glass of whiskey in the other.'"

"And did she?" Karen asked, crooking her arm in mine as we walked down the path leading to Lena Jay and Ernie's abandoned camper van. I figured they weren't going to need it any longer. And there were much finer places in Scotland to haunt than the dilapidated vehicle.

"Did she what?"

"Did Ava Gardner live to one hundred fifty?"

"Sadly, no." I stuck my head in the camper van driving compartment. Perfect, the key was in the ignition.

"How old was she when she died?" Karen climbed in on the passenger side and slammed her door shut.

"Age sixty-seven, I believe." I chugged a couple ounces of whisky, then snuggled the fragile bottle of whisky between the two seats for safe keeping on these wet, bumpy roads.

"Wow. That's young. What'd she die of?"

I started the camper van and was pleased to hear the roar of the petrol engine. "Respiratory disease and pneumonia."

Karen snorted.

I turned on the windshield wipers. The woman was in one of those moods. Oh well, after her brother's untimely demise and seeing all that death and destruction—not to mention a so-called Troglodyte or two—it was important for her to laugh. Better than crying and if laughing at me, rather than with me, gave her comfort, no matter how small, then so be it. I'd suffer the consequences.

After all, Karen and I were in the same boat, camper van, now. Both our brothers were dead. We really only had each other now. An odd twist of fate that her brother died saving us from my brother who had gone mad being held captive for decades while earthlings experimented on him to their hearts' and minds' content. I should show some compassion.

Still, it was going to be a long drive, and the woman could prattle on forever, so I picked a short destination. "Edinburgh, here we come."

I helped myself to a pack of Winstons sitting open on the dash and lit up. Good old, Ernie...